THE CRY OF THE HANGMAN

THE CRY OF THE HANGMAN

Susanna Calkins

SEVERN HOUSE

First world edition published in Great Britain and the USA in 2021
by Severn House, an imprint of Canongate Books Ltd,
14 High Street, Edinburgh EH1 1TE.

Trade paperback edition first published in Great Britain and the USA in 2022
by Severn House, an imprint of Canongate Books Ltd.

severnhouse.com

British Library Cataloguing-in-Publication Data
A CIP catalogue record for this title is available from the British Library.

ISBN-13: 978-0-7278-5033-1 (cased)
ISBN-13: 978-1-78029-820-7 (trade paper)
ISBN-13: 978-1-4483-0558-2 (e-book)

All Severn House titles are printed on acid-free paper.

Typeset by Palimpsest Book Production Ltd.,
Falkirk, Stirlingshire, Scotland.
Printed and bound in Great Britain by
TJ Books, Padstow, Cornwall.

To Alex, Quentin and Matt

ONE

December 1667

The stone face of the churchyard sundial, though aged and worn, proclaimed its timeless warning. *Life passes like the shadow.*

With one finger, Lucy Campion traced each finely etched letter, ignoring the cheerful din of churchgoers released from St Dunstan's long Sunday-morning service. The minister's sermon had been particularly grim, emphasizing the wages of sin, even with yuletide nearly upon them. *Life passes like the shadow. Where fall temptation then*, she wondered.

'That's a magicked piece,' a voice hissed in her ear. 'Why lay your hands upon it?'

Lucy turned to face the old woman, taking in the dark costume of the long-bereaved. The earnestness to her demeanour gave her pause. 'Why do you say that?'

'Can you not see the dead spiders upon the dial's surface? Something ill is coming.'

Lucy flicked the shrivelled arachnids away. 'There. They are gone.'

'Don't be pert, miss. You have an untroubled countenance, I give you that. Do not dismiss the signs of things to come.'

A sudden chill sliced down the back of Lucy's neck and arms as if someone had wielded a knife, and she drew her cloak more closely around her. The woman crept away, edging around the congregants milling about the yard, the burden of her many earthly years causing her to stoop.

Lucy's gaze fell back on the sundial, and she stepped away uneasily. *A magicked piece?* Then she slapped her forehead, berating herself silently. *Oh, Lucy! How can you still be tricked by such words? Have you learned nothing from your time spent with Master Hargrave? Such nonsense is the speech of fools.*

Still apart from the others, Lucy took a deep breath. The

churchgoing crowd was thinning now, though there were still servants and masters alike grasping these precious few moments to mingle and gossip with old neighbours and friends, before going home to their cold noon-time meals. Unlike the local market, full of its buskers' cries and savoury and sweet aromas, the voices in the churchyard were less strident and demanding, and more cloying scents of perfume lingered in the still air. Bodies were cleaner today; most people had likely bathed the night before and many had used aluminium and scented soaps to mask their usual sweaty stench. Most people were wearing their best clothes, looking patched and tidy, and the women had left their aprons hanging on kitchen nails at home. A few women even wore ribbons in their hair and other fripperies, although too great a display of vanity could earn them a tongue-lashing from the minister or their masters.

'Wool-gathering, Lucy?' a woman's voice called from behind her. 'Or are you still contemplating the wages of sin, as the minister bids us to do?' This last said in a teasing way.

Lucy turned to look at the small group who had gathered around her by the sundial. Three were members of the Hargrave household – Mary the cook, her husband John who served as Master Hargrave's manservant, and their maid Annie, who was but a few years younger than Lucy. The fourth was Lach, Master Aubrey's other apprentice. All of them seemed to be snickering at Cook's words.

'No, it's more likely she's thinking about what tract she'll write next,' Annie replied. 'Another murder ballad, Lucy?'

Lucy smiled back at Annie, who'd been like a younger sister to her when they'd both been servants in Master Hargrave's household. It had been over a year since Lucy had left the Hargraves' employment, choosing to apprentice herself to the master printer Horace Aubrey.

'As if the world needs more petticoat authors,' Lach said in his usual mocking way. 'A witless lot.'

Lucy stuck her tongue out at him. 'I publish them as "Anonymous." Who does it harm anyway?'

'I like Lucy's tales,' John said, giving Lach a stern look. They were all used to the bickering between Lach and Lucy. 'She tells a right good story.'

His wife elbowed him in the ribs. 'She ought to write more recipes. Baker's tales and the like. No need to kill him off, mind you, Lucy.'

Lucy chuckled. 'I will see what I can do. Master Aubrey has kindly allowed me to print a few tales of my own, which have fared well.' This last she said pointedly to Lach who shrugged. 'Murder always sells, as you know.'

'Don't know how you have Master Aubrey so tightly wrapped around your finger,' Lach grumbled, kicking a rock.

'Isn't it time for you to become a journeyman soon?' Lucy asked, jabbing a finger in his shoulder. 'Should that not be your first step in striking out on your own?'

When Lach began to grumble about how the plague and Great Fire had delayed his progress, Lucy pointedly ignored him and spoke to her old friends. 'I did not see Master Hargrave today. Is he unwell?' She'd also noticed that the magistrate's son Adam was nowhere to be seen, but she could not bring herself to enquire after him.

'The master woke up feeling poorly, with a bit of a chill. Nothing that some wormwood and rest will not cure,' John said. 'He refused to let me stay home to tend him and insisted that I attend the service with the others. He was sleeping when I left.'

'Oh, I am so sorry to hear he is not well,' Lucy said. Master Hargrave had played a fatherly role to her since she'd first arrived at age fifteen, a nervous chambermaid thoroughly daunted by the prospect of serving in the home of a well-known magistrate. It was her first time in service, and she'd grown up hearing dreadful stories of masters abusing their servants for so much as coughing in their direction or spilling a bit of ale. However, she'd soon found that Master Hargrave, unlike many of his peers, was not ruled by the old adage of 'spare the rod, spoil the servant' and never beat them as other masters might. Instead, she'd found him to be kindly tempered, a figure of logic and calm, not passion and emotion. He'd always looked after his servants benevolently, never seeking to diminish their dignity. She heard that this had been his demeanour on the Bench as well, being well known for his thoughtful and reasoned sensibilities.

He'd been proud that Lucy had taught herself to read by secretly listening to his daughter's tutors, though she did not know that until later. Similarly, she could recall many evenings when he would set the Bible aside, after reading a few obligatory passages out loud to his children and servants, and pull out something from Hobbes or Descartes instead. She hadn't always understood his words and sometimes questions would blurt from her lips, which he would patiently answer. Only later did she learn that he'd been reading those pieces for her sake, believing that a person's station in life did not determine how one might think about important ideas.

When the previous year she had announced her bittersweet decision to leave the Hargraves' employment, he had provided her with a dowry of sorts, in the form of his late wife's silk dresses, which she then sold to pay for her apprenticeship dues. Her own father had died when she was a child, and Master Hargrave had offered a fatherly presence in her life. Indeed, his fatherly warmth toward her had been strong, even before Adam had begun to carefully court her.

At the thought of Adam, a warm flush spread to her cheeks. Almost as if she'd read her mind, Annie gave Lucy a mischievous smile as she answered the question that hadn't been asked. 'Master Adam asked us to keep a hold of you. Said he'd join us in a moment.'

As though she had summoned him, Adam Hargrave pushed open the church doors, Master Aubrey a step behind him.

Lucy's heart skipped a beat when she saw him, just as it had when she'd first spoken to him when she was eighteen. He'd been studying law at Cambridge for her first few years of service, and all their interactions had been brief. *Deliberately so*, he had confessed to her the previous year. Although he'd been intrigued by her charm and bright, curious nature, he had kept his distance, as he did not wish to be one of those terrible masters who took advantage of the women under their protection.

Everything had changed after one of the Hargraves' servants – dear Bessie! – had been murdered and her brother had faced hanging for the crime. They'd drawn together, and an enchanted ardour had surged between them. For a while, Lucy had allowed herself to be blissfully unaware until chilling misgivings had started to set in. *How could a former servant ever be accepted by society as the wife of Adam Hargrave? Who would accept her? Should his wife not be a Lady of Quality?* Fearfully, she had pushed his love away, bewildering them both in the process, and allowed her heart to be moved by someone more befitting her station. She felt a pang at the thought of Constable Duncan, who'd been so kind even as he made his own intentions towards her clear. He'd wanted to marry her, and sometimes that choice had just seemed easier. Adam had left for the colonies, to help establish some new legal codes there and presumably renew his spirit, and had stayed away for several long months. Recently, though, he'd returned, and under his renewed advances, her reserve had begun to crumble.

'Hello, Lucy,' he called, his blue eyes locking on hers as he approached. 'I entreated Master Aubrey to allow you to join us for our noon meal. I know Father's spirits would be raised if you can tell him a few of your true tales.'

'I'll come, too,' Lach declared. 'Everyone knows I tell a better tale than Lucy. Hey, it's true!'

Master Aubrey lightly cuffed his apprentice on the ear. 'Such a rascal! Master Hargrave doesn't want to see the likes of you. Besides, you need to tend to my meal.' With that, the printer dragged Lach away, towards their shop on Fleet Street.

Lucy looked uncertainly towards Cook and John. In a different household, the very idea that the master would invite a former servant to dine with their family would be a laughable outrage. Yet, like her, they were well used to the Hargraves' unexpected take on things.

John's careworn face cracked into an encouraging smile, and he nodded at her.

'All right, lass,' Cook said, giving her a little nudge 'You heard Master Adam. Let's get a move on.' They began to move away.

'Hargrave! Hold on a moment, would you?' a man of noble bearing called out to Adam, his well-dressed servant a few steps behind. Adam stopped, and so did Lucy.

The man did not even glance at Lucy. 'I'd like your opinion on—' he said, before Adam interrupted.

'This is Lucy Campion,' Adam said, pointedly forcing the man to acknowledge Lucy's presence with a startled bow. 'Lucy, this is Richard Newcourt. He is one of our City planners.'

'Miss Campion,' Mr Newcourt murmured, looking sheepish. 'Good afternoon.'

Lucy hid a smile. Ever since Adam had returned from his time in the colonies, he'd seemed focused on narrowing the gap between them. 'Please excuse us, Lucy, if you would. I should like to speak Mr Newcourt for a moment. I'll join you at home shortly.'

'Of course, sir.' After dropping a quick curtsey, Lucy picked up her skirts and ran after the others, linking her arm in Annie's as they walked together back to the Hargraves' home.

As they walked up Holborn, Annie nudged Lucy. 'Master Adam was eager for you to join us today,' she whispered.

'He knows that I care for his father and would wish to visit him during his illness,' Lucy replied, aware that the others around were stifling smiles.

'Certainly, dear,' Cook said, giving her an exaggerated wink.

'It's true,' she insisted. *And he wants to spend time with you himself*, a little impish voice silently added. *Everyone knows he's in love with you. The question is, Lucy Campion, how do you feel about him? For that matter, how do you feel about Duncan?*

'There's no time for that now,' she muttered, once again putting aside the question that had been plaguing her for some time now. Upon reaching the path to the Hargraves' home, she followed the others around to the back servants' entrance that opened from the garden.

'Mary,' John said, abruptly pulling his wife's elbow, forcing her to stop. 'Did you not have the sense to lock the door when we left?'

'I most certainly did,' Cook replied. 'Why ever would you say such a thing?'

John pointed at the door. 'See, it's ajar.'

Cook frowned. 'I am sure I secured it before I left.'

'Look!' Lucy exclaimed, pointing at the door. A long crack snaked down from the lock, with new splinters marring the weathered surface of the door. 'I think someone broke into the house!'

Annie's hands flew to her mouth. 'Oh no!'

'Stay here,' John said, pushing himself in front of the women. 'I'll go and look around.'

Disregarding his order, Lucy and Cook followed him into the kitchen, Annie a cautious step behind.

'Oh my,' Cook whispered, her hand going to her heart. 'Whatever has happened?'

The kitchen was in complete disarray. The lentil and lamb pie that Cook had left out on the counter had a slice taken from it, and there was a plate with crumbs and an overturned cup next to it. Jars of flour and salt had also been overturned, and broken eggs were congealing on the floor. One of the benches that ran the length of the table had been knocked on its side.

'Have we been robbed?' Annie said.

'Helped themselves to a bit of my pie! I should strangle him myself,' Cook declared, moving to right the container of flour. As she did so, her foot slipped on something on the floor.

'What in heaven's name?' Cook exclaimed, staring down at the offending object. It was a carving knife, one that Cook usually stored by the hearth when she was serving roast beef. Frowning, she reached down and picked it up from the floor, eyeing it from arm's length. 'What's this? Blood? I know I wiped it clean.'

'Blood?' Annie whispered, stepping back to steady herself against the kitchen table. 'From an animal? Or—?' Her eyes widened.

Lucy felt a terrible sinking feeling in her stomach. She looked at the others, a sudden realization on all their faces at once. 'The master!'

'I'll check on him,' John called and rushed towards the stairs that led to Master Hargrave's bedchamber.

'Be careful, John,' Cook called. 'The intruder could still be here.'

'I'm going to check the master's study,' Lucy whispered. 'He may no longer be abed at this hour.'

'Lucy, wait!' Annie started to call, but Lucy had already ventured down the hallway.

When she reached the door to the magistrate's study, Lucy hesitated, and then knocked. Without waiting for him to answer, she burst open the door. 'Master Hargrave . . .' The words died on her lips as she took in the scene before her.

The magistrate was slumped at his desk, a brass hourglass lying broken beside him. Blood could be seen on the papers surrounding his head.

'Dear Lord,' Lucy said, her fingers flying to her lips as she took in the magistrate's unmoving form. For a moment, she wanted to run shrieking from the room, but her feet felt nailed to the floor. She tried to scream, but no sound emerged. She swallowed. 'M–Master Hargrave? Sir!'

She forced herself to move to her old master, step by step by step. Finally, she was close enough to touch him. *Please be alive*, she thought to herself as she stretched her hand towards his face. The slightest warmth touched her fingers and then the smallest of groans.

'You're alive!' she whispered, tears falling from her cheeks, gratitude rushing over her. Then her senses began to revive in earnest, and she rushed back to the door. 'Help, help!' she called, her voice at first barely audible, then in louder and more desperate gasping shouts. 'John! Annie! Cook! Come quick! I'm in the study! The master needs help!'

A moment later, she could hear shrieks and a great pounding from all over the house as the others responded to her call and raced to the study. She did not wait until they arrived to act. 'Must staunch the blood,' she whispered to herself, hardly recognizing the hoarse, desperate voice. She tore a bit of fabric from her skirt, gently holding it against his head. The wound looked as if it was no longer gushing, but there was so much blood. Whoever had hit him had done so with force. The broken hourglass said it all.

'Lucy, what's wrong?' Adam called from the hallway as he raced towards her. Then, when he swung into the room, his face convulsed as he took in the scene. 'Father,' he said, sounding strangled.

'He's alive, Adam,' Lucy whispered, reaching her free hand out to him. Blindly, he took it and allowed her to pull him over to his father. 'I promise you, he's alive. I heard him moan.'

'What on earth happened? What is going on?' Adam asked, staring at the broken hourglass. The sand had poured out and mixed with the magistrate's blood on the table, creating a sticky mess. 'Who did this to Father?'

'Adam, I don't know. I found him like this just now.' Her voice choked up as she repeated the only thing that brought any comfort to her in this moment. 'He's alive, Adam. He's alive.'

The others came rushing in then, all stopping in shock as they took in the scene.

'Annie, summon Doctor Larimer! John, fetch the constable!' Lucy cried. 'Mary, please prepare a poultice. I do not know what the physician will need but I have seen him do this for his patients. Head wounds bleed a great deal. The blood need not mean it was a fatal blow. I will keep this cloth pressed to his head to staunch the blood.'

Thus dispatched, all three ran off as charged.

The magistrate's eyes fluttered open for a moment, then closed again, but it was enough to give Lucy hope. 'Pray, do not worry, sir,' she whispered. 'Doctor Larimer is on his way. You'll be fixed up right quick.'

Beside her, she could feel Adam shaking, trying to control himself. 'Tell me everything again, Lucy.'

She took a deep breath, trying to collect her thoughts. 'We arrived a few minutes ago, just before you. The kitchen door had been broken in. When we walked inside, we found the bench overturned, some canisters upended. Even a piece of Cook's pie had been eaten! We also found' – Lucy's hand flew to her heart – 'a knife! With blood on it!'

They both stared down at Master Hargrave's slumped form. Gently, Adam ran his hands down his father's back. 'He couldn't have been stabbed too, could he?' He leaned his father backwards in the chair to check his father's chest and stomach.

'Forgive me sir,' Lucy whispered, moving back the magistrate's jacket so that she could see his shirt. 'I don't see any blood anywhere else,' she whispered in relief. 'Adam, I don't think he was stabbed.'

Adam exhaled sharply. 'I agree. He appears only to have been struck down by the hourglass. We shall have Doctor Larimer confirm this, of course, but I do not see any other source of blood.'

'Whose blood could it have been on the knife? The intruder's? Could your father have stabbed him?' Lucy asked. She looked at each of the magistrate's hands in turn. She had learned from

Dr Larimer how to look at a person's hands when a stabbing had occurred. 'I don't see any cuts. I don't think your father wielded that knife.'

'I don't think he did, either. Father was clearly struck over the back of his head. No doubt taken by surprise while at his studies. I imagine that he was knocked out by that blow.' Adam looked around. 'Things seem out of sorts in here, too.'

For the first time, Lucy observed the state of the room, taking in its uncharacteristic disorder. Master Hargrave's collection of leather-bound texts, usually lined up neatly on the oak shelves, were now in an untidy jumble. Similarly, his papers were typically stacked and sorted or tucked away in drawers and hanging bags; today, there were papers strewn about the desk and floor.

'The intruder must have done this,' he said, clenching his fist. He knelt back down beside his father. 'Please, Father, wake up soon. Tell us what happened.'

Master Hargrave did not stir, although a small tear glistened in the corner of his eye.

A bustle in the hall alerted them that Dr Larimer and his younger assistant, Dr Sheridan, had arrived. Lucy stood up when they entered the magistrate's study. Dr Larimer immediately sank down beside Master Hargrave and began to probe gently at his head. 'All right, old friend,' he murmured. 'I know I promised a visit, but did you have to be so impatient?' Despite his chuckle, Lucy could hear the strain in his voice.

'What happened here?' Dr Sheridan demanded, eying the broken and blood-stained hourglass with distaste.

Adam recounted the facts as they knew them, while Lucy fetched a basket from the kitchen. When she returned, she saw that Dr Larimer had carefully bandaged the magistrate's head.

She began to place the pieces of the broken timepiece into the basket, blinking back tears as she wiped up the sand that had soaked up the master's blood.

Dr Larimer patted her arm. 'He is unconscious, Lucy. Though there is some swelling, the wound does not appear deep.' He looked at Adam and his assistant. 'Let us transport him to his bed. I believe he will rest more comfortably in his own chamber.

The important thing now is to keep a close watch upon him; a head wound is a tricky thing.'

More men's voices could be heard in the hallway. Lucy recognized Constable Duncan's York accent before he stepped inside the study, wearing his customary red uniform, his assistant Hank in tow. Annie and John stood in the doorway, anxiously peeping inside.

Duncan paused, taking in the scene, his eyes resting for a moment on Lucy before he spoke to Adam. 'How does your father fare?'

Although the two men usually bristled in each other's presence, a shared concern today kept their veiled rivalry in check.

'Still unconscious but, as you can see, well attended.' He looked to his servants in the hallway. 'Annie, John, would you please help the physicians move the magistrate to his chamber.' When Lucy started after them, he touched her arm. 'Stay here, if you would. I should like you to explain everything to the constable.'

As the others gingerly moved the magistrate out of the study, Lucy explained all that had happened when they returned from the morning service. Duncan listened with his customary professional air.

'Hank,' he said when she was done. 'Go and speak to the neighbours. Find out if they saw anything.' To Lucy, he added, 'Show me everything.'

Lucy walked Duncan around, pointing to the broken door, the bloody knife on the kitchen table, the overturned pots and bench. Cook was busy making wormwood tea and a poultice for the magistrate and had not yet put things right. Adam walked behind them, silent. If it was a strange thing for her to be taking Duncan around his own home, he did not let on.

Duncan, however, was particularly taken with the pie, staring down at it. So much so that Lucy had to nudge him. 'Constable! I'm sure Cook can give you a piece later,' she whispered.

Duncan gave her a half grin that disappeared when he glanced back up at Adam, who was still just watching them both. 'No, I'm just trying to imagine what might have happened here. An intruder comes in, eats a piece of pie, tosses the kitchen around, attacks Master Hargrave with the hourglass. What is a reasonable order of events?'

Annie came in then. 'Some objects have been stolen,' she said, looking tearful. 'Some silver candlesticks that the mistress held dear, as well as some serving spoons.'

'So this is indeed a burglary,' Duncan mused. 'What about the rest of the house?' He walked back to the magistrate's study. 'What about in here? Anything taken?'

'It is quite a mess,' Lucy said. 'Not the magistrate's customary way at all.'

Adam began to look around at the table. 'Sadly, I can see a few things missing. An engraved silver snuff box. A crystal ink jar, given to him by the King. There was a gold and silver box inlaid with precious stones that Father kept on his desk here. I know it contained a few valuable things, like his pocket sundial and a flea glass.'

'Oh, I know those objects,' Lucy said. 'He used them when studying his maps. I imagine they were quite rare.'

'Expensive too, I'd wager?' Duncan asked.

'Rather.' Adam opened a drawer and frowned. 'Wait a minute.' He opened another drawer, his scowl deepening.

'What is it?' Duncan asked, taking a step forward.

'Both of these drawers are completely empty.'

'What was inside?'

'I'm not completely certain,' Adam said, still staring into the top drawer. 'I think my father may have kept his personal papers here.'

'What sort of papers?'

'Wills, testaments. I think this is also where he kept his memoirs about his time on the Bench. Like the Justice Matthew Hale, he'd been writing down his understanding of the jurisprudence around different interesting cases.'

'Do you think they were stolen by your father's assailant?' the constable asked.

'I can't say for sure. It's possible that my father just moved them himself. Until Father is revived and can shed light on this mystery, I think we must assume the worst.'

TWO

Lucy went up to the master's chamber to see if the physician needed anything.

'Master Hargrave has still not awoken,' Dr Larimer informed her. 'I am hopeful that he will soon. Someone will need to watch over him, especially when he wakes up. Disorientation, dizziness and confusion are quite common after someone has received such an injury to the back of the head. I am hopeful that his memory will be sharp, but as you know, Lucy, sometimes such a blow can elicit amnesia.'

Lucy nodded. That was certainly so. Earlier that year, she'd met a young woman who'd been struck over the head and it had taken quite some time for her memory to be recovered. That woman had other ailments that had worsened her condition, though, and Master Hargrave was still a hale and hearty man, despite his advancing years.

'I will stay with him,' Adam said, entering the room with a small wooden chair. He placed it beside his father's bed, resuming his anxious vigil.

Lucy returned to the kitchen then, to relay the news to the others. Duncan was sitting there, a mug of warm mead before him.

Cook said a small prayer then, to which John added a whispered 'Amen'.

There was a knock at the door and Hank appeared, his hat back in his hands. 'Duncan, I have spoken with the neighbours to discover what they might have seen or heard. Most were still at church when the incident occurred. However, around half past eleven, a Mrs Cornelius Haggerty was home with a bad case of the gout.'

'Oh, she does suffer something terrible from that,' Cook interrupted. 'I've prepared a concoction for her from time to time, hoping to ease her pain. A real shame.'

'She witnessed the burglary?' Duncan asked, turning back to the matter at hand.

'Yes, well, she told me she had just visited the privy when she happened to look out one of her drawing-room windows, which face the street. She told me she'd heard shouting, and then saw two men running down the street, straight past her house. They were coming from the direction of this house, each man carrying a sack.'

'Two men!' Duncan said thoughtfully. He looked again towards the pie and its missing piece. 'What were they shouting?'

Hank shuffled his feet. 'Mrs Haggerty was not certain.'

'Practically deaf, that one,' Cook commented. 'Wonder she heard anything at all.'

Lucy glanced at Annie, who was nervously twisting her apron in her fingers. 'Could Mrs Haggerty describe the men?'

Hank scratched his head. 'It seems that Mrs Haggerty's eyesight is not so good any more, either. She thought one of the men was familiar – a tradesman perhaps who plied his trade on this street. That one was tall and lanky and had brown hair, but that was all she could note.'

Lucy saw Annie's eyes widen. *Why did that strike her so?* 'Were the two men definitely together?' she asked.

'It would seem so,' Hank said.

'What about the other man?' Lucy asked. 'Could she describe him?'

Hank shrugged. 'Not really. "Not a gentleman," she said, but couldn't give much more in the way of detail. Thought he might have been a tradesman too, but she couldn't see any instruments that would tell us what trade he was in.'

'That's not much to go on,' Duncan said, standing up. 'For now, there is little else we can do, until Master Hargrave wakes up. Please prepare me a list of the stolen items. Perhaps we can track them down and maybe discover Master Hargrave's assailant.' He gave them a rueful look, revealing how doubtful he was that the pieces would be recovered. 'Please convey this to the Hargraves.'

'Thank you, Constable,' Lucy said. With that, Duncan and Hank took their leave, and the others sank back down at the table, trying to make sense of all that occurred.

Lucy watched Annie clutching at her apron and looking more

distraught than before. Something was clearly amiss. *What's the matter?* Lucy mouthed at her friend. None of the others seemed to notice.

In response, Annie jerked her head towards the corridor. *Come with me*, she mouthed back.

When Lucy stood up, Annie put her finger to her lips and tiptoed away, tossing a frantic look over her shoulder to make sure that Lucy was following her.

Oh, Annie, what are you up to? Lucy asked herself, as she slipped out of the room.

Lucy followed Annie into the drawing room, shutting the door behind them. 'What is it?'

Instead of replying, the young servant began to pace about, picking at her apron, her eyes reddening with unshed tears.

'You seem distraught,' Lucy said, patting her upper arm. 'Annie, Doctor Larimer thinks Master Hargrave will recover. He just needs a good rest. When he wakes up, perhaps he will be able to tell us what happened.'

'I know,' Annie said, wiping her nose with her sleeve. 'I am indeed grateful that the master's life has been spared. It's just that . . .' She leaned against the sideboard and began to idly pick up objects from its smooth lacquered surface – salt dishes, candlesticks, decanters – and set them back down, all slightly askew. 'It can't be so. Why would he do such a thing?'

'Annie!' Lucy said, more sternly. She grasped her by the shoulders. 'What are you talking about? Do you know something? Tell me!'

Annie's frightened eyes met her own. Leaning over, she whispered in Lucy's ear. 'I think it might have been Sid.'

'Sid? What?' Lucy exclaimed, then quieted when Annie frantically shushed her. 'You think *Sid* was the wretched cur who attacked the magistrate?'

An image of the tall gangly pickpocket arose in her mind. She had known Sid for many years now, first encountering him in a market when he'd stolen a hapless woman's purse before her very eyes. She'd given him a scolding then, but over the years she'd caught him doing many a thieving act and saw him regularly getting pummelled in the public stocks for his misdeeds. He'd grown up an orphan, with no home or family to call his own, which had kept him from service and finding more reputable work.

How had Hank described one of the men? *A tradesman. Tall and lanky with brown hair. Familiar!* That certainly fit the pick-pocket's description.

She began to pace about the room, thinking about how Sid had helped her out of more than one scrape, and she had thought he'd been turning over a new leaf of late. 'I don't believe it. I know he's been short of funds, and too lazy to pursue an honest day's work, but I've never seen him hurt anyone. No matter how bad his circumstances might be right now, I just refuse to believe, Annie, that he would ever have set upon the master in such a dreadful way. Why ever would you think such a thing of Sid?'

Tears filled Annie's eyes. 'I know. I would not like to believe it either.' Sheepishly, she pulled a grey cap out of her apron pocket. 'This is Sid's hat. I am sure of it. See these stitches here? I fixed them when the lining started to pull apart.'

Lucy took the hat, turning it around in her hands, running her finger over the part Annie had patched. She could envision Sid wearing the cap, jauntily pulled over one eye, giving her his mischievous wink. 'Where did you find it?'

'On the kitchen floor. I know it was not there when we left for church this morning. He must have been here after we left.'

She felt a pang, which she swiftly squelched. 'We need to find Sid,' she declared, her hand about to open the door. 'He will surely know what happened. Where's that rapscallion calling home these days, I wonder.'

A faint blush rose in Annie's cheeks. 'He told me he'd been living on Strand Lane these last few weeks. He's been helping the merchants unload their goods at the docks, by the Embankment.' She hesitated. 'Do we need to tell the constable?'

Lucy paused. Duncan was a fair man, willing to listen before taking action. She did not want him to assume the worst of Sid either, since it was the constable who so often oversaw Sid's time in the pillory. 'Maybe it would be better if we just find Sid ourselves first, and then he can tell us what happened.'

*   *   *

'Few souls about,' Annie whispered, clutching Lucy's arm as they walked towards Strand Lane. Cook and John had been so distracted, attending to the magistrate's needs, they hadn't even noticed the girls slip out. Being Sunday, few establishments were open, and the streets were fairly deserted. The rank smell of fish from the Thames was strong, causing Annie to pinch her nose. 'How will we even find Sid?'

'I imagine The Sparrow will be open,' Lucy said. While coffee shops and taverns were expected to be closed on the Lord's Day, inns were usually open so that travellers and wayfarers could get a bite to eat and drink, and chance of respite if necessary. 'I know the innkeeper. He may have heard tell of Sid.'

'I still can't believe Sid would steal from the magistrate. Or hurt him, for that matter,' Annie said, her tone fretful.

Lucy didn't reply. Annie had been saying the same things over and over for the last hour.

'He must have been inside the house,' Annie continued. 'How else could his cap have ended up in the kitchen?'

'How indeed?' Lucy replied, rankled by the same questions.

'What about what the neighbour said? That description sounded like Sid, did it not?'

'It did.' Lucy sighed. 'I should very much like to hear what Sid has to say for himself, before passing judgment.' *That's what Master Hargrave would expect of me. No matter my doubts, let me first hear the man speak.*

They arrived at The Sparrow, a rambling structure that had probably been around a few hundred years. 'Here we are,' Lucy said. 'Let's go in, warm ourselves. Then we can make our inquiries.'

Annie unlinked her arm from Lucy's and took a step back, staring at the inn doubtfully. 'Are you sure this place is *proper*?'

Lucy stepped back too, to appraise The Sparrow with new eyes. She'd first set foot in the inn about a year ago, when she'd sought to discover the identity of a strange man who'd crossed her path. At first, the innkeeper, Mr McDaniels, had not taken kindly to her presence or her enquiries, but when she'd hopped atop one of the great wooden barrels lining the entrance and soon brought a crowd to the inn with her tales, he'd changed his tune. Since then, she'd sold tracts out front a handful of times. Being a goodly sort, Mr McDaniels often invited her in for a pint in exchange, setting her up in a corner away from drunken and lecherous patrons.

'It's quite all right. Mr McDaniels will not let us come to any harm,' she said, drawing Annie's hand back into the crook of her arm. As they walked in, the smell of old mutton and ale washed over her. There were few patrons, mostly old men huddled at tables by the hearth, dribbling into their bowls of barley broth or mash. Nearby sat a young couple, wearing travel-stained clothes. The woman was dandling a babe on her skirts, fatigue weighing down her movements as she tried to keep the infant occupied.

Lucy pointed to a small table away from the others. 'Let us sit here, in that corner.'

The innkeeper emerged from the kitchen then, carrying a plate of sausage and cheese, which he placed in front of the couple.

Lucy hailed him. 'Hello, Mr McDaniels.'

The innkeeper turned around, training his spectacles on her. 'Oh, Lucy! It's you! What brings you here on a Sunday? Aubrey can't be making you sell on the Lord's Day, can he now? I thought he was a God-fearing man!' Here, Mr McDaniels laughed heartily at his joke, and Lucy smiled good-naturedly in return. It was certainly true that Master Aubrey would far rather sell books on a Sunday than listen to a man of the cloth.

'That may be so, but I'm afraid that the Church and City would not approve, nor, perhaps more importantly, the Stationers' Company.' Lucy gave a little laugh, then lowered her voice before getting to the point. 'Sir, we're looking for someone. We were hoping you might know him, perchance even where we might locate him. It's important.'

'Is that so? You're both looking a bit peaked. I should think you would want to rest first,' McDaniels said, his face taking on a calculated expression. Even though their acquaintance was of a kindly nature, he was letting them know that they would not be allowed to loiter in the warm inn for free. 'I'm sorry I cannot offer you a seat by the fire.' He glared in the direction of the old men. 'What can I get you? A spot of mead? Perhaps some cheese to tide you over? Looks like you could use some time to warm up.'

Lucy mentally counted the coins she kept hidden in the pocket beneath her skirts. She'd learned a long time ago that spending a coin or two was well worth the effort when seeking information. 'Thank you, sir. That would be lovely.'

'No "sir" needed for me, Lucy. I'll be back.'

When he walked away, Annie touched the back of Lucy's hand. 'I did not bring any coins,' she whispered, sounding stricken. 'I'm so sorry, Lucy. I did not even think . . .'

'No matter,' Lucy said, reaching inside her skirts to retrieve some silver. To pass the time, she began to tell Annie about what had occurred at this very inn the last time she had sold true accounts out front. Then she saw Mr McDaniels again, carrying in a tray with the two mugs of steaming mead and a tin plate with sliced cheese.

'Here he comes. Let me do the talking.'

Mr McDaniels laid out the mugs and plate in front of them and then pulled over a chair from a nearby empty table, seating himself between them. 'What is on your mind? You said you were looking for someone?'

'Yes, his name is Sid.' Nibbling on a piece of cheese, she described the pickpocket. 'Have you seen him?'

'Sid?' McDaniels laughed. 'Certainly, I know him. Question is, why are two lasses like yourselves looking for a mongrel like him?'

'Oh, we just want to talk to him,' Lucy said, kicking Annie's foot gently under the table. While McDaniels was a decent sort, she'd learned from the constable that it was best to keep details to herself unless it was absolutely necessary to share. 'We haven't seen him for a while.'

'Well, I haven't seen him for a few days either. He fixed one of my windows last week. Practically begged me for work. Said he was trying to mend his ways.' McDaniels raised one eyebrow. 'This your influence, Lucy?'

Lucy shrugged. 'Any idea where he might be?'

McDaniels frowned. 'Last time I saw him, he was working for Mitchell, down by the dock. Helping gut fish. Can't imagine he'd be in on a Sunday, though.'

He could be hiding there, Lucy thought. 'Perhaps. We should check for ourselves,' she said, laying a few coins on the table. She downed her cup and grabbed one last piece of cheese. 'Let's go, Annie.'

THREE

Lucy and Annie trudged over to the area where fish were gutted and sold during the week. The stench was quite strong now and holding their noses didn't help. 'We'll have to have second baths this week, I fear,' Lucy said, sniffing her cloak in distaste.

'I'll have to use all my lavender soap, and maybe even most of my rosemary, too,' Annie pouted. 'I'd been hoping to save it for my Christmas Eve bath. If only I had a sweetheart to wheedle.' She jabbed at Lucy. 'How about you ask for some lovely, scented soap from your two vying suitors. Keep the one from the sweetheart you hold most dear and give the other one to me. I shan't tell a soul.'

Although Annie's words were made in jest, they stopped Lucy short. 'Two vying suitors,' she repeated, a flush rising in her cheeks. 'I suppose that is how it appears.'

'It appears that way because it's true. Master Adam and the constable. Sometimes we think you care for one, but then you seem set on the other. Remember that piece Lach used to sing about the constable?'

As she began to sing the silly tune, Lucy swatted at her. 'Enough of that.'

'We're all so curious to see who you choose. Sometimes I wonder, though . . . do you even know who you like best?' Annie's mischievous smile made the dimple in her chin more evident. 'If I had to guess, I'd say it was—'

Lucy clapped her hand over Annie's mouth to keep her from uttering the man's name aloud. Though she tried hard not to believe in jinxes and charms, her unsettled heart made her love feel ill-fated. 'Never you mind that,' she whispered. She gestured broadly towards an old man with rheumy eyes, smoking a pipe in the doorway of a shack, a wooden cane resting on the wall beside him. 'Let's speak to that man.'

With Annie fiercely gripping her left arm, Lucy hailed the man and asked about Sid. Like McDaniels, the man also seemed to immediately recognize Sid from her description. 'In there,' he said, waving them towards a small shed even more ramshackle than The Sparrow. 'I saw him go in earlier. Didn't look so good, either. Hope he didn't bring the plague back.'

Annie's eyes flashed. 'The plague! He most certainly did not.'

'Come on, Annie,' Lucy said, after murmuring her thanks to the man. Gingerly, she knocked on the door of the shed, straining to hear any movements inside. When she didn't hear anything, she pushed on the door, which turned out to be unlocked. 'I'm going in.'

The shed was dark and windowless, and the light from behind them did not reach all the shadowy corners. Lucy began to move cautiously through the stacks of barrels and crates, feeling her way. 'Sid?' she whispered, her teeth starting to chatter. 'Are you in here?'

From the corner, she heard a small moaning sound.

'Sid? Is that you?' she called.

Edging around the barrels, Lucy looked down to see the figure of a man sprawled across a straw pallet in the corner. 'Sid?' She knelt down beside him, with Annie peering anxiously over her shoulder. 'Sid. It's Lucy. And Annie.'

'What do you want?' Sid snarled, though his voice was weak.

She could see now that he was clasping one arm to his chest, and his face was flushed and sweaty despite the chill in the room. 'What's the matter, Sid? Are you sick?' She touched his forehead. 'Oh dear! You're burning up.' She turned her attention back to his arm, which had been wrapped clumsily in a dirty, bloodied bandage. 'What is this? Are you hurt?' Without waiting for Sid to answer, she pulled his jacket open and opened his shirt, which was caked with mud and blood. He jerked away with a groan.

'Oh no!' Annie cried. 'What happened?'

'He's been injured. Cut somehow. That wound appears deep.' Lifting her skirt, she tore off a bit of her red petticoat, feeling a pang when she heard Annie gasp. This garment had once belonged to Sarah, Master Hargrave's daughter, before she gave up many of her worldly items as a Quaker, and it was made of a finer fabric than Lucy could ever afford on her own. *As if you could be so mercenary at such a time, Lucy!* Swallowing the lump in her throat, she wrapped the torn cloth around the other bandage. 'This should hold until we can get Sid to a doctor!'

'No barber-surgeons!' Sid cried, struggling to sit up. 'They'll take off my arm! I'd rather die.'

'T–take off h–his arm?' Annie said, starting to tremble.

Turning around to face her, Lucy gripped her by the shoulders and gave her a little shake. 'Don't you dare faint, Annie!' Turning back to Sid, she said, 'We're taking you to the physician. No, not a barber-surgeon,' she said, trying to soothe him when he began to struggle. 'I refuse to leave you here. If you aren't tended, you could die. I am not speaking in jest. Do you understand me, Sid?' At the pickpocket's reluctant nod, she continued. 'All right, I'm going to pull you up now.'

Carefully, she pulled Sid up to a sitting position so that he could put his arm around her shoulders. 'Annie, get his other side.'

Together, the women raised the pickpocket to his feet, each taking a side. For a moment, they staggered under his weight. Lucy had a sudden qualm. How would they get him to Dr Larimer's? The physician lived nearly a mile away. They had no money to hire a sedan chair to transport him. *We'll sort it out.* She grunted. 'Let's go.'

As they trudged away from the dock, Lucy could see that Sid was in even worse shape than he had first appeared. He had a great yellowing bruise on his cheek and jaw, and he looked to be in a lot of pain.

Annie began to pelter Sid with questions, despite his poorly appearance. 'What happened to you, Sid? Why were you at the master's house this morning? Why did you steal from him?'

Sid jerked his head up. 'I didn't steal anything!'

'Well, why were you there? Don't deny it! We found your hat.'

'Speaking of which.' Lucy placed Sid's hat on his head, feeling his frozen ears. *Poor lad will get frostbite, on top of his other ailments.*

He gave her a grateful half grin, touching his bruised jaw with a grimace. Then he began trying to explain, sounding both sheepish and defiant at once. 'I came to see you, Annie. I had already been to church and—'

'Liar,' Lucy interrupted. 'You weren't at church today.'

'Well, yes, that was a falsehood,' Sid said, smirking uncomfortably. 'The part about wanting to see you, Annie, was true. When I got there, the door was open, and the pie was out on the table. I wasn't planning to help myself, but I was sitting . . . getting so hungry. I thought you might invite me to your noon meal anyway, and who would it hurt to have a bite early? The pie looked so delicious.'

'The door was open, you say?' Lucy asked, ignoring his boyish pleading. 'You just invited yourself inside? Didn't you think that one of the Hargraves might be home?'

Sid rubbed his head. 'I didn't – I should have thought more. I know the Hargraves are good and God-fearing. I could not imagine them missing the service.'

'Master Hargrave was not feeling well,' Lucy informed him. 'A touch of the ague. He was indeed home.'

'Yes, I discovered that soon after.' He twisted his lips, appearing genuinely distressed. 'I should not have gone inside. The Lord certainly did punish me for this criminal act.'

'What happened next?' she said, bringing him back to the story. He could lament over his trespassing later. 'You were in the kitchen, eating Cook's pie and . . .?'

'I heard a shout and a crash from the magistrate's study. I was quite shocked, and I dropped my fork to the floor. I remember just sitting there, thinking I'd best flee, lest I get in trouble for staying. I was this close to fleeing the house.' He held up his fingers to show a very small space.

'Why didn't you?' Annie asked.

'Something didn't seem right. I thought perhaps someone had fallen and knocked something down.' He took a pained breath. Sweat was pouring from his forehead now. The slow journey was clearly taking a toll on him. 'I forced myself to stand up and tiptoe down the hallway, towards Master Hargrave's study. I thought I could just take a quick peek, make sure everyone was all right and then run away.'

He tightened his grip on Lucy's shoulder. 'When I stood outside the study, I could hear someone inside, opening drawers, moving things around, tossing things to the floor. Who would do such a thing? It was then I remembered how I'd found the back door open and I realized there might be an intruder in the house.'

'*Another* intruder,' Annie said, sounding cross.

'Yes, well, another intruder,' he replied, casting his eyes down in contrition.

'What happened then?' Lucy asked, shooting Annie a stern look. Now was not the moment to scold Sid, no matter how tempting that was. There would be plenty of time later.

'The study door opened, and a man came out, holding a burlap sack. When he saw me, he stopped for a second. I wish I had done something. Why didn't I do something? Except, I froze. He laughed and punched me in the face. Hard. I fell to the floor.' Sid touched his bruised jaw. 'Knocked the sense out of me for a moment, I have to say.'

He took a deep breath. 'I got up, though, and followed him back to the kitchen, thinking I could stop him.'

'Oh, my goodness, Sid! You could have been killed!' Annie cried, true concern surfacing at last.

'I tried to stop him, but I couldn't,' Sid said, flushing slightly. 'I lunged at him, but that's when he grabbed a knife from the rack and stabbed me here.' He pointed to the still-seeping wound on his upper arm, looking gratified when Annie gently patted it with her free hand.

'What happened next?' Lucy said, growing impatient.

'At that point, the intruder ran out of the door. I shouted for him to come back and I tried to keep up with him, but he was already gone. At some point, I must have passed out.' Sid's voice began to grow weaker and weaker, and his steps were getting smaller as they walked. 'I was afraid I'd be blamed for the burglary, since I wasn't supposed to . . .' His last words were indistinguishable.

'He's going to collapse!' Lucy tightened her grip around Sid's waist and looked around. 'Duncan's gaol is closer. We can tend to him there.'

After much exertion, the trio finally staggered the half mile to the makeshift gaol Duncan oversaw on Fleet Street, a stone's throw from Master Aubrey's shop. The gaol had been established the year before, after the Great Fire had swept through the City, destroying most of the major gaols including Newgate. Originally a candlemaker's shop, the constable had outfitted it with several cells, mostly to hold drunks, thieves and other boisterous sorts for brief stints of time.

Panting, Lucy threw open the door of the gaol, to see Duncan and Hank huddled around one of the beer barrels found among the ruins of the original Cheshire Cheese tavern. Ignoring their startled looks, she gestured towards the first open cell. 'In there.'

Duncan and Hank stared as they dragged Sid inside, dropping him on the hard wooden bench. 'Lucy!' the constable exclaimed. 'Is that Sid? Why have you brought him here?'

'Don't lock me up,' he murmured, before promptly passing out.

'What's that vagabond done now?' Hank asked. 'Is he drunk?'

'He didn't do anything wrong,' Annie replied stoutly. 'He's not a vagabond.'

Both Hank and Duncan looked at the servant with pitying eyes. 'Don't know this rascal too well, do you?' Duncan said. Adopting a more authoritative tone, he added, 'Lucy, tell me what's going on.'

Lucy knelt down beside Sid, touching his flushed forehead. 'He was stabbed there,' she said, pointing to the bandage she'd wrapped around his arm earlier. 'We couldn't bear to bring him to a barber-surgeon, so we thought we'd get him to Doctor Larimer's. This is as far as we could get.' She choked back a sob. 'He needs a poultice before his wound fills with pus.'

Duncan knelt beside her. 'How did Sid get stabbed, Lucy?'

She tugged Sid's shirt open. 'He was stabbed by the man who assaulted Master Hargrave.'

'What? How did that happen?'

Lucy quickly recounted what Sid had told them, making an impatient sound when she got to the part about Sid deciding to help himself to Cook's pie.

'Master Hargrave's neighbour said she saw two men racing out together,' Hank commented from behind them. 'Mrs Haggerty didn't say anything about one man chasing the other.'

'You also said she is short of sight,' Lucy replied, carefully unwrapping the bandages as she spoke. 'Perhaps her eyes did not tell her the full tale, or she didn't understand what she was seeing.'

'You believe him, then?' Duncan asked.

'Sid has helped me in the past,' Lucy replied simply.

'Did he offer any description of his attacker?' Duncan asked.

'No, he passed out before he had a chance to tell us everything.'

The pickpocket began to moan then, and his body began to shiver more. 'He's burning up already. Annie, fetch me a blanket.' She pulled back the bandage. 'The wound is still oozing. He needs to be treated. Have you any figwort here? That is what the good Culpepper described for such a wound.'

'No, we have no such medicine here. Let us get him to Doctor Larimer at once,' Duncan replied. 'He must be revived and attended to properly, so that he can tell us what he knows. With any luck, Sid will be able to describe Master Hargrave's assailant and we can apprehend the fellow.'

'Has the magistrate still not woken?' Lucy asked, a catch in her voice. It had been several hours since the attack.

'Not as far as I know. I asked John to send word if he did,' Duncan replied. 'I shall call for a cart to transport Sid. Best if we take care of his injuries straightaway.'

'Has the master's lot improved?' Lucy called to Cook, seeing her outside scouring a pot. Behind her, Duncan and Hank wheeled Sid, sprawled out in their cart. Annie had dropped back, anxiously plucking at her skirts.

At the sight of Annie, Cook scowled but still answered Lucy's question. 'Master Adam is still with him, but he has been revived. He managed a bit of my good beef broth but fell back to his slumbers.' She eyed Sid with disfavour. 'Why have you brought that pickpocket here? In a cart no less? What kind of scrape did he get himself into? He looks taken by the spirits.'

'He's not drunk,' Lucy explained, wiping the sweat from Sid's forehead with a cloth. 'He was stabbed by Master Hargrave's assailant and requires a physician. Is Doctor Larimer perchance still here?'

'Good heavens!' Cook exclaimed. 'Yes, the physician is here. He returned when the master revived a short while ago. They are in his bedchamber.' She waved her hands. 'Go, go! Fetch the physician.'

'I shall need to speak to the magistrate now,' Duncan said. 'Pray lead the way.'

As they transported Sid inside the house, Cook held out the pot to Annie. 'You, girl. Finish scrubbing this pot.' Then something occurred to her. 'If Sid was stabbed here this morning, was he the one who helped himself to my pie?'

Poor Sid! Lucy thought. *What is the pain of a stab wound compared with Cook's wrath?*

'We shall tend to Sid here,' Adam declared a short while later, as Dr Larimer looked over his new patient. 'I know that you are aggrieved that he partook of a meal uninvited, but it sounds as if he also tried to go after the man who attacked my father. We must better understand what happened.'

After a quick flurry of activity, where she informed Dr Larimer of Sid's injuries and a poultice was prepared, Lucy was able to return to the magistrate's bedchamber. Hank and Dr Larimer had remained with Sid, who was resting comfortably in an unused bedchamber that had been intended for the magistrate's daughter.

Master Hargrave, now in his bedclothes, was sitting, propped up by two embroidered silk pillows that had belonged to his late wife. A nearly empty porcelain cup of wormwood tea was on the small table beside his bed. He looked wan, without his customary twinkling countenance. 'Ah, Lucy,' he murmured. 'How kind of you to visit.'

Adam, who'd been sitting on a small bench by his father's bed rose when Lucy entered. Duncan, standing in the corner, coughed slightly.

Instead of seating herself on the bench, Lucy knelt beside the bed, patting the magistrate on his arm. 'Master Hargrave, does your head ache? Shall I fetch more wormwood tea?'

'Lucy, do not concern yourself. I have been soothed by a nice concoction that Cook made for me,' he said. 'I feel much revived. Pray, do not kneel.'

Lucy pulled the small wooden stool over to the bed and sat down, still leaning towards him. 'Sir, what happened? Who attacked you?'

'I was just telling Adam and the constable that, unfortunately, I was bent over my book at the time and did not see my assailant.'

He chuckled ruefully. 'I am rather ashamed to have been caught working on the Lord's Day. I fear that this punishment may be the penance that the good Lord has asked me to submit to.' He rubbed his head.

'Oh dear,' Lucy said, noting the gesture. Despite his light-hearted words, the magistrate was looking far too pale for her liking. 'Was there nothing else you can recall? A sound? A smell, perhaps? Even if you did not see your attacker, perhaps there is something else that might serve to identify him.'

The magistrate's eyes widened slightly. Behind, she heard Adam cough. Sensing a stirring, Lucy looked around to find that all three men were now grinning slightly 'What? What is it?'

'You simply asked the exact same questions as the constable did, before you entered the room,' the magistrate replied. 'To address your questions. I heard a sound in the corridor but, engrossed as I was in my text, I did not make sense of what I was hearing until it was too late.' He sighed. 'With the benefit of hindsight, I realize that my assailant must have slipped into the house and opened my study door with great stealth. Seeing me, he reached for the nearest heavy object, which happened to be that wretched hourglass, and decided to wield it against my poor unsuspecting head.'

Lucy winced. 'I'm so very sorry, sir, that such a blow was struck.' Blinking away her tears, she continued, 'What was the man after? Cook said some items were missing, but nothing overly costly.'

Adam nodded. 'That is so. Cook and I walked around, inventorying what had been stolen while the physicians were examining Father. Mostly small inconsequential things.'

'So, he entered the study,' Lucy said, trying to imagine the scene. 'He thinks it to be empty, only to discover Master Hargrave at his desk, working. He picks up the hourglass, strikes him over the head . . .' She closed her eyes. Reopening them, she continued, 'He then took what he needed and fled the room. Sid had told us he'd heard a crash and jumped up from his meal. They ran into each other in the corridor. Sid realized then that the man was an intruder, and he went after the man, who punches him and knocks him down. The thief then returned to the kitchen where he grabbed the knife. Sid went after him again and was stabbed in the process.' She paused again. *Poor Sid!* 'Despite his wound, Sid followed the intruder out into the road, shouting at him. That was what the neighbour must have seen from her window.'

'Just so,' Master Hargrave said. 'An excellent summary of events.'

'What do you think he was after?' Lucy asked. 'Was it just the items from your desk? I know there were some precious items there. I know some of your personal papers were stolen, too.'

'Yes, I'm rather afraid they were after the latter,' the magistrate said. 'Because anyone with even the most discerning eye might have seized some of the larger, more expensive objects in the room. In the drawing room, too, we do have quite a lot of silver items that would be fairly easy to sell or melt down. Even if the thief was uncertain how much he could take in one bag, surely he'd have taken some of the larger items.' He drained the last bit of wormwood tea from his cup and set it back, rattling, on its saucer. 'Since two of the drawers were emptied of their contents, we might assume that the thief was looking for wills, private deeds, property records, contracts and other legal documents that might be used for a variety of nefarious means. Thankfully, I have them stored elsewhere.'

'What did the thief take, then?' Lucy asked, squeezing her fingers together, hoping it was not anything too important.

'I will have to ascertain this directly, but I believe those drawers mostly contained commentaries I'd written during my time on the Bench, as well as my thoughts on some recent cases.'

'Oh no!' Lucy exclaimed. 'What a dreadful loss. I hope they can be recovered.'

The magistrate clucked his teeth. 'Though the loss is unfortunate, nothing is as terrible as it might have been. I took to heart one of the many lessons of last year's conflagration, making copies of certain documents and storing them in containers that I hoped would preserve them well, should another similar calamity arise.'

'Still, it will be quite a task to reconstruct your thinking,' Adam said. 'To describe your legal reasoning again.'

'That is a sorry thing indeed,' the magistrate said.

'Perhaps I can help you,' Lucy said. 'I can write down your

words and—' She stopped herself abruptly. 'Never mind. I imagine they are full of Latin *ipsos* and *ergos*. I can barely make sense of the Latin tracts we have to set sometimes.'

Master Hargrave patted her hand. 'I do appreciate the thought, Lucy.'

Their conversation was interrupted by Hank poking his head inside. 'Thought you might like to speak to this ruffian.'

Hank pushed Sid into the room, so that he stood at the end of the magistrate's bed, his patched grey cap held tightly in his hand. With his rumpled and dirty clothes, his arm in a makeshift sling, and his cheeks ruddy from a bit of sherry, Sid looked more like the ragamuffin she'd once known, back when he was being pelted by rancid objects in the stocks. His expression was hangdog and ashamed.

Hank nudged his good arm. 'Say it,' they heard Hank mutter.

Sid looked around the room, regaining his customary sense of defiance for just a moment, before a chagrined expression returned to his face when he looked back at the magistrate.

'I am sorry, sir,' he said, his head down. 'I should have caught the intruder. I wish I'd known that he'd struck you, sir. I'd never have given up the chase, had I known.'

'What did the man look like, Sid?' Adam asked. 'My father could not say, as he was struck in the back of his head by the cur.'

'It all happened so fast,' Sid muttered, rubbing his injured arm, now neatly bandaged. 'Slim, taller than me. Not as tall as Master Adam. He was wearing a cap. Couldn't see his hair. He was spry, though. Maybe in his twenties, I'd say. Didn't strike me as a child, I mean.'

'What was he wearing?' Adam asked. 'Could you distinguish his trade? You said he was wearing a cap – what kind of coat?'

'Grey. Serviceable, well made.' Sid rubbed his fingers together, as he tried to recall the texture. 'Finer quality. More of a gentleman's coat, I would say.'

'A gentleman-thief,' Duncan commented.

'Someone could have given him the coat,' Lucy said, thinking how she had received dresses from the Hargrave women after they were deemed no longer fit to be worn. 'From his master, perhaps.'

Adam glanced at Lucy, perhaps following her line of thought. 'Still, it is curious. The thief stole several small objects, of negligible value, while passing up several more expensive pieces. Why would he do that?'

'Perhaps, the other objects were not his focus,' Lucy replied.

'The thief wanted my papers,' Master Hargrave stated, his voice taking on its old dignified magisterial quality. 'But why?'

FOUR

Two days later, Lucy climbed atop one of the smaller barrels outside the newly built Cheshire Cheese tavern on Fleet Street and began to call her tale. 'Gather around to hear the strange news from Kent! Hear how a woman, plagued by the gossipy tongue of her mother-in-law, did take it upon herself to kill her with a poisonous brew.'

On cold, snowy days like this one, she usually did not dare venture far from the printer's shop, for fear that her bag would get caught in the slush and the books inside destroyed. Though the shop was just a little way along the street, Lucy had made sure that her bag was well stocked. The trick was to have related pieces. If she talked about a poisoning, then she also brought along some recipes, since the audience appreciated the joke. On this occasion, she'd also brought along some merriments and riddles as well. Usually, she left the merriments to Lach, because he had a far more jocular side and could sell a well-stuffed bag in a matter of minutes. The murderess from Kent had made a dreadful jest about her mother-in-law before being hanged and the story always brought about a gratified chuckle from the audience.

Within a few minutes, she had a nice crowd gathered about. She was just getting to the end of her tale, detailing how the murderess mounted the scaffold. 'She looked around and said, "It is true that I did poison my mother-in-law, in a most dreadful fashion. However—"'

'Gather round, gather round!' A man's deep, sonorous voice interrupted her. 'Let me tell you the truthful and tooth-ful story of a most barbarous murder committed on the person of Arthur Becker, a silk-man's apprentice on Milk Street, by a false tooth-drawer, one Geoffrey Knight!'

Cut short at the climax of her story, Lucy watched open-mouthed as her audience moved from around her, over to a tall man who was standing on a small crate. *What in the world?* 'Wait,' she cried. 'I did not finish my tale—'

'Sorry, lass!' a biscuit-seller said as he passed. 'I've heard that gent tell a story before. It's not one to be missed.'

Lucy put a hand to her mouth, watching the crowd push and shove each other around. Another bookseller! Infringing on her territory! Usually, they all upheld an unspoken agreement, like a code of honour among knights, where they did not directly compete with one another as they shouted their wares. Even at public hangings, where many booksellers might gather, most tried to distance themselves from each other, so as not to injure the others' coffers.

Who was this rude fellow? Lucy wondered as she hopped off the barrel. As she picked up her little tin pan for coins and dumped the contents into her hidden pocket, she kept an eye on him as the crowd around him steadily grew. Even though she wanted to stalk off and set herself up at another tavern, something compelled her to edge closer as his dramatic story began to unfold.

This bookseller was different from others of her acquaintance. Within a few weeks of starting to work for Master Aubrey, she'd learned that booksellers had to find their own ways to appeal to the crowds. Master Aubrey used his rumbling voice to great effect, assuring his audience that they would soon be privy to a shocking and sensational tale. Lach took a different approach, telling his stories with a twinkle in his eye and a grin on his lips, letting his listeners know that a belly-aching laugh was on its way. Lucy tried to tell her stories energetically, and she'd often been told that it was her own enjoyment of the story that had compelled a person to buy her piece.

This bookseller was clearly used to commanding a crowd. He cut a slim and handsome figure, and with his glib voice and practised movements, he could have been standing on a stage at the Globe Theatre or the Rose. Most surprisingly, he spoke from memory and barely glanced at the tract. '*Tooth-Puller, No Truth-Teller*,' he called. 'Here is a full and most true narrative of the barbarous murder of Becker, who, in great anguish from a rotting tooth, did seek solace from the tooth-puller Knight.' The man's voice dropped into a dramatic stage whisper, as though he was letting his audience in on a secret. 'This tooth-puller had made claims at several ale-houses to be employed as a barber-surgeon and tooth-puller, and that he would provide his service on the cheap, at the edge of London Bridge, London-side.'

Lucy watched the crowd murmur in anticipation. The way the bookseller was telling the story was masterful, she had to admit. He seemed experienced, practised – why had she never seen him before?

'Having found him,' the bookseller continued, 'Knight commanded Becker to open his mouth and did then proceed to carve out the man's tooth, removing a good portion of his tongue and cheek in the process!'

The crowd gagged good-naturedly at the image. The bookseller grinned, his handsome visage causing a few women to flutter and swoon, before he continued. 'Seeing what he had done, Knight grabbed his tools and fled, leaving the luckless Becker to die.'

Again, the crowd responded with gasps and exclamations, fully enthralled by the tale. The bookseller's voice dropped again, so that his listener could grasp the full and horrible implications of what happened next. 'The victim, thus left to die with not a tongue to tell his tale, began to careen after him, wailing.' The bookseller paused, and everyone leaned forward.

'It was then that Guy Donnett, a soap-maker, and his wife ventured by, witnesses to this sorry tale. The tooth-drawer first tried to proclaim his innocence. However, when confronted with the instruments of his unjust trade, as well as the man's blood still across his apron, Knight did eventually confess to killing the man. He then languished in Newgate for some time before his case was heard at trial. Soon after, he was duly hanged at Tyburn Tree, and order was restored.'

The crowd collectively sighed and then burst into great applause. Lucy blinked as the bookseller swept his hat from his head and bowed deeply in one elegant and graceful move. She'd never seen another bookseller do that before.

The gesture moved the crowd, and they surged forward, holding their coins in the air. 'I'll buy that one! A goodly story it was!'

Lucy stayed a few steps away, watching him distribute his tracts and pocket the coins that had been tossed into his cap. She was not the only one lingering either. A few women were still clinging together, coyly admiring his fine form.

He straightened up abruptly, catching Lucy's eye. Abashed to be caught staring, she looked away, feeling unbalanced. Ignoring the cooing women about him, he strode toward her.

She planted her hands firmly on her hips, willing herself not to feel intimidated. 'Quite a tale you told,' she said when he stopped before her.

'Thank you kindly, my dear,' he replied, amusement in his eyes. 'Sorry if I poached on your spot. I did not intend to upstage your fearful tale. Pray, forgive me. I believed you to be done when I began my sorry tale.'

Lucy let that pass. 'I was,' she said, shrugging. 'Most days, people want to hear about a murder.' She held out a copy of *Strange News*. 'Would you care to trade? I have not yet heard of this tooth-drawer's truthful tale.' Such was the courtesy among booksellers to exchange their cheap wares.

'Most certainly,' he said, accepting the tract. 'We have but a few. *The Cry of the Hangman*, which is the lament of an executioner. Here's another one that details the cabinet of curiosities by one collector of natural, artificial and mechanical objects. Here is another of the same ilk, should you like it, that catalogues a set of instructions around all manner of interesting things.'

Lucy accepted the others as well. She'd learned that 'curiosities' were often of interest to collectors and scientists, though of scarce interest to those on their way in and out of a tavern. 'I have not seen you here before,' she said, glancing at the printer's mark at the bottom of the first page. It appeared to be a phoenix coming from the ashes with an *S* to the left and an *H* to the right. 'Nor do I know this printer.'

'We are newly established,' he said. 'My master, Sam Havisham, saw his press burnt down during the Great Fire. It has taken a while to find our way back into this world, as the coins were tight and it took us some time to have a new press made.'

'Many fortunes and livelihoods were destroyed,' Lucy said, feeling an unexpected pang. What would have happened if Master Aubrey's shop had been but a little further east, or if the winds had not turned the fire back in on itself on the fateful third day? His shop and all it contained – presses, pieces, tools and all else – would have been destroyed. Where would he be? Where would *she* be?

The bookseller interrupted her pensive thoughts by giving her a courtly bow. 'Phineas Fowler at your service. Printer and seller of books.'

'Lucy Campion,' she replied, unable to stop herself from dropping a curtsey. 'I work with Horace Aubrey. I'm akin to an apprentice.'

He raised an eyebrow. 'Last I heard, the Stationers' Company was still unwilling to take on female apprentices.' He flashed her a charming grin. 'You wouldn't be lying to me, would you?'

Lucy could feel herself responding to the man's charm. 'Master Aubrey has made this request to the Stationers' Company, but they have not yet acknowledged me.' There was a small boon there, in that the Stationers' Company had been overwhelmed since their Hall was burnt down, essentially operating out of a clerk's home.

'You enjoy the trade so much?' he asked, disbelief in his voice. 'You have no husband or sweetheart who minds you speaking so?' He gestured to the barrel on which she'd stood to tell her tales.

Lucy clenched her hands. 'I have no sweetheart who would say such a thing to me,' she said. Neither man vying for her hand would dare.

'Ah! I see some fur flying. I speak only out of the concern that a woman such as yourself not be endangered. Tut, tut, don't get so upset. I shouldn't like to bring about the ire of such an enticing little thing as yourself.' He reached out for her hand before she could pull it away. 'I do hope to see you again soon.'

'I do not think that likely,' she said, stepping back. The man's flirtatious demeanour was making her feel ill at ease. 'I must now return to my duties with Master Aubrey.'

'Certainly,' he said. He then tipped his hat gallantly, as if bidding farewell to a lady of quality.

Without replying, Lucy slung her pack over her shoulder and made her way down the dirty cobblestone street.

* * *

'There's a new bookseller around,' Lucy called as she emptied out her pack on to the table in Master Aubrey's workroom. She held out the pieces she'd received from Phineas Fowler. 'Looks like a new press, too.'

Lach looked up from inking the typeface, but didn't stop in his quick, practised movements. They were about to run fifty more copies of *The Sign of the Gallows*, a piece Lucy had written about a recent murder she'd found herself caught up in, before breaking down the typeface. Though it was written by 'Anonymous', as Master Aubrey did not wish to bring unwanted attention to Lucy or his shop, Lucy still felt enormous pride in having created another true account that people wanted to hear. It would be a tender moment when the piece was broken down, each type block returned to its case, but she already had stashed away a few copies so she'd always remember the piece. If she was not mistaken, Adam and Master Hargrave had also procured copies for themselves as well, a realization that made her heart warm.

Master Aubrey came over to examine the pieces. 'I don't recognize this printer's device. What did he tell you of the publisher?'

'Just that his master's shop and press were destroyed in the Great Fire. Sam Havisham, I think he said his master's name is.'

'Sam Havisham?' Master Aubrey frowned. 'The name sounds familiar, but I am not certain I remember him. There are many who would call themselves master printers who little deserve the title. With the records burnt and the guild in disarray, I fear it shall be some time before things are put to right. Still, I hope that a goodly order can be re-established before all decorum is lost. I shall inquire at the Stationers' Company next time I am about.'

Books were supposed to be entered into the Company's entry book for review before publication, but after experiencing several long delays, it was clear that the Company's wardens were finding it hard to keep up with all the matters of the guild. They had little time to suppress unlicensed tracts, and neither the justices of the peace nor the Mayor of London viewed this as a priority. Heavens knew there were many illicit publishers printing seditious tracts against King, Parliament and Church, by any number of religious sects that tended to operate just outside the City limits. There were plans to rebuild the Hall, but the Company was in a shambles and it seemed as if anyone could print anything without fear of being disciplined by the scattered and squabbling Company.

Distantly, they heard the church bells tolling the noon hour. 'All right, let us not dwell on our rivals,' the master printer said. He pointed to the baskets containing the cold meat and bread. 'Let us eat.'

Over the meal, Lucy read *The Cry of the Hangman* to them aloud. Lach stopped chewing and Master Aubrey closed his eyes, as they listened to the strange lyrics.

There is a story behind the crimes,
And all my ropes turned to rhymes.
    I and my gallows moan.
For thirteen long years, I've taken those halfpenny wages,
Spending my days, cleaning out cages.
    I and my gallows moan.
Taking the wretched from their gaol,
Parading their sins at the carts' tail,
    I and my gallows moan.
At the hanging tree I have shown great skill,
Allowing their penance, subduing their will.
    I and my gallows moan.
In secret the accursed may pass me bribes,
Although not always enough to save their cowardly lives
    I and my gallows moan.
Excepting when
The thieves and magistrates made a truce,
Saving some criminals from the noose,
Thereby I was of no use.
    I and my gallows moan.
My helping hand there was no need,
To carry out that final deed.
Never so bad was my trade,
When justice was not full made.
    I and my gallows moan.
Though their ghastly corpses invade my sleep,
Righteous justice has been my lot to keep.
    I and my gallows moan.

'Bloodthirsty hangman,' Lach commented.

'Is he craving death?' Lucy asked, reading the ballad again to herself. '"Never so bad was my trade, when justice was not full made." Or is he lamenting that some criminals were set free? Had they not fully faced their crimes?'

Indeed, she'd heard about this very thing not so long ago, when some criminals were illegally set free from Newgate Prison during the Great Fire. Perhaps such an injustice would have been a bothersome thing to the hangman in this ballad.

'Sounds as though this hangman takes pride in his trade, scurrilous as it may be. Heaven knows, I should not like to know more about it.' Master Aubrey pushed the last few crumbs into his hand and shoved them into mouth. 'Let us get us ready for tomorrow, so that we may surpass our newest rivals.'

After they had cleared the few dishes from the table, Master Aubrey went to visit a friend, leaving Lucy and Lach to complete the printing. After they finished hanging up the pages to dry, Lach took the collections of curiosities that Phineas had given to Lucy and began to page through the catalogue of oddities.

Such catalogues were always intriguing. Most of the collections were amassed after their owners took great voyages throughout England and the Continent, and even to the mysterious Eastern countries and the New World. The collection from Phineas inventoried its objects in the common way, categorizing them as natural, artificial and man-made objects.

'I like the collections of curiosities that teach you how to do things,' Lach said, setting it aside and picking up the other catalogue they'd received from Phineas. Some catalogues did not inventory physical objects, but instead offered a collection of curious practices and rituals, as this one did. Lucy found them fascinating as well, and even kept one in her chamber for its droll depictions of courtship rituals, which she peeked at from time to time.

'What kinds of curiosities does it mention?' Lucy asked, still paging through the first one.

'You should definitely study this collection,' Lach teased.

Lucy raised an eyebrow. 'Oh?'

'It explains how to read faster. "An excellent way to teach one to read speedily, and truly, that before could not distinguish their syllables.'"

Lucy peered over his shoulder. 'I *would* like to read faster. Indeed, that is so.' Clumsily, she read out loud. '"Let a scholar, or one that can read well, make a little speck or mark in red ink and at every sentence's end, with blue ink marking hard words with many syllables. Or if it be in a book you would not deface, then take a small pin, and prick little holes at each syllable, which will hardly be perceived."' She shrugged. 'I'll try that later. See if it helps.'

'Look at this one,' Lach said, pointing to another set of instructions. '"How to write any name or mark upon a paper, and then burn it to ashes, yet afterward it may be read plainly."' He set the tract down. 'I'm going to try this one.'

'Sounds like sending a coded message,' Lucy commented, picking up the tract. Over the previous few weeks, she'd learned all about how secret messages could be sent. She looked at the next one. '"How to write secret love letters."'

As Lach got out a candle to follow the instructions, Lucy continued to look through the collection, noting how to detect a magnetized object, how a weather glass can be used to tell change in temperature. 'Here's one that Master Aubrey might appreciate,' Lucy said. '"How to fetch oil or grease out of writings, books, papers or garments." Look at this one! "A merry receipt, being a merry and sure way to catch a pickpocket."' An image of Sid arose in her mind. 'I already know how to do that.' She looked at the next one. *Better keep this from Sid*, she thought. '"How to cheat at cards."'

'Ouch!' Lach exclaimed. 'Ow, I'm on fire!'

Lucy looked up and saw that Lach's sleeve was alight. Swiftly, she pulled him over to the barrel of water that by law they were required to keep by their hearths and doused his arm in.

'Tsk, tsk!' Lucy said, pulling up his sleeve. 'Did you burn your arm? Lach! What will Master Aubrey say?' She examined his arm, noting with relief that his skin was just the slightest pink. 'I'll make you a salve of comfrey for your wound, you dreadful boy.'

'Will you also sew my shirt?' Lach asked, looking like a chastened child. 'Master Aubrey will be angry.'

'As he should be! You know how he is about fire,' Lucy scolded, moving to the kitchen to fetch the salve she'd made recently.

A few moments later, she returned with a small jar of salve. Before uncorking the jar, she held it above her head. 'You must promise me two things if I help you.'

'What is it? Anything? Just tell me!' Lach whined.

'You must do one of my tasks for me, no questions asked.'

'Fine. What's the other thing?'

'You must not write more doggerel about constables or anything similar that relates to me.'

A surprised grin crossed Lach's face. He had not anticipated this request, and she realized too late that she had just opened up to more teasing. 'Oh, I shan't pen more verses about your sweethearts; the piece I already created is already fun enough.'

'Well, you can sing that song while you are fixing the hole in your shirt. You can sing to Master Aubrey when you are trying to explain how awful you look. I won't be helping you more.' With that, Lucy turned and walked out of the room, giggling to herself over how anxious Lach likely was now. 'Serves him right.'

FIVE

'Two more murders for you,' Duncan said, popping his head into Aubrey's shop the next afternoon.

Lucy blinked as she wiped the sweat from her brow. For the last hour she had been setting a political pamphlet on her own, because Master Aubrey was taking a nap and Lach was out selling at Covent Garden. 'What? Who was murdered?'

'A soap-maker and his wife, up by Pye Corner. The wife was killed with a pair of scissors and the man had a basin full of scalding lye dumped all over his head. Happened yesterday.'

'That's quite terrible,' Lucy said, shivering at the image, even as she thought about how she might set up such a story to tell. 'Do you know who killed them? Have you made an arrest?'

'No arrest yet,' Duncan replied. Without waiting to be invited, he seated himself on one of the wooden stools at the table, propping himself up on his elbows. 'No idea who killed them either. The bodies were discovered by a neighbour, who'd been hoping to purchase some scented soap for her bath.'

Lucy sat down on a stool as well. 'Did the neighbour have any idea who had killed them?'

'No. When I enquired around, other neighbours told me they were likable enough folks. Didn't cause any trouble. I spoke to the wife's sister as well, who arrived at their home when she heard. She and the neighbours all seemed broken and shocked by the deaths.'

'A random thief perhaps.'

'No, as it turns out, nothing had been stolen. Their jar of money was still tucked away under their table, untouched,' Duncan replied.

'So, not a burglary gone wrong. You say that she was stabbed and he had lye dumped on his head,' Lucy mused, trying to imagine the scene. 'Could they have killed each other? Perhaps they had a fearful quarrel which led to such a fateful end.'

Duncan stared at her. 'I'll never stop being surprised by the things you imagine, Lucy Campion.'

She shrugged. 'Is it truly so unlikely?'

'Very improbable. They were not killed together, but rather in different rooms. He was seated at his workroom table, while she was found in the kitchen, the scissors still in her back. Both appear to have been attacked from behind, having been caught unawares. He could have stabbed her, but would someone choose to commit self-murder by dumping scalding lye over themselves?'

Lucy inclined her head. 'I should say not.'

'My sense is that the Donnetts' assailant knew them, since nothing appears to have been taken. A personal grudge perhaps. Or maybe revenge.'

'Donnett? That was their name?' Lucy frowned. 'Why is that name familiar to me?'

'Yes, Guy and Mary Donnett.' His expression grew concerned. 'Lucy, don't tell me you knew them?'

'No, I don't think I knew them. Their name is so familiar. Donnett isn't such a common name, is it? Do I know a soap-seller?' She closed her eyes.

A second later she pushed her stool back, causing it to topple to the floor.

'Lucy, what—?'

Disregarding him, Lucy picked up her peddler's pack and began to rummage through it. 'Am I remembering correctly?' She pulled out the truth-teller's tale, running her finger along the lines. Duncan watched her the whole while, wisely staying silent.

'Aha! Look at this!' she exclaimed, shaking the penny piece. 'The testimony in this tale was offered by one Guy Donnett, soap-maker.'

'What? Let me see that.'

When she didn't relinquish it, Duncan came to read over her shoulder. 'The piece was just published recently, but it describes events from several years ago,' she said. 'From before the Fire.'

'That's quite strange,' Duncan said.

'It could be a coincidence—'

'I don't like coincidences. Least not when it comes to murder.'

He pulled on his coat. 'I think I should like to speak to the family again.'

'Perfect. I will join you,' she declared. 'Let me just leave a note for Master Aubrey and fill my sack. I can sell a few pieces at Pye Corner, maybe at the White Horse Inn there.'

Duncan narrowed his eyes. 'Lucy!'

'I'm sure Master Aubrey would be very interested in this coincidence as well,' Lucy interrupted, pulling on her cloak. 'A piece related to this murder would sell in no time. Let us hurry, before it gets too dark.' Lucy had filled her pack and led him out of the door, not giving him any chance to refuse.

As Lucy walked the half mile to Pye Corner at Duncan's side, she hardly spoke. An awkwardness had arisen between them as she sought to make sense of her feelings for the constable after Adam had unexpectedly returned from the colonies. The constable had entered her life in the worst way possible a few years before, bringing news of a murdered friend. But over time, an unexpected fondness and companionship had grown up between them. At first, he'd seemed like a watchful older friend, gently warning her against hoping that she'd ever be accepted at Adam's side. Then their friendship had deepened as they'd found themselves plunged into different extraordinary circumstances, and she'd opened herself up to the possibility of accepting his love.

He's a more suitable match for you, Lucy. She knew that's what everyone believed; indeed, that thought regularly surfaced in her own mind. Despite the dampener she'd given him upon Adam's return, he'd made it clear that he'd not yet given up on her. *He sees my uncertainty*, she thought, a pang striking her. She thought too of the woman whom she'd seen once bringing him a meal in a covered pail. *But he won't wait for you forever.*

Unexpectedly, tears rose to her eyes and she angrily pushed them away.

Catching the gesture, Duncan looked down at her in concern. 'Are you all right, Lucy?'

'Just the wind in my eyes,' she replied. 'That's Cock Lane up ahead, is it not? We must be just about there.'

'That's right.' Duncan pointed at a house near the White

Horse Inn. 'The Donnetts lived just there, above their soap-
making shop.'

Unlike other stores, this shop did not have a shelf that extended
downward from a window. The shop had clearly been a home
before ever being a shop. The Donnetts must have changed it
when they moved in after the Fire.

Someone had strewn rushes in the street and hung black crepe
in the windows, signifying a person of means had chosen to
observe the traditional courtesies of mourning on behalf of the
Donnett family.

At their knock, an elderly servant clad in grey wool opened
the door of the shop, blinking in recognition at Duncan. 'You're
the constable from yesterday,' she said.

'Yes, we had some questions for your mistress,' he replied.

'Wait here, sir. I shall let her know.'

The servant disappeared. Lucy leaned up to whisper in
Duncan's ear. 'The mistress?'

'Mistress Donnett's younger sister. Mrs Bainbridge,' he whispered back. 'I met her yesterday when I made my initial enquiries.
That woman is her attendant. She did not serve the Donnetts.'

'I see. Did the Donnetts not have a servant of their own?'
Lucy asked. That suggested that the Donnetts had not been a
family of means.

'It seems not.'

A moment later, the servant returned. 'Pray, come with me.
Mrs Bainbridge will see you in the sitting room.' She then
proceeded to lead them through the shop, and then into the soap-
maker's workroom. Lucy shuddered as she breathed in the sharp
aroma of lye that still lingered in the air. *This is where Mr Donnett
died*, she thought. A curious thought struck her as they passed
through the workroom. *How hard would it have been to walk in
with a scalding bucket of lye?*

They entered a small sitting room and the servant gestured to
two hard wooden chairs. A woman in her mid-thirties entered the
room from the kitchen, dressed in deep mourning. Her face was
pale and drawn, and her eyes were pink-rimmed from tears.

'Constable Duncan,' she said, glancing curiously at Lucy. 'I
did not expect to see you again. Have you discovered who killed
my sister and her husband?'

'Mrs Bainbridge, thank you for your time. This is Lucy Campion,' he replied, smoothly passing over the gap in Lucy's introduction. 'No, I'm afraid I have not discovered the identity of the killer. However, a matter has come to my attention and I should very much like your thoughts.'

The woman stiffened slightly. 'What is it?'

'I have just recently learned that your brother-in-law and your sister once testified in court during a manslaughter trial. Is that so?'

Mrs Bainbridge sucked in her breath. Clearly, this was not what she'd been expecting. 'The tooth-puller? Wasn't he hanged for his crime?'

'Yes, I believe he was. Can you tell us about it?'

'Not much to say, really. It took place a few years ago, down by London Bridge. We all lived there then, you understand. This was before the Great Fire.' She swallowed. 'I can still recall how my dear sister came to me in tears, telling me how they'd sought out the services of a tooth-puller, on account of her wisdom tooth giving her great pain. They'd heard tell of a man who promised he could do it cheaply.'

Mrs Bainbridge studied her hands. 'When they arrived at the agreed-upon location, the tooth-puller came rushing past them, stuffing tools in his pocket, and reeling as if he'd been well into his cups. There, they saw a man, butchered in the mouth and in deep agony. My brother-in-law, swift of foot and mind, did discern what had happened and tripped the tooth-puller before he could run past us. My brother-in-law then hailed the constable, even as the luckless sot bled to death before their eyes.'

She swallowed again. 'Quite disturbing for my poor sister, I must say. At the trial, we learned that this tooth-puller was a fraud, and that he'd butchered more than one other that day. Unsteady of hand and quick to the drink. The trade, it seemed, was not his own but that of his brother, who had been a barber-surgeon at sea.'

'I see,' Duncan replied, watching the woman closely.

Mrs Bainbridge looked heavenward, blinking back tears. 'My sister and her husband did fulfil their duty, by testifying at that barbarian's trial.'

'Did anyone ever say anything to your sister?' Lucy asked. 'Threaten her for testifying? One of the tooth-puller's kin perhaps? Or a friend?'

'No.' Mrs Bainbridge wiped her eyes. 'I accompanied my sister to the trial and the hanging. The illicit tooth-puller had no one to speak on his behalf. I took that to mean that he had no supporters among his own family. I imagine they were aggrieved that he had besmirched his brother's name.'

Lucy and the constable exchanged a glance. It seemed unlikely, then, that a member of the tooth-puller's family had a grudge against the Donnetts if none sought to support the man during the trial or at his execution. She decided to change tactics. 'Your sister sounds like a good upright woman,' Lucy said, watching Mrs Bainbridge's face closely. She'd learned over time that those closest to the victims were often those most likely to have committed the crime. 'Who might have done such a dreadful thing? Did someone have a grudge against them? A neighbour perhaps? A rival in the soap-making trade?'

'I cannot think of anyone who would hold such a terrible grudge. My sister never mentioned any troubles she might have been having, and I believe she would have told me. They both worked hard, making the soaps that he would sell. It was indeed hard after the Great Fire destroyed their property. I asked why they had set up their home and shop so far away from others, but they said they liked it here.' She pursed her lips.

'You didn't agree with their decision?' Lucy asked.

Mrs Bainbridge stamped her foot. 'Her dratted husband took her away. My sister hardly knows these neighbours; they scarcely gave her the time of day. And travelling so much!' She frowned. 'I never liked that he married her outside the Fleet Prison, instead of at a church. I thought maybe she had a babe on the way when they wed, but she swore she didn't. Indeed, it would have been different if the good Lord had seen fit to bless them with a child, but alas, that was not meant to be.' She sighed. 'He was, despite some faults, a good man and a good husband. He never blamed her for not giving them a child. Not every man would be so patient, I can assure you.'

Lucy looked around. 'Your sister was in the kitchen when she was . . . er, when the terrible event occurred?'

'Yes, it was clear she'd been preparing the meal. She'd told me all about her plans. She'd confided that she'd spent more money than she ought on the beef.' Her voice trembled. 'They didn't even get to eat it.' Her face blanched, big tears welling up in her eyes. 'What am I to do now?' she asked, beginning to wail.

The old servant, who must have been listening at the door, rushed in with a soothing hot drink. 'I think it would be best if you leave now,' she murmured to them after pressing the drink into Mrs Bainbridge's hands. 'The mistress is nearly beside herself with grief.'

They stood up to go, and Mrs Bainbridge caught Duncan's hand. 'Please, find out who killed my dear sister! I shall not sleep until I know.'

'I promise to do my best,' he said, abruptly striding out of the house.

'Duncan, what's the matter?' Lucy called once they were back out on the street. 'You're walking so fast.'

He slowed down to let her catch up but didn't stop completely. 'I don't like this. I believe Mrs Bainbridge truly wants her sister's murderer to be found, but I don't see a clear connection here. Certainly, if the Donnetts' murders had something to do with the tooth-puller's hanging, and the testimony that they provided, I do not see it.' He scratched his head. 'I don't like the coincidence, though. I can say that much.'

'I don't see a connection either. Why *would* someone kill witnesses so long after the trial and execution? What good would it do now? Although . . .' She paused to pick up her skirts to step over a fresh pile of manure. 'Could it be that the Donnetts' names had not been known until the tract was published? That the murderer had not known their names until now?'

'A long-awaited act of revenge? That would certainly point to someone in the tooth-puller's family,' Duncan replied.

'You did say the murders seemed personal.'

'That's true.' He clicked his tongue. 'I suppose it would do no harm to speak to the tooth-puller's family.'

'Will it be hard to track down the family now?' Lucy pulled the tract out. 'Here it says the tooth-puller was late of Miltford Lane.'

'That area was not burnt in the Fire. The family may still be around.'

A sudden gale caused Lucy to pull her cloak tighter. She looked up at the darkening sky. Although the church bells had not yet tolled three o'clock, the sun was rapidly disappearing. A rainstorm was clearly looming. 'I'd better head back,' she said, shifting her heavy pack to her other shoulder. Though disappointed, she could not chance the books and papers being ruined in the rain.

Duncan pulled her hood more fully over her face. 'Yes, hurry back. I should hate for you to catch a chill.'

The tenderness in his voice brought a lump to Lucy's throat. She stepped back and he coughed, the gentle moment ended.

'Well, I'll be off, then,' he said. Abruptly, he turned on his heal, leaving Lucy to stare after him, a confused sadness rising in her heart.

SIX

'I was asked to visit Master Hargrave,' Lucy said when Annie opened the kitchen door the next morning. When she'd returned from the Donnetts' home the previous afternoon, she'd found a note from Adam inviting her to come around when she had a chance. Today, she'd flown through her morning duties and received a grudging consent from Master Aubrey to let her visit the magistrate.

'He'll feel a bit brighter seeing you, Lucy,' Cook replied, as she poured some steaming mead into a mug. 'Pray take him this and tell him some of your stories. That will surely help ease his aching head.'

Lucy tapped on the door to Master Hargrave's study and entered when she heard his assent.

'Ah, Lucy!' he exclaimed. 'I was expecting Annie. Thank you, you may place the mead here.'

'How are you feeling, sir?' Lucy asked, studying him anxiously after she set the cup in front of him. His face seemed more drawn as he rubbed the back of his head ruefully.

'Still got a bit of a lump back there, which is tender to the touch, but I am well and have not been so nauseous.' He pointed to the chess board. 'Sit, sit, Lucy. I fear I've neglected your instruction in this game.'

'Oh, Master Hargrave, sir, do not bother yourself.' Still, she sat at the table and began to set up the pieces. Smiling, she added, 'I suppose this might be the only time you may be less on your guard.'

'We shall see. Do you remember what we discussed the last time?'

'Yes, sir,' Lucy said, moving one of her middle pawns two spots forward. Their play continued for a few minutes, Master Hargrave nodding approvingly.

As she hesitated over her next move, he asked, 'What have you been doing with yourself lately, Lucy? Tell me one of your stories. Yes, you were correct not to move your bishop just now. You would have exposed your flank.'

She moved another pawn instead. 'Well, as it happens, I did learn of two murders yesterday. I even spoke to the sister-in-law of one of the victims about what had occurred.'

'How exciting! Tell me, how did such a thing come to pass?'

Lucy recounted what Duncan had told her about the Donnetts' death. 'There was an interesting coincidence,' she said, pulling *Tooth-Puller, No Truth-Teller* from her pack to show him. Quickly, she narrated the story of the tooth-puller and how the Donnetts had provided testimony against him in court.

'A tooth-puller who committed manslaughter,' he repeated, tapping the arm of his chair. Abruptly, he pushed the chair back and stood up. 'Can it be?'

'Sir? What is it?'

He began to pace around. 'Well, this may be another coincidence – or perhaps not. I believe I attended that tooth-puller's trial.'

'Oh!' Lucy said. 'How astonishing!'

'Not as the presiding judge, you understand, but simply because I'd been gathering my thoughts around our jurisprudence related to manslaughter. I wished to review Matthew Hale's understanding of the concept and I thought this case would be a good one for which to provide commentary.'

'It makes sense you'd be familiar with the tooth-puller's trial, then.'

'That is so. However, my attendance at the trial is not the coincidence that worries me.' He moved over to his desk. 'You see, my commentary on that case was among the papers stolen from me on Sunday morning.'

The image of Phineas Fowler emerged in her thoughts. 'This piece was just printed,' she said slowly. 'Did the thief sell the story to the printers?'

The magistrate scratched his chin as he reviewed the piece. 'That we do not know, though it may be surmised to be so. I can already see that some of these phrasings draw clearly from observations I recorded during the trial.'

'Perhaps the thief sold them to the printer when he realized they had no other value.'

'Perhaps,' Master Hargrave replied. 'Or they were stolen deliberately. At this point, we cannot exclude either the printer or the bookseller you met from this criminal act.' He tapped the bottom of the page, pointing to the printer's mark. 'A phoenix from the ashes. Do you know this printer, Lucy?'

'Mr Fowler told me that his master's press had been destroyed in the Great Fire, and they'd only recently begun printing again. Said his master's name was Sam Havisham. Master Aubrey thought the name sounded familiar.'

'Hence the initials. *S.H.* I see. Not a rogue printer, then.'

'It does not appear to be so, no.'

'This is all quite troubling, Lucy. The notes that were stolen from me not only contain thorough descriptions of the trials, but my personal analyses and conjectures. They are not meant for others to view in their current state, and I am deeply concerned about the consequences of being displayed in this way.'

'I am sorry, sir. Let me inform the constable.'

'In due course.' He handed the penny piece back to Lucy. 'While I am troubled to think that someone might illicitly publish, and profit from, my unvarnished thoughts, I am far more troubled that the Donnetts were murdered so soon after the publication of this piece. What can we make of that?'

'I don't know, sir. The neighbours said they could not imagine anyone who would hold a grudge against such a quiet God-fearing couple. There was no theft involved.' She chewed her lip. 'Besides, Duncan thought the crime seemed personal, not a random attack.'

'Personal?'

'Yes, we thought perhaps one of the tooth-puller's friends or relatives was angry at the Donnetts for providing testimony. Yet Mrs Donnett's sister said no one had expressed any support for the man.'

'That is her say-so.'

'I agree, sir. However, I cannot see a reason for her to lie about such a thing. I believe Duncan plans to track down the tooth-puller's family and see if anyone held a grudge against the Donnetts.'

'That would be a prudent and logical course of action,' the magistrate said, sitting back down.

'We must also locate the bookseller,' Lucy said, feeling heated. 'Demand he tell us where he got the story.'

The magistrate looked alarmed. 'Lucy, you must not follow through on such an endeavour yourself. This is a task for the constable.'

'What is for the constable?' Adam asked, entering the study. 'Good morning, Lucy.'

'Good morning,' Lucy replied, feeling the faintest flush rising in her cheeks. Quickly, she explained what had happened to the Donnetts and handed him the tract detailing their murders. 'It appears that much of this account was drawn from your father's stolen notes.'

Raising one eyebrow, Adam looked to his father, who nodded in confirmation. 'Did the thief steal your notes on purpose, or did he give them to Sam Havisham's shop when he realized what he had stolen?'

'I believe Master Aubrey thought he might enquire about him at the Stationers' Company,' Lucy said. 'He thought he'd be able to discover the printer's whereabouts. Surely the guild would be aware of such things. Then perhaps we can learn how he acquired your notes. I will remind him to do so.' She stood up then. 'I do need to take my leave, sir. I have much to do today.'

'I will walk you out, Lucy,' Adam said, and they walked out of the house together.

When she had pulled on her cloak and faced the chill air, he lightly touched her upper arm. 'Lucy, I can tell you are up to something. Pray tell me you are not planning to seek the printer out on your own.'

'No, I won't do that,' she promised, warmed by his concern. *At least not right now*, she added to herself.

When she reached Fleet Street, she saw a familiar figure walking ahead of her. 'Master Aubrey!' she called, breathlessly catching up with her master. 'Where are you going? I must speak with you.'

'I've some books to deliver,' he said, pointing to his heavy sack. 'Seems my more wayward apprentice has been gone longer than I expected.' Then the twinkle disappeared from his eye. 'Tell me, has Master Hargrave improved?'

'He is much better.' Then she quickly explained everything she had learned about the tooth-puller's tract.

'I truly do not know how you so regularly unearth such mysterious doings,' he said, sighing. 'That is all quite suspicious indeed.' He handed her the sack, giving her an address. 'You may take them in my stead.'

Lucy accepted the sack. 'Oh, I know the place you mean. I have delivered to him before. Master Aubrey, where are you going?'

'I shall go to make inquiries at the Stationers' Company about the printer and the bookseller you met. I'll see what I can discover. Perhaps they'll have the address of the printer's shop.' Then he put his hand to his mouth in a joking aside. 'I promise you. I shall shake the information out of the clerk, if necessary. Then we can find out once and for all how Havisham received the magistrate's private papers.'

Unexpectedly, Lucy caught Master Aubrey's hand and gave it a squeeze. 'Thank you, sir!'

He waved her off. 'Go on with you now. Deliver those materials intact; that's all I ask of you. Don't get into any trouble.'

'Of course not, sir. You know me.'

As soon as Master Aubrey was out of sight, Lucy turned around and walked over to Duncan's gaol. 'I've learned something more about that tooth-puller's account,' she said.

Duncan and Hank looked up from their bread and meat.

'That account came from the magistrate's personal papers.' Quickly, she filled them on the knowledge she'd gleaned as they finished their meal, letting them know that Master Aubrey was going to make inquiries at the Stationers' Company, to see if he could acquire an address for Sam Havisham's print shop.

'That's good,' Duncan said. He glanced at her pack. 'Where are you off to today?'

'Covent Garden. I have a few books to deliver. Why?'

'I heard tell that the tooth-puller's brother, Knight, is now doing his business down by the docks. I'm going there now to see if I can learn anything new.'

'Makes sense that he would set up his shop there,' Lucy mused. 'With such a location, they can ensure trade from the sailors and merchants who've been away, where there are taverns nearby to ease the pain afterwards.' She looked up at him. 'Let me come with you. I can make this delivery along the way and sell the other pieces by The Sparrow. I promised Mr McDaniels, the innkeeper there, that I'd soon return.'

He looked at her curiously. 'Why do you want to accompany me, Lucy?'

'I suppose I am curious. I imagine, too, that Master Aubrey might ask me to write a piece about these murders. The more information I have, and the less I have to invent, the better.'

He gave her a rueful grin. 'It is good to know that I can still get you to accompany me in pursuit of a good story.'

'Well, truth will out,' she replied.

'Indeed,' he said, but did not say anything more after that.

Her delivery made, Lucy and Duncan stood a short distance from The Sparrow, near the Embankment. Everything was bustling and noisy, a far cry from Sunday afternoon when she'd been there last. She looked at the signs overhanging the shops.

'He may not be so likely to advertise in such a way,' Lucy said. She pointed to some playbills that had been posted to a wall, most torn and half shredded from the elements. 'Why invest in a sign when you may need to switch locations quickly? People with aching teeth will learn from their neighbours where to find him.'

'By word of mouth,' Duncan agreed with a wry chuckle.

Lucy rolled her eyes at his unexpected pun. 'Why do I feel I am suddenly accompanied by Lach?' She smiled back at him, relieved that the air had lightened between them. Then she nudged Duncan. 'Look at that woman,' she whispered.

A woman in a grey cloak was stumbling towards them, a red-stained cloth pressed to her mouth.

'Excuse me, miss,' Lucy called. 'Have you perchance been to the tooth-puller? Mr Knight? Might you tell me where to find him?'

The woman, pale and haggard with red-rimmed eyes, pointed backwards. 'Behind the scissor-seller's stall,' she mumbled, her words muffled by the cloth. 'Back there a few steps.'

Lucy and Duncan stepped into the darkened shop. The front

room seemed to be full of scissors and knives, and an old man with spectacles was sitting before a whetstone sharpening a metal instrument. 'Looking for some scissors?' he asked, barely glancing away from his work.

'The tooth-puller,' Duncan replied. 'Knight.'

A woman appeared from the back room and looked them over. 'My husband is with a patient right now.' As if on cue, they could hear a man groaning from the back room. 'It should not take too long if you'd care to wait. Neither of you seems to be in much pain, so the matter does not seem to be so urgent.'

Lucy and Duncan looked around the shop, trying not to be disturbed by the man's moans of pain, although they grew harder to ignore.

Lucy nudged Duncan, pointing at the shelves. 'Scissors,' she whispered. 'Wasn't that how Mrs Donnett was killed?'

Duncan shrugged. 'Many people own scissors. I own a pair myself.'

They continued to try to ignore the anguished screams. Finally, the man uttered one ear-splitting scream and fell silent.

'Is he all right?' Lucy asked the man who had never stopped sharpening his tools.

'Probably passed out.' The man shrugged, then gave her a wicked grin. 'I'm guessing he didn't die. Most survive.'

Lucy ran her fingers over her skirts, uncertain if the man was jesting with her. Duncan did not seem certain either. 'What happens to those who don't survive?'

The old man was kept from replying when the tooth-puller's wife re-joined them. 'My husband said you can come back if you are ready. He's just having a bit of ale right now.'

Lucy followed Duncan into the back room, her stomach recoiling at the sight before her. In the middle of the room was an empty chair with a small table beside it, full of sharp instruments and bloodied bandages. In the corner, a man huddled on a straw pallet, a clenched fist pressed against his face. With his other hand, he was attempting to gulp from a large mug, although the contents were spilling out. He was whimpering, and she could see tears in his eyes.

'Easy there.' On the other side of the room, another man sat slumped on a pillow in the corner of the room. 'Don't waste all my whiskey, will you?'

Mrs Knight bustled past them, picking up bloody bandages and blankets into a straw basket. 'Husband, they want to see you.' She went over to the man on the pallet. 'Time to finish your drink and go on your merry way.'

'What ails you?' Mr Knight said, taking a deep swallow from his mug. 'I hope it's none too hard. I had to pull five teeth just now, and I'm aiming to nap a spell. If it's a quick pull, I can take care of it soon. I haven't had too much whiskey.'

Duncan introduced himself. 'I wanted to ask you about your brother who was hanged for murder two years back.'

The tooth-puller spat on the floor. 'I have nothing to say about that rogue.'

His wife spat too, this one more in the direction of Duncan's shoes. 'Stole my husband's livelihood and nearly took our reputation, too. We had to renounce his brother as a quack!' She shook her fist. 'He's gone now, with the dear Lord in Heaven, I can only hope. His last dying confession was full of remorse, but whether it was remorse at taking a man's life or because he was caught, I was never truly certain. He could be enduring the wages of sin as we speak.'

'Renounced him as a quack?' Lucy asked, seizing on the first part of the woman's speech. Without looking at Duncan, she pushed a coin across the table. 'What happened? I'm curious.'

Mrs Knight took the coin and nodded at her husband, who was still mopping his flushed forehead.

'I'd had too much to drink that day,' Knight said. 'I decided it wouldn't be right to handle the instruments. I don't mind a nip here and there to keep me steady – Lord knows, the work can be dreadful.' He took a long drink to emphasize his point. 'Yet I knew I was too deep in my cups to do right by my patients. A slip of the knife will happen, especially if a person is flailing about or shrieking in pain, but I should have hated to cut out a man's tongue or slice open his jaw, unnecessarily.'

Lucy grimaced, imagining what that would look like. She'd never yet experienced tooth pain severe enough to require a tooth-puller, and she hoped she never would.

Knight set his handkerchief aside. 'My brother, who'd lived

through Cromwell's wars, didn't see it that way. Said we'd lose too much money if we took the day off. He told me that plenty of times he'd seen the barber-surgeons tend to teeth and limbs after several rounds of the spirits. I told him I wouldn't do it, and I thought that was that. My wife and I went home to sleep off the tippling down we'd done.' He sighed. 'To my everlasting regret, I gave my brother a key to the place.' He wiped his forehead again.

Duncan pressed him. 'Go on. What happened next?'

'He did not use my shop for his nefarious doings. I suppose I should be grateful for that. Instead, he stole many of my tools and set up his own dirty shop down by London Bridge. He believed I'd not find out that he'd planned to play the role of tooth-puller in my absence.'

Mrs Knight cursed. 'He damaged two of our best pelicans, too.'

'Pelicans?' Lucy asked. 'Whatever do you mean?'

The woman gestured towards a metal object that resembled a pair of blunt scissors; the curved top part resembled a beak. Lucy had seen pictures of the bird before, in books, though had never seen one for herself.

'I'm sorry that my brother came to such an end, but he brought it on himself. We almost lost our business, though, because I paid the victim's family a goodly sum. That man even had a baby on the way. His wife was so pitiful at the trial.' Mr Knight sighed and wiped a tear. 'My brother lived a fool's life and deserved the fool's end he got.'

'You showed him mercy in the end,' his wife reminded him. To the others, she explained. 'My husband bribed the executioner to add weights to his brother's feet so that he would not suffer for long.'

Lucy's stomach lurched. Bribing the hangman was a common enough practice, given how long it could take a person to die from hanging, even with a broken neck. She put the image from her mind. 'Jack Ketch, I assume?' she asked, naming the famous executioner who'd appeared in many true accounts. For the last few years, Ketch had overseen most of the executions at Tyburn Tree, his notorious bumbling all but ensuring that families of the condemned would pay him the extra bit to keep their loved one from an agonizing and humiliating end.

'No, it was another hangman,' Mr Knight replied. 'Odd thing, though. The day before my brother was to be executed, he came to visit him in his cell at Newgate. I was there, praying at my brother's side. He said he could ensure that my brother died quickly and with little pain. I assumed he wanted some shillings, which I had already set aside. But he didn't want money. He wanted something else.'

'What did he want?' Duncan asked.

'He asked for a pelican.' Mr Knight pointed to the bloodied instrument in the tray. 'Like that one.'

'How peculiar,' Lucy said. 'Did he say why?'

'No and I didn't ask. Thought we were getting off easy. I slipped it to him the next day, while we waited for my brother's cart to arrive. And he delivered, too. My brother uttered just one terrible squawk before he dropped, and death was quick. The crowds booed but I was grateful.' His eyes drifted to a beam on the ceiling, and he mouthed a small prayer. Then he looked back at Duncan and Lucy. 'Now tell me. Why are you asking about my brother after all this time?'

'Two witnesses in your brother's trial were recently murdered,' Duncan said. 'Guy and Mary Donnett. They were the soap-sellers who encountered your brother's victim before he bled to death.'

Mrs Knight closed her eyes. 'Dear Lord, I pray that you protect their souls. I remember how brave they were during the trial.'

'Who killed them?' Mr Knight asked.

'I don't know yet,' Duncan replied. He pulled out a copy of the *Tooth-Puller, No Truth-Teller* tract. Mr Knight flinched when he read the title. 'Have you read this piece?'

'No and I don't want to.'

'This tract was just published,' Duncan continued. 'Within a few days, the main witnesses in the trial were murdered. Such a coincidence is not to my liking.'

The Knights looked puzzled. 'As far as I'm concerned,' Mr Knight said, 'my brother got what he deserved. I am heartfelt sorry for what he did to that man he killed, and I never objected to his punishment.' He swallowed. 'I never objected to the soap-sellers' testimony either – neither did anyone else we know. If anything, their testimony sadly confirmed what I have known for a very long time. My brother – God rest his soul – took the most terrible advantage of people and lacked the skill to relieve them of their pain. He was a good-for-nothing. I still believe, as I did back then, my brother deserved to be hanged for his crimes, and I never gainsaid the soap-makers' testimony.'

'Please go,' Mrs Knight whispered. 'We have tried hard to put that dreadful time behind us. The soap-sellers' deaths, while tragic, have nothing to do with us.'

Stepping back into the bustling street, Duncan and Lucy were both silent for a moment, trying to make sense of what they'd just heard.

'I believe them,' Lucy ventured. 'What would they gain from killing the Donnetts now? They seem to have restored their livelihood and reconciled to their brother's execution. They seemed to be speaking truly when they said they should prefer to keep the past dead and buried.'

'I agree,' Duncan said as he kicked aside a broken wheel lying in their path. 'Now, alas, I do not know how to find the truth.'

SEVEN

'Drat!' Lucy muttered, kicking the press for the third time that morning. Ink had been spooling on to the wooden floor, and she'd already ruined the first run of the broadside she and Lach had set yesterday. She chewed her lip as she worked to ensure that all the type was inked. Unlike most of their tracts, this piece had been commissioned by a group of unhappy citizens who were demanding that the authorities commit to completing rebuilding the areas of the City ravaged by the Great Fire. For months, officials had been warring about how best to finish rebuilding, and this petition, called *To the King, Parliament and Mayor – It is a Just and Notable Time to Rebuild our City*, was designed to persuade the authorities. They wouldn't be selling the petitions themselves but were expected to print and deliver fifty copies in the morning.

'Stupid Lach,' she said, kicking the press again. He was lucky to be out selling instead of dealing with the temperamental printing press, and he probably wouldn't be back until after lunch. 'I'm likely to be printing these into the evening,' she grumbled to herself.

Carefully, she laid another sheet of paper atop the inked type-face and, holding her breath, rolled the top of the press down. This was the challenging part. Press down hard enough so that all the letters made an impression, but not so hard as to overfill the text and make the words illegible.

Unexpectedly, however, the apprentice strolled in through the shop door, his face as ruddy as his hair. 'Sold all my pack,' Lach crowed. His pack had been mostly full of verses and merriments, which usually got the crowds good-humoured and ready to buy. Still, it was impressive and Master Aubrey would certainly be pleased. When she just shrugged, he peered down at the press. 'Looks like you haven't made much progress at all.'

'The stupid press keeps leaking,' Lucy snapped. 'How about you help me figure out what the problem is?'

'Nah, I'm tired.' He sat down on the bench in the corner and leaned down to pick up the stone jar that Master Aubrey kept covered with a cloth. 'Saw the new fellow today,' he commented, pulling out the purse he kept hidden under his shirt. 'The bookseller.'

'You mean Phineas Fowler?' Lucy exclaimed, setting down the ink ball. 'Where did you see him?'

Lach raised his eyebrow at the sudden barrage of questions. 'Why so interested? I knew that your head would turn at the sight of a handsome fellow, but now you're going willy-nilly after this one, too! Whatever would Master Adam say? Or the constable for that matter?'

'Stop teasing!' she demanded, cuffing his arm lightly. 'Tell me where you saw the bookseller. Quickly!'

'Tut tut, such violence,' he said, rubbing his arm. 'I'll tell you in a moment.' He opened his purse and uncorked the jar, and then, with painstaking slowness, emptied all the coins inside. He looked pleased as he listened to the plunk-plunking they made as they bounced against each other and against the stone. 'Yes, I dare say Master Aubrey will be quite happy with my take.'

Lucy crossed her arms and began tapping her foot. 'Cease this dilly-dallying. Speak, Lach.'

'All right!' he exclaimed, setting the jar on the ground with a loud thud. 'I saw Fowler over by The Three Geese alehouse, having a pint. He invited me to join him, so I did. I also traded him a few of ours for his new piece.'

'Is he still there?'

'Doubt it. He left when I did. No, I don't know where he went.'

'Did he say where their press is located?'

Lach shook his head. 'Didn't ask.'

'Oh, Lach. Why didn't you? Don't you remember what Master Aubrey told us last night at supper? About how the Stationers' Company only had a record of Master Havisham's press from before the Great Fire? He had no apprentices listed either.' Lucy wanted to shake him. 'Honestly! Have you completely lost your wits? We thought it was odd that they were selling books without being licensed.'

'I guess I wasn't paying attention,' Lach mumbled, looking a bit sheepish. 'Fowler seemed a good enough fellow. Even paid for my pint.'

With a sigh, Lucy realized that the conversation was going nowhere. She decided to change tactics. 'Show me the piece he gave you,' she ordered.

'Why should I?'

'Because Phineas received that other tract from Master Hargrave's assailant. We don't know if he knew the *Tooth-Puller's Tale* was stolen from the magistrate's personal papers, but I'm not certain that I can give him the benefit of the doubt.'

To her surprise, Lach hung his head. 'I suppose that's true.' Sheepishly, he handed her a simple folded four-page tract, which she then smoothed out.

She read the title, stumbling over the Latin pronunciation. '*Digitus Dei*.' She then read the lengthy subtitle that followed. '*Or a Treacherous Murder, Strangely Detected, by a pointing finger. Wherein the suspicion, apprehending, arraignment, trial, confession and execution of Ruth Owen, late of Charing Cross, for poisoning her employer, the widowed gentlewoman Mrs Joan Jennings.*'

'Ah, the corpse's pointing finger,' Lach said. 'Why do killers never understand that their victim's body will accuse them, even after death?'

Lucy began to pore over the piece. 'With much lamenting, the victim's grown children described the woes and pitiful cries of their mother as she died, following much retching and paroxysm of the stomach. Ugh, sounds painful.' Lucy continued to peruse the story, sometimes reading a passage out loud. '"Suspecting that their mother's maid, one Ruth Owen, harboured ill will against their mother, and seeing how their mother had grown steadily sicker over a span of three months, they did demand an inquest upon her death."'

'No need to read it to me. I've already read it,' Lach said, moving toward the kitchen. 'I shall see what the larder yields for our noon meal today.'

Lucy stuck her tongue out at him and continued to read silently. The inquest revealed that the elderly woman had indeed died of poison. The murderess, her servant Ruth Owen, had hoped to receive a goodly bequest upon her employer's death. Owen did not acknowledge guilt until she'd spent several days at Newgate, and then she broke down in confession when queried by the presiding judge.

A few minutes later, Lach stepped back into the shop, wiping the crumbs from his mouth. He'd already eaten his share of bread and cheese. 'You're still reading?' he asked in mock surprise, poking her shoulder with his index finger. 'Honestly, you need to practise that trick for reading faster.'

She batted him away, still reading the tract under her breath. The last bit was far more hard-going than it had begun, surprisingly ending with a summation of the law surrounding confessions and planned murder. There was a question about the legality of a coerced confession, which she read aloud. '"How can we know that such a confession is true and good, if the accused was deprived of the basic necessities while in Newgate?"' A good question, to be sure. She returned to reading out loud, ignoring Lach's exaggerated sighs. '"Such is the question of a so-called noted magistrate, whom we shall simply refer to as T.H."'

T.H. Lucy froze. '"A so-called noted magistrate?" T.H.?' She stared at the paper. 'Thomas Hargrave? Could this tale be another piece stolen from his private collection?' She ran her finger over the lines, continuing to read. '"Surely, though, T.H.'s opinion surely runs counter to what other learned justices have said. Perhaps T.H. is but a quack?"'

A flush of indignation washed over her. 'How dare they refer to Master Hargrave in such a way?' Crumpling the tract in her hand, she stood up. 'I must show this to Master Hargrave at once.'

Lach pointed at the stack of blank paper beside the printing press. 'We need to finish printing the petition first.' He opened the press and picked up the inking ball. 'Let us begin.'

Over the next four hours, Lucy and Lach worked tirelessly to print out fifty acceptable petitions. They had a good rhythm going that Master Aubrey even remarked upon when he saw them. 'Such diligence,' he said, looking at them both sceptically. 'Why are you two working so well together?'

They both shrugged at the same time but didn't reply. Master Aubrey continued to watch them, his brows furrowed. 'I tell you, it's strange to see you acting thus. Has a demon possessed one of you?'

They both exclaimed at the same time, pointing to the other.

'Her!'

'Him!'

When Master Aubrey sat down with a tankard of ale, Lucy brought him *Digitus Dei.*

'Let me show you something,' she said, pointing to the section that discussed *T.H.* 'I think the author is referring to Master Hargrave.'

Master Aubrey read the section, frowning. 'It does seem that someone has an axe to grind against the magistrate,' he replied. 'Why speak of him in such a fashion?'

'Sir, I must share this with him. He needs to see this. The petitions are all finished.'

'Supper first,' Master Aubrey said sternly.

'Yes, sir.'

Lucy raced through the rest of her chores and preparing their evening meal. Only after the dishes had been cleared did Master Aubrey wearily wave Lucy off. 'You are free to see the Hargraves,' he said. As she walked out of the door, she heard him mutter, 'As if I could stop that girl anyway.'

Thankfully, the evening curfew had been lifted, as had the rule on carrying lanterns, so Lucy was able to make her way through the streets fairly quickly, slipping a little in the slushy snow left from the morning's dusting. Skirts still in hand, she burst into the Hargraves' kitchen a few minutes later, startling Cook as she pulled a savoury pie from the oven.

'Lucy! What in the world?'

'I've no time to explain,' she said, taking off her cloak and hanging it on a peg. 'Is Master Hargrave in? I must speak to him at once.'

'Well, yes, but—'

Lucy was already halfway down the corridor leading to the magistrate's study. She reached for the doorknob, about to push her way in, when years of training pulled her up short. She straightened her cap and smoothed her skirts, and then, taking a deep breath, she knocked on the door in her customary way.

Adam opened the door. 'Lucy? What's wrong? What are you doing here?'

Master Hargrave was sitting at his small table, a mug of mead in front of him. They'd evidently been enjoying a quiet conversation before she'd entered. He looked up at her, his careworn face appearing troubled. 'Lucy?'

She placed *Digitus Dei* in front of the magistrate. 'Master Hargrave, this tale – is it another from your personal papers?'

Frowning, the magistrate returned his spectacles to his nose while Adam leaned in over his shoulder.

The magistrate read the subtitle. '*Wherein the suspicion, apprehending, arraignment, trial, confession and execution of Ruth Owen, late of Charing Cross, for poisoning the widowed gentlewoman Mrs Joan Jennings.*' He stopped reading. 'Hmm . . . A servant poisoning her employer in Covent Garden? What of those surnames. Owen? Jennings? Indeed, they do strike me as familiar.' He looked up at Lucy. 'What has put you in such a state, my dear?'

Lucy opened the true account to the third page, pointing to the commentary from the author about the 'so-called notable' magistrate with the initials T.H. 'I think . . .' she faltered, unable to finish the thought.

Master Hargrave patted her hand. 'Never you mind, Lucy. I understand what it is you do not wish to say.'

'Preposterous!' Adam said, his eyes running over the piece. He pounded his fist on the table in a rare outward display of anger. 'How could he call you such a thing?'

'A quack?' the magistrate commented, now reviewing the last few pages with a furrowed brow. 'I have no illusion that this is the first time I have been called such a thing, and most likely worse, by the criminals I condemned.'

'Father, these words are not made in jest,' Adam said, an angry red suffusing his cheeks. 'These words are made by an enemy. One who wishes to drag your good name and reputation through the muck.'

The magistrate, by contrast, still looked his usual calm and temperate self, if a bit paler. 'Could this have been what my assailant wished for? To share my observations publicly? To make a mockery of me? Do I have such an enemy?'

'No!' Lucy exclaimed. 'How can that be?'

The magistrate gave her a half smile, before resting his jaw back on his fist. 'That may certainly be so. It may also be, as we've said, that our thief was simply of a more opportunistic bent, seizing the opportunity to sell the accounts when he discovered they lacked any other value.' He sighed. 'I am fearful of the harm that may be incurred, however, should more of my commentaries come forth to the public's eye.'

EIGHT

Over the next two days, Lucy moved among the fish and meat markets, pubs and playhouses, braving sleet and wind, hoping to catch sight of Phineas Fowler as she called her true accounts and strange news. She knew Duncan and Hank were keeping an ear out as well, as they rounded up drunks and thieves in the usual way. *He has to still be out and about*, she thought, trying to dismiss what would happen if the bookseller never surfaced again. What if they never caught hold of the man who had assaulted and stolen from Master Hargrave?

Right now, she was standing by a pipe-maker's stall, giving her voice a break. It was almost time to return to Master Aubrey's. As she rubbed her hands over his small fire, a rag-maker passed by, chuckling. The pipe-maker hailed him, clearly knowing him. 'Say there, friend,' he called. 'I could use a laugh. Mind sharing, would you?'

The rag-maker rested his bags full of dirty clothes and held his hands over the open flame as well. 'Just heard a bookseller tell the most humorous tale—'

'Bookseller?' Lucy interrupted. She knew Lach was not supposed to be selling right now, since she was out of the shop. 'What did he look like?'

The two men glanced at her in surprise, but the rag-maker humoured her. 'I suppose he's a good-looking enough fellow, I'll give you that. Was that why you're seeking him? A bit too much swagger for his own good, if you ask me.'

'Blond? Slender? Tall?' Lucy asked, her heart racing.

The rag-maker grinned. 'That's him! He's over by The Three Geese. Your sweetheart, I'm supposing?'

This is where Lach first met him. It has to be Phineas Fowler, she thought, grabbing her belongings. *There's no time to alert Duncan.*

She scurried over to The Three Geese, slowing down when the tavern came into sight. Still panting, she could see Phineas

Fowler out front, dressed handsomely in a purple coat and black hat. She tiptoed closer just as he began to call another true tale, being careful to keep hidden behind the crowd that had gathered close to hear him.

As before, Phineas's voice carried easily over the din of the crowd around them. 'Hear how the Wheel of Justice did turn!' he called, his words rhythmic and tuneful. 'Listen to the true tale of a cooper, one Tom Allen, who did commit murder in his neighbour's house. Hear how this order was righted upon his execution.'

The crowd still leaning in, he then proceeded to explain how the cooper, exhausted from his day of making casks and tubs, went looking for his wife when he discovered her missing. Phineas gave a salacious grin. 'He did soon discover her, in the bed of his neighbour, a man who ran a blossom-catching stall, just two doors away.'

As Phineas spoke, Lucy watched him. There was no denying his skill in the way he staged himself before others. Even though the story had been told as a true account and not as a ballad, he added a mournful song to his retelling, his lovely tenor voice drawing more than one tear from a lady's eye.

Should I follow him when he's done? Lucy wedged herself behind a woman holding a basket of apples on her hip.

She'd hoped to stay hidden, but when it was the final call for pennies, the crowd dispersed more quickly than she expected, exposing her to his view.

'Miss Campion!' he called, hurrying toward her.

She muttered an oath. This was not going as she hoped. She straightened her back as he bent before her in an elegant bow.

'What a pleasure to see you again. I dare say I did not expect to see you again so soon. Pray tell, did I swindle you of your customers again?' He put his hand to his heart and leaned closer. 'I fear I have committed another injury. Such an offence was not my intent.'

'No,' Lucy said, stepping back. 'I sold a few pieces before you began to call.' *Now is the time to learn more about him,* she thought. She looked up at him with what she hoped was an admiring gaze. 'I was wondering. Were you an actor, perchance? You seem to have said all the words from memory.'

Phineas puffed out his chest, looking thoroughly pleased. 'Indeed, I was. My parents were in a troupe of travelling players. When I was but a lad, before the Lord Protector saw fit to close the theatre and protect us from such merriments' – this with a twist of his lips – 'I performed on many stages in my early years.' He smiled at her. 'You are quite a joy to watch as well. Although . . .'

'Although what?'

'If you try looking up more when you tell your stories, I think your voice would carry better. You do better when you do not appear to be reading. You've seen actors on the stage, have you not? Even the female players have learned this trick to ensure that their words can be heard in the furthest reaches of the theatre.' He looked at her earnestly, the gallantries dropped. 'I do not say this to offend, I hope you understand. You have a lovely, charming presence.'

'Thank you, I am not offended,' Lucy replied. Indeed, such advice should not be ignored. 'I see you have another new offering.'

He handed her one of the pieces he'd just been selling. 'Another good one, with which I am quite willing to part.'

Lucy read the full title out loud. '*The Wheel of Justice Turned – the True Tale of a Cooper, Tom Allen, who did commit murder in his neighbour's house, with order righted upon his execution.*' Then she tapped on the printer's device of the rising phoenix. 'I see that you have not provided a location for your press. Have you no shop?'

He put his hand to his chest in mocking apology. 'Indeed, we do not have such a store. At least none so fine as Master Aubrey's.'

'Have you been to our shop?' she asked, forcing herself not to step away. Something about the idea that he'd been inside Master Aubrey's workspace bothered her, but she wasn't sure why.

'Indeed, I have.'

Then before she could lose her nerve, she asked, 'The pun in the title – did you come up with that yourself? Or was it perhaps Master Havisham?'

'It was me.'

'Did you write the rest of the piece? How did you hear about it?'

He studied her for a moment. 'Let me ask you, do you write the pieces you sell? Or does Master Aubrey?'

'Master Aubrey does write a few, but certainly many accounts are brought to us.' No need to tell him that she had written a few herself now, although published anonymously, of course. Why share such a secret with a man she barely knew. 'You? Where do you get your stories?'

He rubbed his chin thoughtfully. His tone stayed even when he replied, 'Why do you ask?'

'Call me curious.' She smiled when she spoke, hoping to disarm him.

He smiled back at her. 'I see. Well, we have a partner who provides the stories. He is acquainted with my master. He drops the stories off with him, and we set and sell them.' That was a common enough practice to be sure. *Was this the man who had stolen Master Hargrave's personal papers?* There was no way of knowing if Phineas knew the pieces had been stolen. *He could be printing and selling them in good faith.*

'I see,' she said, smiling straight up at him. 'They are very vivid accounts. Of course, you are quite the entertaining teller of tales.'

Phineas bowed his head at the compliment. 'They don't come to me in a form that I can readily sell. I have to spend some time writing them to make them more appealing to our audiences.' Unexpectedly, he took a step toward her. 'Now you are buttering me up. I quite enjoy such compliments coming from you, but should I wonder if you are trying to steal some business from me?'

'What? No! Of course not!' Lucy replied, feeling flustered, before she realized Phineas was speaking in jest.

'Good, I should not like it if you stole from me.' His grin had tightened, and his eyes lost their warmth.

Lucy stiffened. Seeing this, he returned to his charming self. 'Well, I'm heading in for a pint.' Unexpectedly, he lifted a strand of hair away from her face. 'Would you care to join me?'

Startled, she jerked away. 'N–no, thank you. I must be heading back now.'

Just then a blonde woman came up and tucked her hand in Phineas's elbow. Smirking at Lucy, she gazed up at the bookseller. 'Dearest, what mischief have you been up to now?'

'Mischief? None. I am just conversing with a fellow tradesman. Letitia, allow me to introduce—'

The woman waved her hand in front of his face. 'I am terribly sorry, Phineas, but I *must* have a word with you. I'll take that pint you offered *her*.' With that, she quickly pulled Phineas inside the tavern before he could utter another word.

Lucy leaned back against the chilly stone wall of the tavern, feeling as irritated by Phineas's hangdog expression as she was by the high-handed behaviour of the woman. Besides, now she'd lost her opportunity to follow Phineas back to his shop, and it was certainly too cold to wait until he left the tavern. *I suppose I can at least tell Duncan where I saw the bookseller*, she thought, hurrying over to the constable's gaol. *He can follow up with Phineas Fowler himself.*

As she prepared a stew for supper later that night, Lucy perused *The Wheel of Justice Turned*. Earlier, neither Duncan nor Hank had been at the gaol when she'd stopped by, forcing her to return to Master Aubrey's shop, feeling discomfited by a lack of answers from Phineas Fowler.

As she read, she sought any references to the magistrate. Like the other tracts that Phineas had printed, this true account was similarly wrapped in legal commentary composed by a legal scholar. She didn't realize she'd been biting her lip until she reached the end, only relaxing when it was clear there were no direct references to the magistrate, let alone anything casting him in a bad light.

Still, it was curious how Phineas had received these stolen accounts. What connection did he have to the thief? From what she understood, there were still a number of missing accounts that had not yet surfaced, meaning more publications were likely forthcoming. 'I wager we'll see him again soon, when he has the next one ready to sell,' she said, adding a few scraps of yesterday's ham to the bubbling pot.

'Almost time for supper, Lucy?' Will asked, entering the kitchen. Her brother stripped off his coat, boots and hat, and laid them by the hearth to dry. It must have been raining and she had not realized.

'Does your ladylove not cook?' Lucy teased, batting a long wooden spoon at her brother before she used it to give the pot a quick stir.

'Celia does indeed cook, but I fear she'd want to cook for me all my days, should I stay any longer at her home,' Will said as he settled down on the kitchen bench.

Lucy rolled her eyes. 'Is that so bad?'

'It is.'

Will looked away from her, and she ladled out a bowl. Her brother was not likely to commit to any woman enough to wed, and even if he did, she wondered if he would still be devoted to one love. Years ago, the woman he'd loved had been murdered and sometimes Lucy feared he'd never get past that pain enough to settle down.

Perhaps sensing her thoughts and seeking to ward them off, he knocked on the table. 'Quite a ruckus going on at the constable's gaol,' he said. 'Don't you want to hear about the constable's doings?'

'She's only got eyes for Master Adam now,' Lach said, walking into the kitchen with Master Aubrey.

Lucy squawked and tried to bat Lach with the same spoon she'd just used to ladle the soup. He neatly sidestepped her, pulling out three bowls and setting them on the table before joining Will on the bench.

'Is that so?' Will studied Lucy. 'Adam is a good man, I grant you that. I will never forget what he did for me. I would not be sitting here today, watching the two of you bicker, if it had not been for him coming to my aid during my trial.'

Lucy lowered her head. A day did not go by that she did not remember her desperate state when Will stood accused of murder.

'I hope that act of kindness does not mean you are forever beholden to him, Lucy,' Will continued, his voice growing gruff. She glanced up at him, taking in his troubled brow.

Her eyes returned to her hands clenched tightly in her lap. 'I do not feel beholden to him, Brother,' she whispered. How could she put into words what Adam meant to her?

'I know that he cares for you. I know he would provide well for you. But . . .' He sighed. 'We are not of his station.'

They all fell silent then, the crackle of the fire filling the room. For some reason, the sound reminded her of the night London went up in flames. It was that same fateful night that Adam declared his love, not caring what society would say of their attachment. A sadness flowed over her then. He would not be happy to know of her doubts.

Master Aubrey coughed, breaking the quiet. 'What was going on at the gaol? What's this ruckus you mention?'

Will seized on the change of topic. 'A brawl, that's what. I saw Hank get bashed over the head, too.'

'What!' Lucy exclaimed, her momentary melancholy forgotten. 'Is Hank all right?'

'Oh, he's got a thick noggin, I have no doubt. Looked like the constable was getting everything under control. He's a tough one, too.'

'You didn't help him?' Lucy asked.

Will clucked his tongue. 'I most certainly did. I helped wrest the men apart. Got myself a bruise to show for it, too.' He pulled back his sleeve to show a purpling bruise.

Lach whistled and Master Aubrey nodded approvingly.

'Oh dear. I must know that they are all right,' she said. More to herself than the others, she added, 'I shall run over after supper and bring them some stew. We have plenty to spare. Some good warm victuals may be just what they both need.'

Master Aubrey shook his head in mock despair. 'All that the lass just said, without so much as a "by your leave". I sometimes wonder who is the master here?'

'Forgive me, sir,' Lucy said, smiling brightly. 'May I please take some stew to the gaol after supper?'

'As if I can even stop you. A more stubborn lass I never have seen.'

'I brought you some stew. Bread, too,' she said to Duncan, entering the gaol. She set the covered basket down in front of where he was slumped, Hank at his side. Both men looked haggard, and she could see two sullen men staring at her from inside the two adjacent cells. One was a younger blond man, perhaps in his early twenties. The other looked to be more middle-aged, with a beard that was starting to grey and a protruding stomach.

Since the gaol was well lit by candles and lanterns, she blew her own lantern out and set it aside. From the basket, she pulled out two bowls and spoons and began to serve them the stew.

'What are you doing here, Lucy?' Duncan asked, watching her.

'Will told me there had been some trouble here earlier. A brawl. I thought I'd bring you something nourishing to eat.'

'I'm mighty grateful to you, lass,' Hank said, picking up his spoon with a bandaged hand. 'We are fine, as you can see.'

'Thank you kindly for this, Lucy,' Duncan said, wrapping his hands around the warm bowl. 'Thanks are indeed due to your brother. He bounded in here, like nothing was the matter, knocking the heads of those two dolts there. At that point, we were able to tear them apart and put them in their separate cells.'

'That man stole from me! Him! Smith!' the younger blond man shouted, pointing at the other. 'I don't know why I've been treated this way!'

'I most certainly did not steal from you, Allen!' Smith returned, his face red and sweaty. With more years and pounds to his frame, every move seemed a bit laboured. 'You attacked me! Constable, I want this man arrested for assault!'

'I've yet to sort it out,' Duncan said quietly to Lucy. He gestured to the younger blond man. 'Mr Allen here claims that Mr Smith stole from him, and when he denied it, he took a swing at him. That led to the brawl and me bringing them both here to settle their fight.'

Although he'd kept his voice low, both men heard it anyway. 'He stole my hoop driver!' Allen shouted, shaking at the bars. 'I know it was him!'

'I did not! Why would I? I've got one of my own.'

'Who else but a cooper would need a driver?' Allen shook his fist. 'Explain that to me!'

The men began exchanging insults again.

'Muckspout!'

'Lubberwort!'

'The driver belonged to my father!' Allen exclaimed. 'I demand that you return it at once!'

'Your father? You mean the man who killed his wife? Your own mother? Oh, I know all about that!'

Lucy and Duncan exchanged a puzzled glance.

Smith looked at them. 'Oh, you didn't know about this sordid tale? His father, Tom Allen, killed his own wife in cold blood a few years ago. As members of the same guild, we were friends and companions. At least we were before Tom committed murder and was hanged for his crime. My wife doesn't take kindly to us consorting with a murderer's kin, like this brat here.' He paused. 'To think that I'd steal his father's tool when I have plenty of better ones myself. What a preposterous notion.'

'Pretend you don't have it, why don't you!' Allen exclaimed. 'The truth will out!'

Hank made a threatening gesture to both of them. 'Quiet yourselves!'

Tom Allen? A cooper? Lucy clapped her hands to her mouth. 'I don't believe it.'

'What is it?' Duncan asked sharply.

She drummed her fingers on the barrel that served as a table. 'I'm afraid we have another coincidence.' She stood up then, standing a foot away from Allen. 'Your father was the cooper who found his wife – your mother – with the neighbour? A blossom-seller, I believe? That's what led him to the murderous act, was it not?'

'How could you possibly have known that?' Duncan asked.

Allen gave a pained shrug. 'I suppose you've read that wretched tale that's been circulating about my father's crime. Anyway, what of it? Smith stole the driver and that's that.'

'Was the driver valuable?' Lucy asked, feeling beads of sweat forming on her forehead. Something was starting to nag at her.

Allen shook his head. 'My father prized the driver, but I admit it was old and fragile. I never used it myself, but I kept it hanging on the wall with my other tools, to protect it from being broken.'

'That driver was practically useless,' Smith said. 'I say again, whyever would I have stolen such a piece? If I had wanted to use a driver, I'd have taken one of the better ones off my own worktable. Why would I break into Allen's workshop and take that cheap tool? Even Allen has better tools himself – just ask him. Don't know why I was even locked up.'

'You were locked up for disorderliness,' Hank replied. 'Public drunkenness.'

'What do you expect? He attacked me on the way out of the tavern. Of course, I was a little worse the wear for imbibing a few spirits. Maybe I taunted him.' He turned back to Allen. 'You can search through my belongings when we get home. I swear to you that I didn't steal it. Please, I need to get home. My wife has been ailing something awful since the birth of our third baby, and I need to tend to her.'

'Your wife's travails didn't stop you from being in the tavern, did it now?' Lucy muttered.

Smith hung his head. 'That is so and I'm sure the good Lord will require my due penance.'

Allen looked stricken. 'I didn't know Mary wasn't faring well, or the babe.' He paused, before speaking in an uneven nervous spurt. 'When we get home, I'll have my Anna send over something nourishing for your supper. Your wife will get better, right quick.' Then he called over to Duncan. 'Look here, Constable. I'm dropping my charge of theft against my neighbour here. I am convinced he didn't take my tool. I'm willing to let bygones be bygones, if he is.'

'I am,' Smith replied. 'I should not have kept you from the guild's activities out of spite. We were angry at your father for his terrible act, but the son should not have to bear his father's deed.'

Hank and Duncan looked at each other and shrugged. 'Long as you keep your fists off each other and do not visit another alehouse on the way home.'

After duly promising, the men left. They weren't quite arm in arm, but there was a friendliness to them now that was unexpectedly warming.

'Well, this was certainly odd,' Lucy said, pacing around the small area outside the cell. 'This is now the second act of violence that occurred after a tract was sold by Phineas Fowler. Another coincidence? I don't care for it.'

'There is nothing similar between these events,' Duncan said.

'Other than that there was recently a true account published that related to them in some way.'

'Divine providence at work,' Hank commented.

'I suppose,' Lucy replied, as she bade them farewell. Something continued to nag at her, though, as the lantern cast long shadows around her during the quick walk home.

Setting her chamomile tisane down on the edge of the small table in her bedchamber, Lucy pulled out the pieces they'd received from Phineas Fowler so far. Three of the accounts came from Master Hargrave's stolen papers, which she spread out in front of her. The fourth and fifth were the catalogues of curiosities, which she set to one side.

She pulled the candle closer, being careful not to splash any of the hot melted wax on to the accounts or her wrist. She tapped on the first, speaking out loud. 'Here we have *Tooth-Puller, No Truth-Teller*. After this tract was published, two witnesses mentioned in the trial were murdered.' She laid it in front of her and picked up the next one. '*The Wheel of Justice Turned* was published, and then, a few days later, the murderer's son gets in a nasty brawl with a neighbour after his father's cooper's driver was stolen.'

She remembered what Hank had said. 'Divine providence? How can that be?' She stood up and leaned against the shuttered window before sitting down again. 'No one was murdered after this account was published, that is true. It was just a theft. Yet we would never have known of the theft if the brawl had not come to the attention of the constable and Hank.' She sighed. 'Maybe this is just a coincidence.'

She picked up the third account, *Digitus Dei*, and read it again. The account was straightforward enough, detailing how Ruth Owen had poisoned her elderly female employer with arsenic over a number of months, until the widowed Joan Jennings died a most terrible death. Like the others, the crime had occurred several years ago, over by Charing Cross, an area that Lucy knew reasonably well.

'I wonder . . .' She broke off before she could say the half-formed thought aloud. Then she said it anyway. 'Is it possible that something did happen after this account was published?

Should I go and find out?' She rubbed her forehead. 'Is such a deed too fanciful to pursue? What would I do? Speak to Mrs Jennings's surviving kin? What would I say? "Pardon me, has something odd happened to you since an account about your relative was published last week?"' She bit her lip. 'Of all the foolish, hare-brained ideas!'

She stacked the accounts into a pile and blew out her candle. As she lay in bed, she could still smell the faint scent of burnt tallow. The curious idea, once she'd conjured it, was now impossible to ignore. 'It wouldn't hurt to make some general enquiries, that's for certain. I'll likely have a good laugh at my own expense later.'

She turned to her side, trying to find a good spot on the pallet. 'I'll just go to Charing Cross tomorrow and poke around a bit. Perchance, there's nothing to discover. On the other hand, perchance there is.'

NINE

The Strand was bustling the next morning, the markets in full movement, sellers hawking their wares from shop fronts, stalls, carts, peddler packs, and baskets. The strong aroma of the butchers' market wafted over her, and she pinched her nose. She stopped in at a baker's stall, the sweet cakes and buns offering a welcome respite.

Christmas is less than a week away. That means it's almost time for mince pie, she thought, her mouth watering. When she was a child, mince pie had been banned by Oliver Cromwell, although she thought she remembered her mother making it for her. This was one of those furtive traditions that prevailed despite the law, since most authorities looked the other way. It was not until she began to serve in the magistrate's household, a few years after the ban had been lifted by the King, that she truly experienced the delightful flavours of Cook's mince pies.

Looking around, she saw that the wood and coal had all been surrounded by bricks, one of the new requirements that City officials had imposed on new businesses since the Great Fire. She pointed to the sweet buns. 'I'll have two of those.'

As she handed over a coin, she made her enquiry as carefully as she could, offering up a quick prayer for forgiveness over the lie she was about to tell. 'Say, do you know the widow Joan Jennings, perchance? When I told my mother I'd be in this area, she said I should visit her if I could. Only I do not know her exact address.'

The woman's faded blue eyes blinked slowly. 'I do not think I know her. But my memory is not nearly as sharp as it once was.'

'Ma, you knew the widow Jennings,' her son interrupted, looking up from the dough he was kneading. 'Don't you remember? She was killed by her servant more than a year ago.' He came over, slapping the white flour from his hands before reaching out to accept the coin Lucy held in her outstretched hand.

'Oh, how awful,' Lucy said, trying to sound shocked. 'Can you tell me what happened?'

The baker studied her. 'Try the bun, would you?'

Unable to resist, Lucy bit into the soft warm bread in delight. 'Mmm, delicious,' she said.

'We've got the best buns around,' the baker said. 'Perhaps you need to purchase a few more? For family members.'

Lucy was about to demur, but then she realized the baker was giving her a meaningful look. Taking the hint, Lucy put another coin on the table. 'I'll take another six,' she said, patting her pocket ruefully. *At least this may help me get some information now.*

Evidently satisfied, the baker began to wrap up the buns. 'Mrs Jennings lived up the road a little way. Above the old furniture store,' he said, far more talkative than before. 'Her niece inherited the place, since she had died childless. She moved in there and soon after rented the first floor to a furniture-maker.'

'What happened, do you know? What caused her servant to do such a thing to her employer? An older widow, at that?'

The baker shrugged. 'Who's to say? I do remember that Mrs Jennings could be quite cross. On more than one occasion, I can recall her striking her servant, that miserable Mrs Owen, with her walking stick. That was before, when Mrs Jennings still accompanied her servant to market. We saw the old widow so rarely in the last six or so months of her life. Mrs Owen would always smile when she bought the buns, saying that no matter how unwell Mrs Jennings felt, she always could find a way to eat them. We know now, of course, that Mrs Owen had been poisoning her with arsenic.'

He sighed and then waved his hands towards Lucy. 'Off with you now. I've satisfied your curiosity and I have business to tend to.'

Lucy walked over to St John's and saw the furniture-maker's shop in the middle of a long row of three-storey brick and stucco buildings. There were several wooden chairs and tables out in front, advertising the obvious skill of the artisans who had crafted them. A few had embroidered seats, which suggested this was where men and women of quality would shop.

She walked slowly over, wondering if she should go inside, perhaps talk to the furniture-sellers. What would she say? The baker said they had moved in after Mrs Jennings died.

The other option would be to use the tactic she'd sometimes employed, to begin selling and hoping to draw in someone who could share useful information. But that wouldn't work this time. She couldn't very well begin selling here on the street. She didn't want to bring the wrath of the furniture-sellers, who might not be happy if a crowd barred access to their wares. She walked past the house as she thought about it, and then turned back around.

As she passed by the second time, an elderly servant came out, shaking the dust from a blanket. Lucy decided to take the chance. 'Good morning!' she called. 'Is your mistress about? Mrs Jennings?'

The servant squinted. 'Eh? What's that you say? The mistress? Mrs Jennings?'

'Yes, ma'am. I was enquiring after her.' Improvising, she added, 'I used to live this way, but have not in a very long time. My mother always spoke very fondly of Mrs Jennings and I thought I'd pay my respects, if she is at home.'

The servant frowned. 'No, Mrs Jennings is not at home.'

'I see,' Lucy said, frantically wondering how to continue the conversation.

To her surprise, the servant, who had been thoroughly appraising her, continued. 'My mistress, Mrs Jennings, died two years ago. If you mean my new mistress, her niece Mary Jennings, well, she is out making calls.'

Lucy paused. She had convinced the woman to talk, but she wasn't sure where to go from there. 'I am very sorry to hear that your mistress passed away. Could you tell me what happened?'

The woman shifted ever so slightly, suspicion falling over her face as she started to turn away.

Lucy changed her approach. 'My goodness!' she exclaimed. 'I just realized . . . I heard tell of a woman who'd been poisoned on this street. Was it Mrs Jennings?'

The servant's suspicious face softened under Lucy's guile. It was far easier to confirm someone's knowledge than to give them information from the start.

At the servant's nod, Lucy continued. 'I just hadn't realized – you must have been here then. You must know all about it.'

Now the woman's eyes lit up, clearly excited to have a new audience, the fear of being labelled a gossiper clearly gone. After a swift glance around, the servant stepped closer. 'I most certainly was! Such a tragedy!'

'I heard tell it was another servant,' Lucy prompted, lowering her voice.

'That hateful woman! Mrs Owens. She'd served as cook and had been adding arsenic to my mistress's meals. Mrs Jennings was an invalid, you see, and took a tray in her room most days.'

Without any more prompting from Lucy, the servant launched into the murderous tale, detailing the particularly horrific details of the mistress's final agonizing moments, as the poison finally claimed its victim.

'Has anything unusual happened since?' Lucy asked carefully, not sure how else to phrase the question.

'Praise the good Lord, nothing like that will ever happen again,' the servant said.

'Where is the murderess now? Claimed by the Tyburn Tree?'

'Indeed. Her daughter tried to claim that her mother was innocent, but we all knew the truth of the matter.' The servant spat. 'That's what I do, every time I see the insolent miss.'

Seeing that the woman was about to return to her work, Lucy offered her one of the buns she'd bought from the baker. 'Oh, Mrs Owen's daughter still lives nearby? She has not moved?'

'Where is the daughter of a murderess going to move? She has no other family. She works for a fishmonger, last I heard.' She swallowed the bun in three bites. 'I warned Mr Black about her. "Like mother, like daughter," I told him. "I won't buy fish from you, if you let her stay. She'd murder us all, I wager." He said that he needed the help, even from a murderess's daughter.' She licked her fingers and picked up her stick. 'Pfft.'

With that, she began to beat the rug in earnest, the dirt and fur causing Lucy to sneeze as she walked away.

The task identifying Mr Black's stall in the fish market proved far easier than Lucy expected. During the winter, there were fewer standing stalls, and by hanging back and listening to the fishmongers greet their regular customers, she soon figured out which one was his.

Right away, she noticed a young woman with black hair tucked loosely under her cap, sullenly slicing open fish and preparing them for sale. *Could that be Mrs Owen's daughter?* Lucy wondered. *What will I say to her?*

She watched the woman as she blew on her chapped red fingers and stamped her feet to keep them warm. There were small pots of burning coals nearby to help warm the stall, but today the winter chill was upon them. Idly, Lucy wondered whether the Thames would freeze over again as it had done the winter before.

'Next! Miss, what can I get you?' Mr Black called, looking at Lucy. Although she hadn't planned to purchase any fish, she pointed to the perch. 'One please.' *I can poach it later, with a little beer and some herbs for the broth*, she thought. *Master Aubrey will be pleased. Lach, too, though he'd never tell me so.* At least that coin she could get back from Master Aubrey.

'Wait over there,' he said, pointing to the end of the stall where the woman was. 'Elsbeth will get it ready for you.'

Lucy watched as the woman expertly removed the fish's entrails. 'You've got quite a natural way with the fish,' she said in an admiring tone.

'I suppose,' Elsbeth muttered.

'You must have worked here a long time,' Lucy continued, trying to draw her into a conversation, but the woman just shrugged.

A customer behind Lucy spoke up then, her words dipped in spite. 'I know exactly when Miss Owen here started working for Mr Baker. Happened right after your mam was hanged for poisoning her mistress, wasn't that it?'

Her cackle abruptly broke off as Elsbeth held up her fish knife. 'My mother paid for her crime! Tyburn took her and you know it!' she exclaimed. 'I have paid a deep debt for my mother's crime, too. Everything we owned was taken as reparation for her deeds.' Tears began to form in her eyes. 'Indeed, I only had one thing from my mother. Two embroidered combs for her hair. She wore them to her execution, and I took them from her hair myself. I would not part with them, no matter who begged me for them!'

She wagged her finger at the customer, who had now taken

several wary steps back. Others passing by the stall stopped as
well. Not seeming to care about the ruckus she was causing,
Elsbeth began to stab at the fish with her knife. 'Can you imagine?
I was left with only her combs. Then someone stole them from
me! Just this week! Now I have nothing! Nothing, you understand! Nothing except this job and a rush mat to call my own.'
Tears began to roll down her cheeks. 'Why must you bring up
such a thing when I am trying so hard to put this terrible tale
behind me?'

The customer drew herself up. 'Well! I never! I don't think I
want the daughter of a poisoner preparing my fish.' She sniffed.
'I shan't be coming back.'

Her departure drew Mr Black's ire. 'Enough, woman!' he
shouted at Elsbeth. 'I hired you because you work hard and you
keep quiet. I can throw you out just as easily if you do not mind
your manners.'

Elsbeth paled. A sense of dismissal hung in the air.

'You've done a wonderful job,' Lucy exclaimed. 'Look how
well you prepared the fish. I shall get a second perch, since
you've gutted it so well.'

Elsbeth gave her a startled glance, but Mr Black looked pleased.
'All right, all right. Let's not delay, I've got other customers
waiting.' He rubbed his hands. 'Shaping up to be a good morning's take, after all.'

As she handed Lucy the fish, Elsbeth gave her a tremulous
smile. 'Thank you,' she mouthed.

'I am sorry that your mother's combs were stolen,' Lucy
murmured in return. 'Were they very expensive?'

'They were the finest thing I own, which isn't saying much,'
Elsbeth said, looking downcast. 'I should say, though, that only
one was taken. I found the other as I'd left it. I looked and looked,
and it never showed up. I remember removing them before I
slept, and the next morning one was gone.' She shivered. 'Who
would take but one comb?'

'Who indeed?' Adam asked later that afternoon. He and Lucy
were standing together in the Hargraves' drawing room as she
had recounted how she had met Mrs Owen's daughter earlier.
He'd been none too pleased when she'd told him of her private

enquiries, but his curiosity, like hers, had been piqued. 'Why take one comb from a pair? The woman must have simply misplaced it, I'd wager.'

'Perhaps,' Lucy said. She was about to explain why the petty theft bothered her when they heard the magistrate's voice coming from down the hall.

'Thank you, Sidney, for stopping by,' he was saying. 'I shall look into this deplorable business at once. Pray, do not let it overcome your thoughts.'

As Master Hargrave and his guest began to pass the entrance to the drawing room, Adam stepped forward. 'Father,' he called.

'Ah, Adam, you are home,' his father said. 'You remember Justice Allerby, of course?'

Like Adam, Lucy recognized the magistrate's guest. He was slightly built, bespectacled and sickly-looking. Over the years, Mr Allerby had joined the Hargraves for an occasional evening together, and he had always seemed quiet and reflective, appearing to weigh everyone and everything around him. She'd always found him pleasant enough, and he always courteous, if a bit detached. Today his pallor was even more grey than usual, and she wondered if he had been ill.

Adam extended his hand in greeting. 'Of course, sir. Are you enjoying your time away from the Bench?'

The justice murmured something in response to Adam and then turned to Lucy. She could tell he was about to utter some customary words of greeting, but then he closed his mouth, taking in her countenance and form. His perusal felt more questioning than rude.

Master Hargrave coughed slightly. 'Allow me to introduce—'

'Your servant,' Allerby interrupted, his tone measured. He continued to take in her appearance, before glancing at Adam. 'Lucy, if I recall?'

'Yes, indeed. Lucy *was* our servant. What a memory you have, Sidney!' Master Hargrave said, clapping his friend on the back. 'Such an eye for faces.'

Adam shifted then, so that he had positioned himself in front of Lucy in a protective way. His father continued. 'This is Lucy Campion. She is now a printer's apprentice, working for Master

Aubrey over on Fleet Street.' Then, unexpectedly, he added, 'We're quite proud of her.'

Heat rose in Lucy's cheeks at Master Hargrave's words and she gave him a quick appreciative smile.

'I see,' Allerby replied, looking puzzled. 'Our world has turned upside down these last few years. It no longer surprises me that a female servant could become a printer's apprentice, and cavort so familiarly with her former master's family. I feel keenly that the natural order of things has been disrupted, and I am eager to see the world righted once again.' *With servants and women back in their rightful places.*

Lucy could feel Adam stiffen beside her, and she touched his arm ever so slightly. She did not wish him to offend his father's friend. Seeming to receive her message, he simply asked, 'What brings you here today, sir?'

'Did you not tell Adam about—?' Allerby asked Master Hargrave but stopped abruptly when he glanced at Lucy.

Master Hargrave gently pulled his friend into the drawing room, reaching for the decanter of sherry on the sideboard. As he poured the sherry into a small glass, Lucy overheard him, though he spoke quietly. 'No, I haven't told Adam yet about these bothersome doings. Let's tell them now.'

Allerby stiffened. 'In a servant's presence? Thomas, have you lost your senses completely?'

'Sidney.' Master Hargrave's low tone, though courteous, had taken on a slightly warning quality, as he pressed the sherry into his friend's hands. 'Lucy, as I just mentioned, is no longer my servant. More importantly, you should know that not only do I trust Lucy wholeheartedly, but I have found her mind to be sharp and clear. There has been many a time when she has provided me with perspectives and ideas that I would not have thought about myself. Besides' – he glanced at Adam – 'she's quite like a daughter to me.'

Thoroughly humbled now by overhearing even more praise from Master Hargrave, Lucy looked down at the floor. Adam nudged her. 'You've clearly won over my father,' he whispered. Then, in a regular speaking voice, he called to his father. 'Sir? Of what bothersome doings do you speak? Pray, bring us into your conversation. Perhaps we can help.'

'The cur who stole my personal papers has now resorted to blackmail,' Master Hargrave explained, his lip twisting with uncharacteristic anger.

'What?' Adam exclaimed, as Allerby downed the sherry in one long gulp. 'Who would dare blackmail you?'

'Alas, we do not know. Both Justice Allerby and I received messages earlier today. He came to consult with me about it and that's when I told him about last Sunday's theft.'

'What did the message say? Father, show us!'

Master Hargrave pulled a sheet of paper from his inner jacket pocket and passed it to Adam. Without asking, Lucy peered around his arm to read it as well.

The script was uneven, with many of the letters ill-formed. The handwriting of someone who had not been trained at a university. *Or intended to look that way*, Lucy thought to herself.

> Hargrave. Pay ten pounds by six o'clock in the morning of this nineteenth of December in this year of our Lord 1667, lest we tell the world of how you assisted in a Grave Miscarriage of Justice.

'Oh dear,' Lucy murmured.

> That you knew of the Truth and allow S.A. to suppress it and allow a murderer to go free without inducing much in the way of forfeiture or punishment.

'S.A.?' she said. 'Oh, Sidney Allerby.'

> Payment to be left behind the barrel by the sign of the black hart on Drury Lane. Do not think to set upon us, or we will be forced to set upon YOU.

'Ten pounds,' Lucy exclaimed. 'Such a sum! By six o'clock tomorrow morning? Whatever are you going to do?'

'Well, we won't pay the blackmailers, Lucy,' Master Hargrave replied, giving Allerby a firm look. Without asking, the man went back to the sideboard and proceeded to refill his glass again, downing half of it again in one gulp.

'Not because we can't muster such funds but because we won't,' Master Hargrave continued. 'We have not done what we have been accused of so maliciously. Once we give in and pay, I believe we could be hounded our entire lives. The blackmailing thief knows no such solace in his work. He sees there always fleece to be shorn from his victims.'

Lucy nodded grimly. Such a thing made sense. Why would a blackmailer, desperate for easy funds, ever give up such a lucrative source of income?

'Father, why did you not tell me?' Adam asked, touching his arm.

The magistrate gave him a tired smile. 'I did not see there to be anything to be done. Such a thing should not be borne. I have dealt with many threats of this nature throughout my lifetime, and I saw no reason to succumb to such an obvious attempt to exploit me.'

'Who brought you the note?' Lucy asked. 'Was Annie able to describe him?'

The magistrate shook his head. 'I questioned her to no avail. Apparently, someone had slid the note under our front door, in the early hours of the morning, likely before the tradesmen were out and about. She found it when she went to stoke the hearth.'

'What "miscarriage of justice" could the blackmailer be referring to?' Adam asked, and then read one of the lines out loud. '"That you knew of the Truth and allow S.A. to suppress it and allow a murderer to go free without inducing much in the way of forfeiture or punishment." What "truth" do they think you and Justice Allerby suppressed?'

'Sidney and I were just discussing this. The warning is so vague that it could very nearly mean anything.' He glanced at Allerby again, who was looking pale, sweat beading on his forehead.

'Are you unwell, sir?' Lucy asked him. 'Shall I ask Cook to make you a warming tisane?'

'No, thank you, Lucy,' Allerby said, dabbing his face with a linen. 'I shall be leaving soon and will rest later. Perhaps have another drink.' He looked forlorn and sad. 'I hardly know what to do myself.'

Master Hargrave scowled again. 'I suppose there is little else we can do, except to call the blackmailer's bluff. I have already spoken to Constable Duncan, so we must hope he can catch this blackmailer when he comes to collect the money in the morning. I wonder now if the blackmailer and Sam Havisham are working in concert. At the very least, they both seem to be working with the thief who stole my papers.' He turned back to Lucy. 'If I recall correctly, didn't you say that Master Aubrey intended to make enquiries about Havisham's press at the Stationers' Company?'

'Yes, sir,' Lucy replied. 'He discovered that Havisham had not registered with the Company following the Great Fire, so there is no record of these latest tracts. Nothing that they sold these last few weeks was properly licensed.'

'A rogue press,' Master Hargrave mused. 'Hidden somewhere. London? Westminster? How can we know?'

'I suspect the press is not so far from Fleet Street,' Lucy said. 'I see Phineas Fowler at many of the same sites where Master Aubrey likes me to sell.'

Master Hargrave rubbed his beard. 'That may prove useful.'

Lucy nodded. 'Perhaps catching one will lead us to the other.'

TEN

'Hasn't the constable returned yet?' Lucy asked, peering out of Master Aubrey's shop towards the gaol. A light snow had begun to coat the ground, catching the dim afternoon sunlight, adding a shining beauty to the otherwise foggy, dirty street. 'He should have been back by now, shouldn't he? Did he return and not tell me?'

'You're letting in cold air,' Lach grumbled from the workbench. He and Master Aubrey were looking at different woodcuts, trying to decide which one worked best for the Christmas recipe collection Lach had put together. 'Besides, that's at least the fifth time you've checked in the last hour.'

'I just need to know if he and Hank caught the blackmailer!' she replied. 'Maybe it will turn out to be Phineas Fowler. Or Havisham himself.'

'Didn't Duncan tell you he'd stop by when he had news?' Master Aubrey asked, warming his hands before the hearth. 'Shut the door, lass. Be patient.'

'Be patient?' Lach snickered. 'Lucy?'

Lucy glared at him but shut the door and resumed pacing around the wooden floor. Master Aubrey and Lach continued to set the broadside together, although Lucy could tell they were going more slowly than usual. 'You're waiting on the constable just as I am,' she said accusingly. After pacing a few more minutes, she threw open the door for the sixth time, not caring about the others' tepid protests.

This time, however, Duncan was standing there, his fist raised as though about to knock on the door. 'Oh, Duncan,' she cried, practically dragging him inside. 'What news? Did you catch the blackmailer?'

His shoulders sagged as he pushed his hood off his face and began to stamp his feet on the thrush rug at the shop's entrance. 'We did not.'

'What happened?' she asked. 'Did he get away?'

He brushed some snow off his coat. 'We never even saw him. No one came at the appointed time to pick up the money. Hank and I watched the spot for several hours, to no avail.'

'Obvious what happened,' Lach snickered. 'He saw you watching and fled. Your red coat will stick out anywhere.'

'We did keep ourselves a goodly distance away,' Duncan replied, but he sounded doubtful. 'I kept my cloak pulled around me, so that my uniform would not stick out.'

Lucy tapped her fingers lightly on the table. 'It does seem odd that a blackmailer would go to the trouble of trying to get money and then not follow through.'

'There's truth in that.' Duncan closed his eyes. 'I do recall a moment where a woman wearing a white knit cap and a tightly drawn cape approached the location. I remember feeling certain that we would see her retrieve it. We braced ourselves for pursuit, in case she tried to flee when we apprehended her.'

'What happened?'

'Nothing. She resumed her previous pace and continued on.' He rubbed his forehead. 'Could that woman have been the blackmailer? Or perhaps simply hired by the blackmailer to retrieve the package? If I had thought about it, I would have had Hank pursue her to make some enquiries. Now I am not certain at all.'

'A woman with a white knit cap?' Lucy repeated, trying to imagine the scene. 'Not a lot to go by. What happened next?'

'We waited for the rest of the morning, and no one else came even close to the package. Finally, we gave up and have just now returned. I knew you would want to hear the news, so I came here directly. Hank is back at the gaol.'

'What will happen now?' Lucy asked. 'Will the magistrate's privacy continue to be violated, since the blackmailer did not accept the payment?' She angrily pushed away a sudden tear. It was all so unfair.

Seeing the gesture, Duncan sighed. 'I don't know,' he replied. 'We will see if the blackmailer communicates again with Master Hargrave. We may have a better sense of what we are dealing with then.' He put his hand on the door. 'Well, I must be going.'

Why did he suddenly look so forlorn? Lucy wondered. *He couldn't be as sad as she was about the insult to Master Hargrave.*

'We have just made some mead,' she said, wanting to comfort him. 'Let me bring you a jar, to warm yourself on your way.' Quickly, she ladled some into a jar and pushed the stopper in tightly.

He accepted the mead with an appreciative but still sad smile. Upon opening the door, he stuck his bare hand out. 'It appears to have stopped snowing for a minute.'

Before he could take a step, Lucy tugged on his arm. 'Duncan! Wait!'

Pausing mid-step, he looked down at her. 'What's wrong?'

'Look at that.'

Two footprints, rapidly disappearing in the lightly blowing snow, could be seen on the ground, at the threshold of the shop.

'Footprints? What about them?'

'Look at how they're positioned. I think someone came and stood at our door just now, but did not enter the shop.' Lucy stuck her foot out to compare with the print. 'They are about the size of my shoe,' she said. 'Belonging to a woman, I would think.'

They looked up and down the street at the different figures scurrying about to take shelter from the growing winter storm. It was impossible to know who might have been at the door.

'A customer who changed her mind?' Duncan asked.

'Perhaps. Or someone who wanted to eavesdrop on our conversation.' Lucy shrugged. She'd done such a thing herself, in order to acquire titbits, so she would not deny the possibility. Still, it was disconcerting.

'That's far-fetched, Lucy, even for you,' Duncan replied, but she could see a faint look of anxiety in his eye.

'I suppose,' she said. 'I might be imagining things.'

When he left, though, she leaned against the door, trying not to feel unsettled. Had someone been listening to their conversation?

'Thank you kindly!' Lucy called to the crowd as she caught pennies in her little straw basket the next morning. She'd sold most of the pieces in her pack, which included the Christmas recipes they'd printed the day before. *I'll best you yet, Lach! Master Aubrey will be so pleased.* She was so intently imagining her victory over Lach that she did not notice the long shadow now looming over her.

'Mind if I keep your crowd?' a teasing voice asked. 'You gathered it so nicely for me.'

Phineas Fowler! Lucy stood up too quickly, causing her to be instantly light-headed. The bookseller put a steadying hand on her elbow, grinning down at her in his customary way. 'You'll want to hear this story, I think.'

'W–what? Why?' Lucy asked, but Phineas had already begun to call. 'Gather round, gather round! Hear the true confession of one magistrate, late of the King's Bench!' He turned to wink at Lucy. 'This magistrate who did allow a most grotesque miscarriage of justice!'

'What is this tale you tell?' Lucy called, but there were already people crowding between her and Phineas and she found herself being pushed back. 'Who are you talking about? What magistrate?'

'Tell us!' the crowd began to clamour, sensing something sensational to be forthcoming.

Still using his deeply resonating voice, Phineas read off the full title of the true account. *'The Magistrate's Confession, Or, Foiled No More – A True Account of how a Magistrate who did know a Certain Truth of Murder did seek to Repress it.'*

Lucy edged closer, her heart beating faster as Phineas's words flooded over her. 'Hear how one Henry Fortenberry, a player with the Swan Theatre, did kill another player, Winston Scott, whilst they were playing together with foils, before an upcoming performance.' Putting his hand to his mouth, he uttered a stage aside. 'Stabbed him through the heart, he did!'

The crowd murmured a bit. 'Took the play to heart!' one man called out, to a general guffaw.

'Indeed!' Phineas said, his grin widening.

'Such misfortune,' another woman added, her gleaming eyes belying her sympathetic tone.

'Should have liked to have seen it!' another man said. He then pantomimed looking at an imaginary sword in his hand and then around at an imaginary audience in shock. 'That blood seems true!'

Another loud guffaw from the crowd followed.

Phineas raised his hands to regain the audience's attention. 'A misfortune, you say? A bit of bad luck for the player? That is how it seemed, to spectators and jury alike.' He raised his voice, and the crowd followed along, clearly mesmerized. 'Indeed, even the jury was convinced that Fortenberry had intended no malice when he killed Scott. As such, the judge set the man free. Everything was right again . . . or was it?' He looked around at the crowd, an exaggerated questioning look on his face as he fell silent.

At his prolonged silence, a hush grew over the crowd, and everyone leaned forward in anticipation. Like everyone else, Lucy strained to hear what he would say next.

'The answer is "No!" Everything was not right at all,' he said. 'As with any of the great tragedies that play out on these players' own stages . . . this man's death was no accident! Moreover, both the presiding judge and another sought to hide that incendiary knowledge from the jury.'

There were audible gasps and much shaking of heads and fists from the crowd. Judge and jury were supposed to restore order out of disorder; they were not expected to bring injury to the process.

Phineas raised a clenched fist. 'That's right, my friends. A murderer went free that day! Rather than facing the hangman's rope, he was released. His only requirement was to pay for Scott's burial costs.' He paused, commanding silence among the general sense of indignation. 'Moreover, that same night, he performed in the dead man's place, taking on a plum role that brought him many accolades and much praise. He said it was to *honour* his departed friend, but such an honour did benefit him greatly.'

The crowd gasped and stirred, with many *oohs* and *aahs*. This was the type of gossipy reveal they fed on. Lucy could already see people pulling out another coin to purchase the piece.

But Phineas was not done. 'That we know of this miscarriage of justice is another trick of fate,' he continued, his words bringing a hush to the crowd. 'As you will learn in this true tale, a *second* magistrate recorded the confession of the presiding magistrate! Moreover, he even informed the first corrupt magistrate that many points made during the trial had not been explained satisfactorily either by the murderous player or the victim's family. He did not voice his concerns, and the trial was decided in the defendant's favour, allowing a murderer to be set free.'

The crowd began to shake their fists in anger, and Lucy could sense a rise in animosity. Criminals were not supposed to be allowed to roam free and benefit from their crimes, especially not murders. The idea that justices would allow such a travesty to occur was clearly stirring their imaginations and their sense of wrath. Phineas looked around in satisfaction.

He's provoking the crowd on purpose, Lucy realized, taking a step back. The rising anger around her was making her palms itch.

'Who were those judges, you ask?' Phineas said, slowly baring his teeth. 'Those lying and duplicitous magistrates who dared to upend justice in such a fashion?'

The crowd leaned forward, sensing another reveal.

Phineas looked around, his gaze falling briefly on Lucy, who had pressed her knuckles to her mouth. 'Perhaps I dare not say aloud.' He waved a handful of the penny pieces around. 'You may, however, throw me a penny, to discover for yourself those judges who've subverted the truth.'

The crowd gave a collective exhale but began to dig into their pockets for a spare coin.

Giving a low chuckle, Phineas continued. 'You may ask yourself, why did two such reputable judges do such a dishonourable thing? Did someone pay them? Alas, that I cannot say.' He raised both hands. 'I can assure you this. The truth will out.'

Without thinking, Lucy found herself elbowing her way through the crowd and planting herself in front of Phineas. 'Where did you get this terrible story?' she demanded, her hands on her hips. 'I demand that you tell me at once.'

The bookseller winked at her again. 'I told you before. I have a partner who provides these true accounts,' he said, emphasizing the word *true*. 'Now, if you'll pardon me, I must attend to my customers.'

Lucy remained planted in front of him. 'What gives you the right to say such things?' she asked. Her voice was shaking in rage and pain. 'To lie about such honourable men!'

He raised his eyebrow. 'Why are you sure they are honourable? Do you know them? What make *you* so certain?'

A man roughly pushed her back. 'Aw, don't you have your own tracts to sell?' He threw a couple of pennies in Phineas's cap. 'I'll take two of that confession.'

For a moment, Lucy stood there, stunned, getting jostled from all sides as Phineas easily sold the pieces, one by one. Suddenly, he only had two left.

Lucy grabbed one from his hand and pressed a coin at him. 'I'll take one of those!'

He raised an eyebrow but accepted the coin. 'I'll be eager to hear what you think.'

'I was here first,' a plump older woman said angrily, shoving Lucy in the elbow. 'You'll give that to me or get a fist in your eye.' The woman drew her arm back to strike Lucy, but somehow got pushed to one side, allowing Lucy to duck and slip away.

Once she was a goodly distance from the crowd, she skimmed *The Magistrate's Confession*, her puzzlement and confusion growing with every line. Her heart beating hard, she looked back at Phineas, who was still accepting coins from the eager crowd.

Should I keep an eye on him and discover the location of his shop? Or shall I alert Master Hargrave that this disreputable tract has been published about him?

Her feet decided for her, as she found herself practically trotting towards the Hargraves' home, skirts in one hand, pack in the other. 'I just hope he's at home,' she said. 'Although . . . however will I tell him?'

Being direct is best, Lucy decided, holding up the account to two very startled-looking Hargraves. They were seated together in Master Hargrave's study. 'Here is the p–piece they wanted to b–blackmail you with,' she said, stammering from trying to catch her breath after the cold run. 'Phineas Fowler called this *The Magistrate's Confession.*'

'*The Magistrate's Confession?*' Master Hargrave repeated, stretching out his hand for the account. 'I suppose that's sufficiently direct.' He gave her a troubled smile. 'Don't fret, Lucy.'

Gulping, she handed the penny piece to the magistrate. 'I don't believe a whit of it, sir.'

Adam pulled his chair over so he could read over his father's shoulder. Lucy stepped back, watching the men peruse the account together. Neither spoke, although their jaws tightened in tandem.

Finally, Master Hargrave pushed back from the desk, heaving a great sigh. 'So this was the "miscarriage of justice" the blackmailer was referring to,' he said. 'I wondered if this story might come to light.'

'You do not seem surprised, sir,' Lucy exclaimed. 'It is not true, is it?' Then before he could reply, she bowed her head, a sudden lump forming in her throat. 'Nay, I know it is not. Forgive me for thinking such a scurrilous claim to be true, even for a moment.'

Master Hargrave studied her face. 'Ah, Lucy, I should be most sorrowful if I ever destroyed the good faith you have in me. Rest assured, I would never suborn perjury or allow such a travesty of justice to occur.'

'Father, can you explain this charge that has been levelled against you?' Adam asked. 'As Lucy noted, you do not seem to be astonished. I know that it must have drawn from your personal papers, of course, but what did you write that could have been construed as a confession of a travesty of justice?'

Master Hargrave stood up and moved over to the window, gazing out towards the street. After coughing slightly into his fist, he began to speak. 'You may remember that I began to collect examples of differentiation in different types of homicide. Homicide, both involuntary and voluntary, manslaughter, justifiable homicide and so on. I was also interested in which cases were inducing forfeiture or pardon.'

'I remember,' Adam replied.

Master Hargrave gestured towards *The Magistrate's Confession*. 'I sat in on this trial and I remember it well. Allerby was presiding. As I recall, the trial revolved around two players rehearsing a duel on stage, to be performed in that afternoon's performance. As I understood it, as the two players cast their foils around, Mr Fortenberry accidentally struck a fatal blow that brought about Mr Scott's untimely death.' He stroked his chin. 'As I recall, too, even as the victim lay dying, he did not blame his friend.'

'The other players believed there to have been an unfortunate accident,' Lucy said, remembering what Phineas had told the crowd. 'As did the jury.'

Adam frowned. 'It does indeed appear a case of involuntary manslaughter – two players, practising with swords before an upcoming performance, with one ending up killing the other. A misfortune to be sure, but that seems to have been an accident.'

'Yes, that is so,' his father replied.

'Moreover, the victim himself did not suspect his friend of malice. It is not surprising that others would not believe it, either,' Adam said. 'The jury was no doubt easily convinced.'

'Indeed, that is exactly right,' his father replied. 'As I recall, the jury took very little time to decide, coming back with a verdict of involuntary manslaughter. Their judgment, confirmed by Allerby, determined that Mr Fortenberry had not intended to kill Mr Scott. Instead, they all agreed that he had been the recipient of an unfortunate feint left that put Mr Scott in the way of Mr Fortenberry's sword.'

'Why would they blackmail you on this, then?' Lucy asked. 'What is the "true confession" they claim you have made?'

Master Hargrave coughed again. 'I surmise that what they refer to as the "true confession" is those questions and thoughts that I scribbled down during the trial. My intention, you understand, was to transform those jotted notes into a legal commentary about the effectiveness of different lines of inquiry, when bringing a case against a defendant.'

'What was it you wrote, Father?' Adam asked.

'I am trying to recall the particulars, as it was a few years ago now that I took those notes.' Master Hargrave rubbed his jaw. 'Something the theatre owner said bothered me. He had alluded to how fortunate it was that Mr Fortenberry had prepared for Mr Scott's role and was able to perform that same night.'

'No one had questioned how the crime had directly benefited Mr Fortenberry,' Adam said.

'Precisely. I remember writing something to that effect in my notes on the trial. I remember, too, that Mr Fortenberry said that he would make amends to Mr Scott's wife – who I recall being quite comely even in her distress as she sat silent at the trial – and that he would take care of her.' He glanced at Adam who nodded.

'Mr Fortenberry might have had designs on Mr Scott's wife

as well as on his role,' Lucy said, tapping her fingers on the table as she worked it out.

'It was just a small intuition, a hunch that occurred to me in the moment,' Master Hargrave explained. 'I would not have relied on such a hunch to make a legal decision when I was on the Bench, but I might well have posed such a question to the witnesses. Allerby did not stop the testimony to pose such a question. I remember being surprised that he did not comment on either of these potential motives as reasons why Fortenberry might have wished to kill Scott and pass his murder off as an accident.'

'Why do you suppose that Master Allerby did not probe those motives more?' Lucy asked.

Master Hargrave looked troubled. 'I cannot say for certain. I should have thought he would have been more attentive to such incriminating details. I remember, too, feeling quite disappointed that my friend had not taken the opportunity to press Fortenberry in more detail.' He rubbed his jaw. 'I may have indicated as much in my commentary about the case.'

Lucy recalled how the other magistrate had appeared pale and shaking when she'd seen him the other day. How he'd downed several glasses of the magistrate's wine in quick succession. *Could he have been drinking during the trial?* She couldn't quite bring herself to ask the question so bluntly. 'Was Master Allerby in his regular faculties at the time?'

Master Hargrave looked startled and then more reflective as he pondered her question. Once again, he seemed to understand the intention behind her words. 'He did not adhere to a model of sobriety and virtue to which most justices strive.' He brought his fist down on the table. 'But I can say, with confidence, that Justice Allerby did not suborn perjury and neither did I. As far as I can discern, no falsehoods were spoken during the trial.' He sighed. 'I'm afraid, however, that my scribbled speculations will be used erroneously and serve to damage the reputation of both of us.'

'Allerby is not identified by name, and only your initials are mentioned,' Adam said, touching his father's shoulder.

'I wonder . . . Why would the blackmailer not have assigned blame more clearly?' Lucy asked. 'Why did they refrain from injuring you?'

'Perhaps this *Confession* was intended to be more of a warning,' Adam said. 'To illustrate their hold over you. It may be that we will hear from them again.'

'I agree. One would think the blackmailers would contact me again with a new demand – and a new threat,' Master Hargrave replied. 'I cannot imagine that they have given up on their quest for illicit gains.'

'Pardon me, sir,' Lucy said, smoothing her skirts. 'In your personal papers, are there more . . .?' Her voice trailed off.

Master Hargrave finished the question Lucy could not bear to ask. 'Are there more commentaries that could prove injurious to me or other magistrates?' He frowned. 'Sadly, I imagine the answer is yes. We must get my papers back as soon as we can, before more shameful allegations can be publicly made.'

Although his tone was steady, Lucy could tell that the magistrate seemed deeply wounded. She wanted to pat his arm the way she would Annie or even Sid, but with the magistrate she did not quite dare. 'Phineas Fowler is the key,' she said instead. 'We must learn who has been providing him with Master Hargrave's records. Since Master Aubrey said that the Stationers' Company had no address for Havisham's shop, I wanted to follow him today when I saw him, but I thought it more important that I bring the piece to Master Hargrave.' She stopped when she realized that father and son were staring at her, aghast. 'Don't you see? We have to know where Havisham's shop is to stop him from printing such vile pieces.'

Adam found his voice. 'Lucy!' he exclaimed in a strangled tone. Standing before her, he gripped her shoulders and shook her gently. 'Tell me you will not do such a dangerous thing!' His eyes were intent as he gazed down at her. 'To follow him on your own – oh, Lucy!'

'I–I won't,' she agreed reluctantly. Inside, her thoughts were raging. *To stop Phineas Fowler from publishing such awful pieces about Master Hargrave, we must find the home of the rogue printer! From there, we may discover the identity of the heinous blackmailer.* She searched Adam's face, still etched with concern. *Forgive me, Adam. I know where your heart lies, and why you say what you say. But I will do everything I can to stop these scurrilous attacks on your father, and not even you can stop me.*

ELEVEN

ach cleared his throat for the fourth time in as many minutes. He was seated across the kitchen table from her, having finished sopping up the last of the gravy with their hard bread. Master Aubrey was out front with a customer but had given them leave to eat their noon meal.

Lucy didn't look up. At her request, the magistrate had returned *The Magistrate's Confession* to her, and she was still studying it now, wondering if there was anything new to learn. So far, nothing had come to her, although she clenched her fists every time she read the demeaning words about the magistrate's alleged corruption.

When he cleared his throat for a fifth time, Lucy finally stopped ignoring him. 'Do you need something to soothe your throat?' Stacking their plates and cups, she removed the dirty dishes over to the basin to be washed later. 'Some honeyed mead should do the trick.'

'Nothing wrong with my throat,' Lach muttered.

'Then why are you coughing?'

He pulled out a piece of paper from his pocket and pushed it toward her. 'Here's a piece I've written. See, er, what you think.'

'A piece?' Lucy raised her eyebrow.

He scowled at her. 'Just a bit of nonsense. Read it.'

'"Two men courting a lass,"' she read. '"One a gently-born lawyer, the other a constable" – Lach, what is this nonsense? Why do I feel the need to box your ears?' She crumpled the paper, ignoring the apprentice's quiet snickering.

'What's he done now?' Master Aubrey asked, entering the kitchen. He sat down at the table and Lucy went to fill up his bowl with the rest of the stew. 'Never mind that. I have a question for you, Lucy. What more do you know of the murder of that soap-maker and his wife?'

Lucy set the bowl in front of him and resumed her spot across from Lach, who was now glaring at her. 'Why, very little, sir.

Only what Constable Duncan mentioned when he told me about the crimes the other day.'

'Harrumph. Do I have to spell it out for you? Their murders would make for a most exciting true account. We could sell it easily.' He spread out his arms dramatically, as if welcoming a great imaginary crowd.

'I suppose that's true, sir,' Lucy said, playing with the feathered end of a quill.

'Do we know who murdered them?' Aubrey asked, his eyes still gleaming. 'Perhaps they have made an arrest.'

'I do not think they did,' Lucy said. 'I think Constable Duncan would have informed me if they had.'

'See,' Lach crowed from the corner. 'It's just as I wrote in my piece.'

'What?' Reluctantly, Lucy smoothed out the paper she had crumpled in her fist. '"The constable, so beguiled by this silly lass, did tell her details of all crimes, making him an—" Lach!' she exclaimed. 'Tell me the meaning of this!'

'The meaning is clear,' Lach muttered. 'You're just saying it wrong. Taking all the fun and merriment out of the piece.'

'We can't publish this!' Heatedly, she pushed the paper in front of Master Aubrey, who picked it up with interest. 'We can't.'

Master Aubrey read it over, snorting under his breath, and ending with a broad chuckle. 'Not bad, Lach. What tune is it set to?'

'"Cuckolds All in a Row",' Lach replied, his mischievous grin spreading fully across his freckled face.

'Master Aubrey!' Lucy exclaimed. 'You can't publish this doggerel.'

'Why can't he?' Lach countered. 'We'll sell heaps, I know it.'

'If it does not please you, Lucy, then give me something better,' Master Aubrey said, grinning at them both. 'Go to that soap-maker's home. See what else you can find out and write me a good true account. Lach, you go with her.' He rubbed his hands together, looking like a mischievous child. 'I have a good feeling about this.'

Lucy and Lach spent the next twenty minutes bickering as they walked to Pye Corner. Although they had both protested, Master

Aubrey had insisted that Lach accompany her, much to his annoyance.

'I don't know why he insisted that we write this true account. Lots of people prefer jests and merriments to murder.' Lach gave her a little shove. Before she could completely stumble to the ground, he grabbed her arm, restoring her balance. 'We aren't all so grim.'

'I know that.' Lucy glanced at him. He seemed more out of sorts than usual, which was saying a lot. 'Master Aubrey was just teasing you, Lach. I believe he will allow us to set your merry piece. Even though I was not so fond of it myself.'

Lach snorted. 'The crowds will love it; just wait and see. I'll sell more of it than any murder ballad.'

'Perhaps,' Lucy replied. 'We're almost there.'

Lach slowed down, his scowl returning. 'I don't know what we're supposed to do now. Go to the Donnetts' family and say, "Tell us all the details of your sister's murder"? I bet she throws you out on your ear when you ask. I would.'

'Yes, you're right,' Lucy said, sighing.

'I am?'

'It is indeed a terrible thing to ask questions about how someone died, especially when it is a loved one. I can't imagine that Mrs Donnett's sister would have more to say than what she already told me when I was with the constable.' They stepped aside to let an old woman carrying two heavy baskets of rags pass them by. She looked as if she were made of rags herself, since everything she wore was grey and tattered.

Lucy continued. 'It would be better to find a gossipy neighbour or shopkeeper. *Someone* has to know *something* to help us get a better sense of the truth of the tale.' She pointed to the White Horse Inn. 'I had planned to sell there the other day, when I was here with the constable, but then we left to avoid the rainstorm. Perhaps we can ask a few questions to the people who gather. Maybe talk to them afterwards. That's worked for me in the past.'

'Sounds like a lot of work. How about I just go in and have a pint?' He flashed his usual grin. 'I can keep an ear out. Get the latest gossip.'

Lucy glared at him. 'You're trying to get out of work.'

'You have your way, and I have mine.' He handed her his

pack. 'Master Aubrey made me pack some more murder ballads. Sell them if you wish.' With a chuckle, he grasped the iron handle of the old wooden door and disappeared inside.

'Easier without him irking me anyway,' she muttered before beginning her customary call. 'Gather round, hear the story of a murder must vengeful!'

Within a few minutes, two women had gathered at her side. One was an elderly well-dressed woman who was leaning heavily on the arm of a much younger woman. At first, Lucy was relieved, because once a few people had gathered, more were likely to follow. However, her high hopes disappeared when the older woman began to loudly interrupt her.

'What's all this?' the older woman said. 'Eunice, what's she shouting about?'

'Grandmother, she is a bookseller. She is about to tell a tale.'

Gamely, Lucy began to tell the story, but she'd barely said two sentences when the insistent questions began again.

'What did you say? What did she say?' the woman prodded her granddaughter. '*What* did the wretched thief do? I can't hear her properly.'

'She said that he hid all the lanterns so no one could find him in the dark.'

'In the *what*?'

'In the dark!'

Lucy tried to keep telling the tale, but the older woman's loud interruptions were getting harder to manage. Other people who'd wandered by to listen to her tale began to disperse, until the two women were the only ones who remained. Lucy looked mournfully at her empty basket. *It looks as if Lach will have the last laugh today after all.*

'I'm afraid we lost you your business,' Eunice said, looking chagrined.

Ruefully, Lucy nodded. A quick look at the darkening sky suggested that it was about to rain, making it nearly impossible to sell anything. *How will I find out about the murders now?*

Unexpectedly, the older woman prodded her granddaughter and pointed at Lucy's pack. 'Eunice, dear. Buy one from the poor girl. You can read it to me later.'

'Let us take several, then,' the granddaughter said, pulling out her purse. With a relieved giggle, she added, 'With the rain coming, it will be a nice way to pass the time, even if I have to shout in her ear the whole time. My grandmother adores strange and terrible accounts like these.'

'I see,' Lucy said, as she gratefully accepted the coins. It was high time to get to the point of her venture. Crossing her fingers behind her back for luck, she said, 'By the way, I heard tell of two murders that happened here recently. A soap-seller and his wife, was it?'

'Eunice, what did she ask?' the grandmother demanded.

Eunice leaned down and shouted into her grandmother's ear. 'She's asking about the murder of those soap-sellers!'

'Oh!' The grandmother's eyes gleamed in sudden excitement as she exchanged a glance with Eunice. 'The Donnetts, wasn't it? Yes, we heard about that. A strange tale indeed.'

Seeing the older woman's smirk, Lucy grew more hopeful. Perhaps she'd happened on the right people. She decided to proceed carefully. Even though the two women seemed interested in gossiping about the murder, the real trick was to convince them to confide what they knew without making them feel poorly for wagging about the misfortunes of others. The pursuit of a pious nature had stilled many an uncharitable tongue. But ask the right way, and the gossipers didn't even think twice about what they were spilling to a willing audience.

'A sad tale,' Lucy commented, looking at a loose thread on the sleeve of her cloak. 'I heard they were a lovely God-fearing couple.'

'A God-fearing couple, Grandmother!' Eunice repeated. To Lucy she said, 'We saw them a few times in church, but they kept to themselves. Who would have thought they would come to such a terrible end?'

'The Donnetts made lovely soaps,' the grandmother said. 'Made soaps for my niece's wedding, they did. Everyone quite enjoyed the gift. An honest flowery scent it was. Tragic that we won't have such soaps any more.'

'That is so,' Lucy murmured.

'I hear Mrs Donnett's sister has taken on the shop,' Eunice said. 'Perhaps she'd be willing to sell off the stock. I don't think she plans to continue the business, more's the pity.'

'Do you have any idea who might have murdered them?' Lucy asked, trying to bring her back around.

'What's that?' the older woman asked.

'She wants to know if we know who murdered them!' Eunice shouted, her loud words causing Lucy to inwardly groan. This was far less discreet than her usual way of making enquiries.

'Why in heaven's name would we know such a thing?' the grandmother asked, sounding more curious than outraged. Then she sniffed loudly. 'Truth is, we hardly knew them. They kept themselves from us.'

'They weren't very sociable,' Eunice added. 'They didn't take to us and we didn't take to them.' She lowered her voice. 'I used to think it was because of Grandmother, you know. Some people cannot take the shouting. But even when Grandmother was not around, they were not very friendly.' She returned to the loud voice she'd been using before. 'I never saw them with any companions. Is it any wonder that they found themselves killed?'

A few drops of rain began to fall then, and Eunice led her grandmother away, both clucking their teeth over the Donnetts' misfortune.

Lucy stared after them. It was clear that both women believed that the soap-makers had brought their fateful misfortune upon themselves for having failed to be more sociable with their neighbours. *Why had they held themselves apart?* Lucy wondered. 'I'll never get enough details about their murder this way,' she said.

She was just reassembling her pack when an older man resting heavily on a crutch appeared before her. 'Buy me a pint, lass, and I'll tell you what I know about the Donnetts' murders. Better than that piddle you just heard.'

Lucy squinted her eyes. The man looked downtrodden and hungry. 'What do you know?'

'It's not for discussing outside in broad daylight; that I can tell you.' He raised and lowered his crutch. 'One pint. That's all I'm asking.'

Lucy looked around. There was no longer anyone on the street to overhear, but he might walk away, leaving her with no tale at all. Wasn't that why she'd come here, in search of the story? Master Aubrey would not be pleased if she came back empty-handed. Besides, Lach was inside.

'All right, then,' she said, pulling open the tavern door. 'One pint. Your story had better be worth it.'

'Indeed, it is, lass. I promise you that.'

Lucy spotted Lach right away, staring down into his pint. She was struck by how downcast he looked. *What is ailing the lad?* she wondered. She vowed to tease it out of him later, but right now she was curious to hear what the man would say. 'Over there,' she said, pointing to Lach's table.

At her advance, Lach's melancholic expression became a questioning look as he took in Lucy's companion. 'This is Lach,' she said, sliding into a stool at the table. 'He works with me at Master Aubrey's.'

'I'm Master Aubrey's *real* apprentice,' Lach clarified.

Lucy kicked his ankle under the table and then gestured to the serving maid to bring them two ales. 'This man, er—'

'Addison,' the man supplied, seating himself carefully on the bench, tucking his injured leg under the table. He accepted the ale that Lucy pushed towards him.

'You have your drink. Now tell us: what do you know?'

He took a deep sip of the ale. 'All right, lass, all in good time!'

'I heard nothing was stolen from the shop,' she commented. 'That means the murderer wasn't there to rob them.'

'I don't think they were killed by common thieves,' Addison agreed.

Lucy tapped her fingers on the table, giving him a pointed look. He took another long sip, and finally began. 'I was at the Donnetts' shop, several days before they were killed, thinking I'd bring some soap to my family. I live on the other side of the White Horse Inn, but I'd never stopped in their shop before.'

'Did you know the Donnetts already?'

'Seen them at church most Sundays, of course. I'd never passed the time of day with them. They weren't the friendliest sort.' Addison then began to talk at length about all the new congregants who'd been attending his church since the Great Fire. 'I can hardly ever get a pew now with my family and—'

'You stopped in their shop. What happened?' Lucy asked, curtly breaking into the man's reminiscing.

He pinged the glass with his fingernail. 'A man was nosing

about, and Mr Donnett was none too happy about it.' Sitting back, Addison let loose a long and satisfied burp.

'That's it? What happened?' Lucy grimaced as the rank stale smell wafted towards her nose, and she waved the stench away. 'What do you mean, that the man was "nosing about"?'

'He was asking a lot of questions. How long had they lived there? Did they have any children? Had they always been soap-sellers? Questions like that.'

'Did Mr Donnett seem to mind?'

'At first, no. Then he appeared to be getting more cross every time the man spoke.'

'Good at eavesdropping, aren't you?' Lach muttered. Lucy kicked him under the table again.

'I wasn't really paying attention at first. I wanted to buy some soaps for my daughter and wife – they've been angry with me for so long,' Addison said, rubbing his cheek. 'I just came home drunk a few times and my wife said she'd toss me out on my ear, saying that I was a good-for-nothing just because it's been hard for me to find work and—'

'You were telling us about the man you saw in Mr Donnett's shop,' Lucy interrupted again. Truly, was it impossible for the man to stick to the point of the tale? 'Then what happened?'

'Ah, yes. Well, the man kept picking up different soaps, and then laying them back in their barrel. He kept saying, "What a nice shop, Mr Donnett. What nice soap, Mr Donnett. How nice that your business is doing so well? How nice that you have such a beautiful wife."'

Lucy and Lach exchanged a puzzled glance.

'What of it?' Lach asked.

'It was the man's tone, you see. He sounded angry. I could tell that he was baiting Mr Donnett for some reason. A man knows when another man is being goaded.'

'What about Mr Donnett? Did he answer the questions?'

'Yes and no. None of the questions were of the sort you'd really want to answer. He told the man to take the soaps he wanted and just leave. Didn't seem to expect the man to pay either, which seemed odd to me.'

'Did the man leave?' Lucy asked.

'Yes, he did. Without taking any soaps either. Since he hadn't taken Mr Donnett up on his offer, I took a few myself.'

'The Donnetts must have known the man,' Lucy commented.

Addison took another deep sip. 'Well, I can't say anything about Mrs Donnett since she was not there, but I do believe that Mr Donnett knew the man. He looked nervous.'

'Why do you think this man had something to do with their murder?' Lach asked. Lucy glanced at him in surprise. She'd been about to pose the same question herself. 'Sounds as though the man was just interested in the Donnetts' life.'

Clicking his tongue, Addison considered the question. 'I suppose because he brought to mind a man I knew when I was a soldier in Cromwell's army. That man was pleasant, as you could imagine, to our superiors. No matter what they made us do, the muck they made us fight in, he was always so pleasant and polite. "Yes, sir." "If you please, sir." Then one night . . .' He shuddered.

'One night, what?' Lach pressed.

Lucy leaned forward, a chill of expectation running over her.

'The soldier just snapped like a twig.' Addison looked down at his drink. 'Slit the throats of all our commanding officers, as quick as you please.'

'What?' Lucy gasped, while Lach just gaped at him.

'When the alarm was sounded and the rest of the solders all woke up, we found him there, playing with his knife, a foolish smile on his face.' He pressed his knuckles to his lips. 'It was his tone, you see, that reminded me of the man in the shop. The pleasant-sounding questions that weren't so pleasant at all. Of course, I didn't realize it at the time. It only occurred to me a few days later when I heard the Donnetts had been murdered. I just know that it was *that* man.'

Lucy frowned, not sure what to make of Addison's story.

'Can you tell me anything more about their murders?' She gestured towards her pack. 'I've been asked to help write a true account.'

The man tapped on his empty mug. 'I'm a bit too parched to talk. Perhaps if this was refilled, it would be easier to say.'

Lucy flagged down the servant and ordered another round.

Pulling out a pouch containing a small jar of ink, her quill and a scrap of paper, she painstakingly wrote down some key details of their deaths. All the while, Lach looked out of the dirty tavern window, watching the people scuttle by. The rain that had been threatening earlier seemed to have abated. Finally, when she'd eked out all the details she could, they bade him farewell and left.

'See, Lach. It wasn't so hard to get the information we needed,' Lucy crowed on her way back. 'Master Aubrey will be greatly pleased, don't you suppose?' She jabbed Lach in the ribs.

His response lacked much fervour. 'I suppose.'

'What's with you? Why are you so surly? I told you, Master Aubrey will publish your piece soon enough,' Lucy said.

'I just don't like talking about murder,' Lach grumbled.

Was that a tear in his eye?

Without thinking, she grabbed his arm. 'Lach! What is it?'

'Sometimes you are too nosy for your own good, Lucy,' he said, jerking his arm free. 'I don't wish to be in your company any longer.'

Lucy stared at him. There was no jesting or laughing evident in his tone. This boy she'd known for several years was looking now like a complete stranger. She raced after him and grabbed his arm. 'Lach! What on earth is the matter?'

'You told me once that a good friend of yours had been murdered!' he spat out.

An image of her dear friend Bessie emerged in her mind then, forever young and sweet. She pushed the image away. 'That is so. What of it?'

'Well, I knew someone, too.' He began to walk away again.

'Someone . . .' Realization dawned and she caught up with him again. 'You knew someone who'd been murdered? Who?'

'My mother.'

'Oh, dear Lord in Heaven, Lach. I am heartfully sorry.'

He grunted, continuing to walk at a fast clip.

'W–when did it happen?'

'I was not yet apprenticed to Master Aubrey. Indeed, I can scarcely remember it now.' His lie hung in the air between them. He abruptly pulled away then, leaving Lucy with both packs and staring after him.

*   *   *

When Lucy entered the workroom a few minutes later, she found Lach already seated at the workbench, setting his piece. His eyes were still red-rimmed, and he suddenly reminded her of a kicked puppy.

She knelt down beside him. 'Lach?' Her voice was soft. 'I'm truly sorry about what happened to your mother. Indeed, I'm sorry, too, for having asked you about it.'

'Go away.'

Master Aubrey came in then and glanced from one face to the other. His jovial expression faded. 'What's wrong? What happened between you two? Not another fight.'

'There's nothing wrong. Doesn't everyone "love a good murder"?' Lach exclaimed, slamming his hands down on the bench. Then, without saying another word, he stomped out of the room.

Master Aubrey stared after him in astonishment and then turned to Lucy. 'What was that all about?'

'His mother was murdered!' Lucy said, tears filling her eyes. She sank down on the bench. 'When he was a child. He told me, just now. Shouted at me, actually. I never knew anything about it! Did you?'

'Oh, that dear, poor boy!' Master Aubrey said, slapping his head. He sat heavily on the bench beside her. 'I suppose I hoped he would somehow have forgotten. He never talks about it. He was only a wee one at the time. A few years later, his father brought him to London when he was just seven, and he became apprenticed to me when he was twelve.' He sighed. 'I never knew his mother, but his father said she was a lovely mischievous lass, with bright red hair like Lach.'

Lucy wiped away a tear. 'Such a dreadful thing. Do you know what happened?'

Aubrey shook his head sadly. 'A thief, passing through the town, from what I recall. As I recollect, her murderer was never caught and brought to justice.'

'How awful!' She stared down at the floor, her throat and chest aching from unshed tears. 'Poor Lach. No wonder he does not like to sell murder ballads and true accounts.'

'That is likely so,' Master Aubrey said, mopping his glistening forehead.

'Why do we create such pieces?' Lucy whispered, Lach's rebuke still piercing her thoughts. She hugged her knees to her chest. 'Why are people so entertained by death, especially murder?'

She held her breath, but Master Aubrey did not appear to be startled by her blurted remark. 'Ah, Lucy! From time to time, I have asked myself this very question,' he said, the long creases in his jaws pronounced in his face. 'I'm not sure if my answer will satisfy you or not. Would you like to know what I think?'

'Please,' she whispered.

'Our stories help people make sense of tragedy and disorder. While we write our pieces to entertain, we do more than that, do we not? We show when justice has been achieved, as well as the consequences of wrongdoing – is that not so? Yes, we show the terrible side of humanity, but we also show the place of goodness, righteousness and justice in the world.'

Lucy sat back. She'd never heard Master Aubrey speak this way before. Although the printer did not have the measured countenance of Master Hargrave, or the fervent eloquence of Adam, his words provoked swirling new thoughts. She realized that he was waiting for her to reply. 'That is so.'

The conversation apparently over for the printer, he patted her hand. 'Why don't you make Lach a tincture. Bring him some more apple pie?'

Unsure if it would work, Lucy prepared a tray and knocked on Lach's chamber door a while later. He opened the door a crack, and she could see his eyes were still puffy, and his face looked unusually pallid. She held out the tray, and after a slight hesitation, he took it.

'Thanks, Lucy,' he said gruffly. Then, with the faintest grin, he added, 'I'll eat it, even though you are the one who made it.'

TWELVE

After finishing her evening chores and checking to make sure that all the candles were blown out and the coals banked, Lucy brought the lantern up to her bedchamber. Taking a seat at her small table, she stared down at the paper before her, not sure how to start the story of the soap-sellers' murders. The murder of Lach's mother still weighed heavily in her thoughts. *Poor, poor lad.* She blinked back some tears. *To lose his mother in such a terrible way.* 'I understand now why he prefers jests and merriments to murder ballads,' she said with a sigh.

Master Aubrey's words still hung over her as well, about how their pieces helped show order restored and wrongdoings righted. She forced herself to put Lach out of her thoughts and focus on the matter at hand – how to best tell the tale. As always, she began by pondering a title. 'True News? A True Account of Two Most Horrible Murders?' She bit her lip. 'The Soap-Makers' Dirty Demise?'

She began to outline the basic details of their deaths. For this alone, Addison had earned his two pints, providing many details about the Donnetts and their deaths that Lucy had not learned when she had spoken to Mrs Bainbridge, and which Duncan did not seem to have known. 'A soap-maker and his wife did brutally leave this mortal coil, following their most terrible deaths, killed by person or persons unknown. Guy and Mary Donnett, by all accounts a goodly God-fearing couple, were employed at Pye Corner, by the White Horse Inn, industriously labouring over their scented soaps, when they were killed.'

She tapped her quill on the paper a little harder than she intended. To her dismay a drop of ink rolled down the nub unexpectedly, leaving a round inch-wide stain on her paper. Carefully, she blotted the ink to keep it from spreading further and sat back, trying to imagine the scene. 'Mrs Donnett was likely killed first, as she had been advanced upon from behind, the sharp scissors plunged into her back by her assailant. Her husband, in the other room, had no knowledge of the sorry affair, it would seem, for he, too, was taken by surprise when the stringent lye was dumped over his head.' She paused. 'He likely did not perish immediately, and his shrieks and shouts would have been heard easily by anyone else in the house at the time.' She scratched her forehead, before continuing to write. 'There were no neighbours or those who would conduct business in the shop on hand, so the killer likely took a quiet moment to complete his most terrible deed.'

She tapped the end of the quill on the table. Here she needed to introduce some speculation. 'Could it have been a neighbour, not wishing to pay for such delightful, scented soaps?' She pushed back an errant strand of hair that had fallen from her cap. 'Perhaps it was a customer, angry that an order had not been delivered?' What about the man Addison had told her about? Hastily, she wrote more. 'Perchance a customer, believing the soap to be of an inferior quality, did take it in his hands to strike Mr Donnett and his wife down. A neighbour by the initial A did report that he saw an altercation of late between Mr Donnett and a customer a short time before, but little else is known.'

Lucy hesitated. Had Addison been struck by the customer's behaviour at the time? Or was he only remembering after the fact? No one could know the truth of it, at least not yet. Besides, would such a trivial situation warrant such an unforgivable end? Nothing was stolen, no monies removed, nothing was broken. Indeed, the crime shows that this was not an act of common theft. Instead, everything was left in remarkable order.

She stood up and began to pace around the room, trying to think about what to write next. 'No, this crime was personal,' she said, tapping on the wall. 'The hostility was very great. What could have inspired such rage and violence? A family affair? A troubled past?'

She sat back down. The Donnetts had, after all, once given testimony at court about a murder they had witnessed, which resulted in a man being hanged. Could it be a case of long-awaited revenge?

She brushed the feather end of the quill over her cheeks. What was it that Mrs Donnett's sister, Mrs Bainbridge, had said that day? She'd been disappointed that her sister had married outside Fleet Prison, instead of a church.

Why else get married at the Fleet? Lucy tapped on the table. Couples who got married at the Fleet did so for privacy, especially if they did not want acquaintances or family to hear of the banns, in case someone did not approve the match. *I thought my sister might have been with child when she wed, but she swore that not to be true. There never was a babe, after all this time.* So the reason was not a child out of wedlock.

Who else got married there? Nonconformists who didn't want to marry in church. Except that she'd not heard anything about the Donnetts being Quakers or belonging to any of the other sects outside the Church of England. Who else?

She tugged on another loose strand of hair. 'Couples with great age differences,' she said softly. Guy Donnett had been forty-six when he died, Mary had been twenty-seven. A twenty-year age difference was not so uncommon, especially when it was the husband who had years on the wife, although some brows might have been raised at the time.

She continued to think. Perhaps the Donnetts had thought someone would protest their marriage. One of them could have been in debt or have legal troubles and did not want to draw attention to themselves. Or one of them could have been married before. That was certainly a cause for a more clandestine wedding, if they did not want bothersome in-laws harassing them.

Dipping her pen in the ink, she added a few more lines in which she speculated upon their marriage, alluding to what Mrs Bainbridge had confided about getting married at the Fleet. She then returned to expand upon the motivation of revenge.

Lucy had a slight pang writing that last part. It had been clear when she'd spoken to the tooth-puller's family that they had not sought revenge for their brother's eventual execution. 'I have to say something to whet our reader's appetites,' she said aloud, Master Aubrey's wagging finger appearing in her mind. 'Or else it won't sell at all.'

Early the next morning, Lucy wiped her sweating forehead as she walked toward St Giles-in-the-Fields. Despite the winter chill, she was getting quite warm from the exertion of carrying a pack full of heavy books, which Master Aubrey had asked her to deliver to his old friend Grier Larkin. Her mind was just as heavy. Lach still seemed out of sorts, even after Master Aubrey had rubbed his hair and cheerfully informed him they'd be setting Lach's piece shortly, as soon as Lucy's true account of the Donnetts' murders was completed.

The crackling sound of branches caused her to look warily around, suddenly on alert. Unlike ladies of the upper classes, she wore no fine clothes or jewellery when she travelled, and so rarely attracted the attention of thieves. Still, she remained alert in case someone pursued her for more nefarious purposes.

'Who's there?' she called, spotting a movement behind a low stone wall that may have once marked the edge of a property. Her hand moved to the side of skirts, where she kept the knife that both Duncan and Adam had separately urged her to carry when travelling alone.

In response, an ill-sounding dog howled. She frowned. What manner of dog was that? She braced herself, trying to decide if she should flee or stay still.

Then, to her relief, Sid stepped from behind the wall, looking sheepish. 'I didn't mean to frighten you,' he said. 'I was just having a bit of fun.'

'I've got deliveries to make, Sid,' she said, resuming her gait.

He scrambled after her. 'I can see that. Where are you going?'

'St Giles-in-the-Fields.' She glanced at his arm. 'Has your wound healed?'

He flexed a muscle. 'Strong as an ox,' he declared, though she could tell he was hiding a grimace. Sid reached over and took her pack, hefting it over his shoulder. 'Let me accompany you for a spell.'

They continued on in silence. Sid's face was puckered in a frown and he appeared to be deep in thought.

'Something on your mind, Sid?'

'Is the magistrate still doing poorly? Or has his lot improved?'

'He is doing well enough. Close to his regular form.' She sighed. 'Despite maintaining his usual steady calm, I fear that the loss of his personal papers has caused him deep distress.'

'Is that so? I mean, it is distressing, of course,' Sid replied.

'Especially since we know the thief sold them to a printer. All his hidden thoughts have been made visible to the public in a way that does not serve him well. He was writing his own discussion of events,' Lucy said, a surge of sadness and indignation coursing over her. 'To top it all, he is being blackmailed by someone seeking to besmirch his fine reputation. It's all terribly unfair.'

Sid swore. 'Ah! Why did I not knock his assailant down when I could? Why did I not run faster and tackle him that day?'

'Sid! He stabbed you and yet you still raced after him. Do not berate yourself. You did what you could.'

'That may be so. Still, when I see the trouble that fellow has caused, it makes my blood boil.'

Lucy had a sudden memory of her first time meeting Sid, when he was pocketing a poor woman's money that she'd intended to use for supper. If his former self could hear him now, she did not know what he would make of Sid today. 'I know,' she agreed. 'This upsets me, too. Master Hargrave does not deserve this. Nor do those publishers deserve to profit from stolen goods.'

'We have to find that bookseller,' Sid declared.

'I agree. We know the bookseller is Phineas Fowler, and the master printer is Sam Havisham. But the Stationers' Company has no record of his press since before the Great Fire. I had thought that the next time we saw Phineas out selling, we could simply follow him.' She crossed her arms. 'Only the Hargraves made me promise that I would not follow him if I saw him. They are fearful that I would get myself into a tricky spot.' She stopped in the middle of the street before one of the fancier homes, which suggested a man of means lived there. 'I think this is where I must make my delivery.'

Seeing a servant out front beating the dust from a blanket, she confirmed that it was Larkin's home and explained her presence there. As she was being led inside the house, she could see Sid still standing outside, a troubled look on his face.

'Master Aubrey had all of the titles you requested except one,' Lucy said to Master Larkin after she was led into his study by a pocked-face maid. She began to remove the books one by one, and the scholar began to peruse them eagerly.

'Very good, very good, Lucy,' he said, seeming pleased. He

pulled out his purse and carefully counted out some coins. He held up another shilling and laid it beside the others. 'For your troubles.'

'Thank you, sir,' she replied, picking up her empty sack. 'We shall bring the last book when we acquire it.'

She was about to leave when he called her back. 'If I recall correctly, Lucy, you used to be employed by my old friend Thomas Hargrave – is that correct?'

She dropped a small curtsey. 'Indeed, sir. He was a wonderful master and there is much I learned from him. He helped me secure my current position working for Master Aubrey, when there were no ladies left in his home whom I could serve.'

'I see. Good man, indeed,' he said. 'A shame his name has been vilified in such a fashion.'

With a sinking feeling, Lucy watched Master Larkin as he gingerly picked up a familiar-looking tract from his desk and held it out in disdain. 'Have you seen this dreadful piece? *The Magistrate's Confession.*' He scowled. 'Those of us who know him well know that he was both honest and honourable when he served as a magistrate.'

'Yes, sir,' she said. 'All lies.'

He exhaled heavily. 'I do not believe these allegations, either. Thomas is one of the finest men I know.' He rang the bell on his desk to have the maid show her out. 'Unfortunately, there are others who will believe this account. I am rather afraid that my dear friend's name will be dragged through the mud, and there may be little anyone can do, should any more such terrible allegations appear.'

Larkin's words shook her. Even if the magistrate's true friends knew the allegations to be lies, there were far more people who were willing to believe them to be true. *Could we write a defence of Master Hargrave? Perhaps some former judges could speak to his honesty and virtue? I'll see what Adam thinks.*

To her surprise, she found Sid still waiting where she'd left him. 'Why are you still here?' she asked, glancing at the sun. 'I don't have time to dawdle. Besides, don't you have work to do, Sid?'

'Tell me what that rotten bookseller looks like. That Phineas fellow.'

'Why?'

'I was thinking about what you said,' he replied. 'How the Hargraves made you promise not to go looking for the bookseller on your own. Nothing is keeping me from looking for him, is there?'

'I suppose that's true.' Perhaps that would help solve at least one of their problems, if Sid could be dispatched to follow Phineas. Her eyes narrowed. 'What will you do when you find him? Tell me exactly.'

'I'll tell the constable at once. I promise.'

'You'll tell me, too.'

'Fine. Now tell me what he looks like.'

Lucy then described Phineas Fowler, with as much detail she could muster.

'Studied him closely, did you?' Sid said, handing her back the pack. In a girly, high-pitched voice, he said, '"Handsome man, blond, striking green eyes, slender build, the voice of a player." Your description has much to be desired.'

Annoyed, Lucy began to walk back in the direction of Master Aubrey's shop, her steps quick and tight. She'd had enough of Sid's foolishness for one day.

Sid easily matched her pace as he walked alongside her. 'Please, Lucy. I truly feel that I let the Hargraves down when I allowed that man to escape my grip. To think that those printers and blackmailers are now taking advantage of the magistrate, after he was injured.' There was an unexpected catch in his voice that caused her to look up at him in surprise. 'I should like to prove myself capable. I want the Hargraves to think well of me, as they do you.' He clenched his fists. 'I want to track down that printer so that we can bring the magistrate's assailant to justice once and for all.'

A lump rose in her throat at his unexpectedly heartfelt words.

When she didn't reply, he pressed on. 'To be honest, I don't think I can find him without you, Lucy – even with that, ahem, helpful description. You've seen him selling several times now, have you not?' At her nod, he continued. 'That means you have a better sense of how to find him. You know where he'd want to sell, at any given time, would you not?'

'Certainly. Any London bookseller would have a sense of it.'

'Let us work together to find him. I know the Hargraves are concerned about you getting in harm's way, but I promise I would keep you safe. Once we locate Phineas Fowler, we can just follow him. Maybe he'll go to his home or to his printer's shop. Then we can tell the constable. Please, Lucy, allow me to help.'

Lucy hesitated, thinking about her promise to the Hargraves. She wouldn't really be breaking that promise, would she? After all, she wouldn't be alone, and working together might make it easier to inform the constable of Phineas's whereabouts. Certainly, the sooner they found him, the sooner she could return home to set the tract about the soap-sellers.

'All right,' she agreed. 'This afternoon, I'm to first sell at the Falcon. After that, I'll be done and I can meet you at the Cheshire Cheese, around two o'clock or just after.'

THIRTEEN

Gulping down some cold mutton and a bit of mash, Lucy waved to Master Aubrey and headed over to the Falcon. She had brought two true accounts of murder to sell, which she hoped would not take too long. As she walked the half mile to the tavern, she thought about how she would set the soap-seller's piece later that afternoon. Master Aubrey wanted to read it over before she set it up, but she wanted to be ready if he had questions about which woodcuts and type she planned to use.

When she arrived at the tavern, it did not take her long to get started. 'Gather round, gather round!' she began to call. 'Hear the true and most terrible story of a murder . . .'

She was still at the start of her story when a man strode up to her and ripped the account right from her hands and began to tear it up in front of her.

'Hey!' she exclaimed. 'What are you doing?'

'You should be ashamed of selling rubbish like this!' he exclaimed. 'These are all lies! Have you no conscience?'

Lucy stumbled back from the man's fury, casting about the crowded street for help. Although a few merchants were watching the man from their shops and stalls, no one appeared ready to step forward to assist her, avoiding her eyes.

Then the man, who looked to be about her own age, reached down and picked her pack from the ground and held it up high. 'More lies!'

'Leave that be!' She tried to grab her bag back, but he held it up, high above her reach.

He grinned down at her malevolently. 'Why should I allow you to profit off the misery of others?' He began to slowly turn the bag upside down over a puddle, muddy with slush.

Realizing his intent, Lucy grabbed his arm. 'Stop! Please! This is my livelihood.'

'What do I care about the livelihood of someone like you?' He then dumped the bag into the puddle and stepped on it, so that it became submerged in the muddy water. 'You call yourself truth-tellers but all you do is peddle lies! True accounts!' he scoffed. 'You don't know the damage you reap!'

Lucy grabbed his arm as he started to stalk away. 'How dare you ruin my wares? You must be accountable for the damage you have wrought!'

The man shook her off violently, so that she was knocked to the ground with some force.

At this point, the onlookers began to murmur among themselves in an uneasy way. They were not bothered by a man shouting at a young woman, but to see her assaulted by a stranger was another thing altogether.

A burly man set down a crate he'd been carrying and stood in front of him. 'How about you leave the lass alone?'

'Stay out of it,' her abuser replied, squaring his shoulders.

A large matronly-looking woman came to stand beside the man. 'We came to hear a good story. No need to stop the lass when she's just trying to make a living. Get on with you!' With meaty hands, she pushed Lucy's assailant backwards.

A wall of men and women suddenly formed, protecting Lucy from her assailant until he had no choice but to slink away. For her part, Lucy stood still, stunned by what she'd just experienced. She'd suffered her share of abuse since she'd become a bookseller, but never had anyone attacked her for selling penny pieces. Why was that man so angry?

'You all right now, miss?' one of her protectors asked, and she smiled weakly at the woman.

'Yes, thank you all,' she said.

The rest nodded or tipped their caps in acknowledgement, drifting back to the market and businesses around them, the quarrel already forgotten. Lucy stared at her sodden penny pieces forlornly and began to pick them up, hoping at least a few might be salvaged. Master Aubrey would not be pleased when he saw the ruined stock.

Heaving the sodden pack over her shoulder, she began to limp home. Her hip was hurting from where she had landed on it. *Another lovely bruise.* She rubbed the painful spot, trying to decide if she should tell Master Aubrey what had happened. He was a soft-hearted soul underneath his bluster, and she knew he'd be incensed if she told him. At the same time, she did not want him thinking she could not handle being alone on the streets. *I'll tell him I slipped in the puddle*, she decided, even though the painful scolding she would receive would be far worse than the physical pain she'd just endured.

Still lost in thought when she reached the juncture where Fetter Lane met Fleet Street, Lucy did not even realize someone had been calling her name. She looked up at Sid dully when he appeared before her, looking anxious.

'Hey! Didn't you hear me calling you?' Sid asked, ducking down to peer into her face. 'That bookseller is over at the Cheshire Cheese.'

She blinked. 'Oh, Phineas is there?' Squinting, Lucy looked towards the Cheshire Cheese. She could see a crowd had gathered in front of the newly built tavern but couldn't make out Phineas himself. 'What? Are you sure?'

'I think it's him. I was waiting for you and he showed up. Truly, Lucy, I am impressed by your fortune-telling!'

'No fortune-telling involved – just common sense,' she replied, batting at him. 'This is a good time to be over at the tavern, before people head home from their shops and stalls. I didn't think he'd really be there; that was just where I was intending to sell myself.'

'Well, let's go!' He grabbed her arm, and then let it go, looking startled. 'Why are you all wet? It's not been raining.' Then he looked at her more closely. 'Lucy! You're filthy! Why do you have mud all over you?'

Lucy sighed. She must look a sight. 'Someone knocked me into a puddle.'

He frowned. 'Why weren't you more careful? You must be freezing.'

'Never mind that now. We can't miss out on Phineas Fowler. Let's go!'

His fleeting concern was replaced by his earlier fervour, and he began to run down the street towards the tavern.

'Sid, wait! Slow down!' Lucy called. 'I don't want him to see me! He'll know who I am.'

Sid slowed down, stopping behind a haymaker's cart. 'Stay behind me,' he said in a hoarse whisper. 'Is that him?'

Lucy peered out at the bookseller from behind Sid's back. It was definitely Phineas, his blond hair tied back with a black velvet ribbon. Even though they were beyond the edge of the crowd, she could easily hear his distinctive voice, relating the *Tooth-Puller's Tale*. As always, his audience was entranced, their eyes wide, mouths agape, delighting in his every word. An elderly woman, clutching a basket full of dried flowers, seemed particularly entranced.

'Yes, that's him,' she confirmed.

'He's a good fellow!' Sid said, unable to contain his admiration. 'That's a master storyteller to be sure.'

For some reason, Sid's comment rankled and she jabbed him hard in his ribs. Recognizing Phineas's customary flourishes and climactic moment, she added, 'I think he's about done with that tale.'

Sure enough, Phineas finished up then, to the collective sigh of his audience. He began to collect the coins efficiently, passing out the tracts. As the audience drifted away, Fowler looked inside his pack, a satisfied smile on his lips.

Lucy stayed hidden behind Sid's frame. 'I'd wager his pack is empty now,' she whispered. Then she tugged on Sid's arm. 'He's leaving!'

Slowly, they edged forward, keeping an eye on Phineas as he moved.

'What's he doing now?' Sid muttered.

Phineas had stopped in front of the old flower-seller and bought a bouquet of the dried flowers wrapped gaily in a red ribbon. The woman stared at the coins and gave a deep painful curtsey. Phineas nodded at her before turning away. The woman clutched his sleeve, holding out another bouquet, gesturing wildly. She must have been mute, because they could only make out inarticulate noises coming from her mouth.

'She's trying to make him buy another,' Sid whispered.

'I don't think so,' Lucy replied.

As they watched from their careful distance, Phineas pressed the woman's bony hand. Then they heard him speak. 'Madam, I do not require a second bouquet, but I thank you kindly for listening so carefully to my tale.' Holding the posy to his nose, he inhaled deeply. 'One bouquet is all I need.'

'I wonder who he got the flowers for,' Lucy whispered. 'Oh, he's moving again.'

Keeping a cautious distance behind, they began to follow him. They could hear him whistling and his step was jaunty. 'He seems gladsome enough,' Lucy said. 'Likely sold all his pieces.'

He caught the eye of several passers-by, including a comely young woman who gave him a coy smile as she passed. Phineas stopped abruptly, causing Sid and Lucy to throw themselves into a doorway so they would not be seen if he looked down the street. His attention was solely on the young woman. 'For you, miss,' he said, extending the flowers toward her with a flourish.

Sid snorted softly and Lucy rolled her eyes, expecting that he would press his advantage as she accepted the flowers with wide eyes and stammered thanks. Then, when she began to shyly introduce herself, he cut her off abruptly. 'No thanks necessary,' he said, and continued on.

Perhaps we misjudged him, Lucy thought curiously as they traipsed after him. Phineas continued his walk, turning on to a street near Embankment. Akin to other streets that had not been touched by the Great Fire, it was full of homes and shops hanging on top of each other. Sid and Lucy reluctantly stayed close to the storefronts and stalls, so they could dart easily into a doorway if necessary.

Hope no one throws slops out, Lucy thought, glancing from time to time at the upper windows, in case someone decided to dump out a basin.

'Look. He's going inside,' Sid whispered. Sure enough, Phineas had disappeared into one of the narrow buildings. There was no sign above the door and no wares outside to indicate that it was a shop, so they could not follow him inside. They could not very well walk into a private home without suffering the consequences.

'Maybe that's where his press is,' Lucy whispered. 'Let's wait to see if he comes out.'

For the next fifteen minutes, they waited, but Phineas did not come back out.

'I can't wait much longer,' Lucy said finally. She gestured ruefully at her sodden pack. 'I will have to explain this to Master Aubrey.' Then, as she was about to go, Sid grabbed her elbow, pulling her back out of sight.

'Lucy,' he whispered in her ear. 'Look at that man!' He pointed to a stocky figure walking down the street. 'He's the fellow who attacked Master Hargrave!'

'Who? Where?' Lucy exclaimed. 'That man? Are you certain?'

'Yes! Reasonably so. Let's see what he does.'

The man strode up to the building that Phineas had entered, swinging open the door without knocking. They heard him shout something when he walked in, but his words were not clear.

'He has to be Fowler's partner,' Lucy said. 'Now we need proof. Come on!' Catching hold of Sid's arm, she dragged him across the narrow street. The shutters on the front windows were mostly closed, but cracked a little to let in air and light. Carefully peeking in, she could see Phineas sitting at a table. Behind him, Lucy could see a small printing press and familiar shelves full of type and woodcuts, separated by cases and drawers by font and type.

We found it! she mouthed at Sid.

The man who had just entered was slightly out of view. 'How did you do?' she heard him ask, his voice gruff.

'Sold everything I brought with me. Gamel, where's my new piece? I've been waiting.'

Gamel came into view then and Lucy edged back, still able to see through the narrow crack where the shutters were hinged to the wall. She could see him hold out his hand towards Fowler. 'I'll take my portion of the money now, though, if you would.'

Phineas dumped some coins out on the table and pushed half towards Gamel. 'Here!' he said. 'I'll take a new piece, if you please.'

From the inner pocket of his jacket, Gamel pulled out a folded piece of paper and handed it to Fowler. When the bookseller opened it, Lucy could see lines of elegant handwritten script.

A long silence ensued as Fowler perused the papers. 'All right, Gamel. This will do for a true account.' He sighed. 'Why not just give me all the pieces at once? Let me decide which ones to sell next. Let me just pay you a tidy sum and we can dispense with this piecemeal business once and for all.'

'In good time, Brother,' Gamel replied.

Brother? Lucy exchanged a startled glance with Sid. Squinting, she studied both men. She could see now there was a similar cut to the jaw, but Gamel was far less slender. With his cap off, she could see he was balding too, though Lucy sensed he might be the younger of the two.

A sense of indignation washed over her. Phineas was not just acquainted with the man who had accosted and stolen from Master Hargrave but was linked to him by blood. She forced herself to turn back to the scene playing out before her.

'Is this your way of keeping the upper hand?' Phineas clenched his fist. 'Does it amuse you that I must grovel every few days for a new tale to publish? Does it amuse Father?'

Gamel snorted. 'While it is not without some pleasure to see you humble yourself before me, it is not my choice to be so stingy with these accounts. Father has insisted that you only receive one piece at a time.'

'He wants me beholden to you.'

'Perhaps.' Gamel's voice had grown louder as if he was moving towards the window.

Sid put his finger on his lips, urging Lucy to stay silent. Lucy nodded, acknowledging the warning.

They heard him sigh. 'I don't know why you look so disturbed, Phineas. You've long known Father's temperament. You know what he wants.'

'I still do not understand why . . . Wait! Is Father still . . . building his collection?' His voice sounded strangled. 'Gamel! Tell me he is not!'

'Do not worry, Brother. I shall make sure you can print his collection soon. Perhaps that will end this, in a way that is well and good for him.'

'I have nothing more to say to you, Gamel. I think you'd best leave so I can work.'

Sid jerked his head towards a collection of wooden crates near a horse trough. He dragged Lucy over to hide just in time, as Gamel strode out of the door. Fortunately, his eyes were directed forward, and he was not looking around, so he did not see the pair of them where they hid.

'I'm going to follow him,' Sid murmured, and before she could grab him, he stood up as soon as Gamel was a few feet away.

'Wait!' Lucy whispered. 'Take heed! That man is dangerous! He stabbed you! And brutally attacked Master Hargrave!'

'Don't care,' Sid muttered in return. 'I'm doing it for Master Hargrave.' Without waiting for her to respond, he took off after Gamel, who was already halfway down the street.

Lucy moved back towards the window and this time cautiously peeked inside. She could see Phineas seated at a low wooden table poring over some cramped parchment, a quill in his hand.

'I can include this. This part as well,' she heard him mutter. 'Make it a folio. Let's see, shall I call it *A True Account*? Or *A Most Terrible and Monstrous Tale*? Or *True and Barbaric News*? What a story!' she heard him mutter. 'Or how about *A True and Just Monstrosity: Woman Kills Midwife After Giving Birth to a Cat*?'

He looked as though he would be busy working on the piece for a while. Two giggling servants passed by on the street then, giving Lucy a curious look as she passed. Lucy straightened up from the window and stepped away, trying to appear as if she'd not been eavesdropping. There seemed no reason to spy on Fowler further and she couldn't risk being caught. *At least we found Fowler's press*, Lucy thought, still stunned by what she had just learned. 'We need to tell Duncan.'

'I found Phineas Fowler and the location of his printing press!' Lucy exclaimed triumphantly as she walked into the gaol. Hank and Duncan came out, brushing away the last of their crumbs from their afternoon meal. 'You can arrest him now!'

'Lucy, what is this about?' Duncan asked, standing up.

Quickly, Lucy described what she had just witnessed between the Fowlers. 'Go and arrest him, Constable.' Then, feeling chastised by his raised eyebrow, added, 'Please, if you would.'

Duncan looked thoughtful. 'I don't think I should arrest Phineas Fowler – at least not yet. Perhaps it would be better if I spoke to him first.'

'Why not arrest him?'

'If we arrest Fowler now, we will lose the chance to go after his brother Gamel for stabbing Sid and assaulting Master Hargrave. From the conversation you overheard, it sounds as though his father played some sort of role in this as well, which we should not discount. I worry that if we go over now, without more evidence, then we might show our hand.'

Lucy sighed, realizing the truth in his words.

Perhaps recognizing her frustration, Duncan sought to soothe her. 'Besides, you saw the printing press. The man has settled in, it seems. Why don't you show me where they are? After that, I can keep an eye on them myself.'

Although she felt a little disappointed, what Duncan was saying made good sense. A little patience could go a long way in bringing the Fowlers to the punishment they deserved.

The delicious smell of mince pies washed over Lucy as she walked into Master Hargrave's kitchen a short while later, causing her mouth to water. Cook and Annie were seated at the table, shaping shells to hold the sweet Christmastime pie. As she breathed in the aroma of fruits and spices, Lucy forgot why she was there.

'Lucy?' Cook prompted. 'Is there something we can do for you?'

'Oh! I need to speak to Master Hargrave.'

'Lucy?' Adam asked, entering the kitchen 'I thought I heard your voice. What brings you here?'

'We found Phineas Fowler!' she exclaimed. 'Sid and me!'

Adam frowned. 'Lucy! You promised that you wouldn't follow the man.'

'Sid was with me the whole time. I swear he never saw us.' She described how she and Sid had followed the bookseller back to his shop. 'I already led Duncan to the place so he and Hank can keep an eye on him.'

Worried that Adam's tight lips meant he was angry, Lucy pressed on. 'I wanted Duncan to arrest Phineas on the spot, but he said it was too soon.'

'I agree with the constable,' he said. *Was it hard for him to say that?* Lucy wondered. 'It would have been premature to arrest Fowler, when it sounds as if his brother – Gamel, was it? – was the one who struck down my father.'

'Sid followed Gamel when I went to speak to the constable.' She glanced at the window. 'I wonder what he's doing now. I'm hoping he did not do anything foolish.'

'Oh, that dratted Sid!' Annie complained, scrunching her apron in knots. 'Why does he always have to get himself in trouble?'

'He's not in any trouble right now, Annie,' Lucy said. 'Maybe he will acquire some new knowledge about Gamel.' She looked back at Adam. 'We already learned something interesting about the magistrate's notes.'

'What did you learn?' Adam asked.

'Gamel only seems to give Phineas one trial record at a time, every few days. My guess is that he is allowing Phineas to work off one record at a time, giving him time to write and print the piece. From the conversation, it seems his father told him to do it that way. I suppose he wants Phineas to be beholden to him, although I cannot fathom why.'

'I see,' Adam said. 'Was Sam Havisham at the shop?'

'I didn't see him,' Lucy replied, moving away from the hearth now that she was sufficiently warmed. 'Adam, may I speak to your father? I overheard Phineas talking to himself about the piece Gamel had given him. Perhaps we can see if your father recalls this piece as well.'

'Let me take you to him.'

A moment later, Lucy and Adam were seated with the magistrate, and Lucy was trying to recall what Phineas Fowler had said as he read through Master Hargrave's notes about the trial. 'I heard him say that a woman killed her midwife after she gave birth to a cat. Do you recall that case?' Lucy asked.

The magistrate uttered a grim chuckle. 'A difficult case to forget. A woman, who'd become delusional during her labours, indeed believed she'd given birth to a cat.'

'Gave birth to a cat?' Annie said, having followed them to the study, holding a tray of warmed mead. 'Like Agnes Bowker?'

Lucy nodded. She'd shared the ballads of Agnes Bowker who, depending on which ballads a person read, either had actually been delivered of a cat instead of a babe or was so afflicted in her mind that she only believed she had done so.

'Indeed,' the magistrate replied, apparently also recalling the tale. 'The case was another odd one. Only this woman sought revenge on the poor witless midwife, striking her down with her own knife.' He accepted the steaming mug from Annie. 'As I recall, the murderess had just given birth. Poor woman. She must have been half out of her mind from the pain when she gazed upon her infant. The witness testified that the babe made a mewling sound, and she mistook the babe for a cat.'

'Babies can sound like kittens,' Annie commented. 'My ma said something like that once.'

The magistrate raised an eyebrow. 'I do not recall if either Adam or Sarah made such sounds. Anyway, back to the case at hand. Apparently, the woman also suffered from a regular nervousness and then, in her disturbed state, did plunge one of the midwife's own tools into her chest, before anyone had the wits to stop her.'

'What a dreadful tale,' Lucy exclaimed. 'What happened to her?'

'She was of course arrested and brought to Newgate, with no respite from childbirth. Separated from her child, whom she came to realize, when her terror subsided, was not a cat.' He tsk-ed at the memory. 'She was quite pitiful during the trial, trembling violently the whole time, clearly stricken down by remorse. The remorse, not only for what she had done to the midwife, but to her own precious child, who would grow up in another woman's family.'

'Surely she was not found guilty of murder?' Lucy asked. 'Would she not simply have been taken to Bedlam, to live out her days with other similarly afflicted sorts?' Though truth be told, having visited Bedlam herself once, she could not imagine a sorrier fate.

'Perhaps she should have been sent to Bedlam – that may well have been the sentence I would have handed down, should I have presided over this trial,' the magistrate said, gazing out of the window. 'However, during the trial, while she remained agitated, it was clear that the confusion had cleared in her mind and she no longer believed she'd given birth to a cat. Moreover, the midwife was a well-respected member of the community, with many connections among the nobility. By contrast, the murderess was quite the opposite – the unmarried daughter of a rat-catcher.'

'A rat-catcher's daughter?' Annie murmured. 'No wonder she dreamed her babe a cat.'

'They did not believe the woman because she was poor and unmarried?' Lucy asked, her lip curling at the magistrate's claim.

'That was certainly part of it, I'm afraid,' Master Hargrave replied. 'However, the case was clinched when another witness stepped forward, claiming she'd been outside the bedchamber when the birthing was happening. She claimed that the midwife had asked the woman several times to provide the name of the babe's father and she had refused.'

'Must she provide the father's name?' Annie asked.

'Midwives have the right to refuse service to a woman in her travails if the name of the father is not known,' Lucy said thoughtfully, an odd piece of information gleaned from the many murder ballads she'd read these last few years.

'That is so,' the magistrate replied. 'According to this witness, the woman refrained from speaking until the pain had grown so immense that she shouted out a man's name and begged the midwife to help her. After the babe was safely born, the witness claimed that the woman killed the midwife to keep the name of the babe's father a secret.'

He sighed. 'I remember thinking at the time that the witness's testimony was likely coerced or at least paid for by one of the midwife's more powerful friends. This new testimony gave the jury a new angle to consider – now, instead of sending the woman to Bedlam, they could conclude the killing to be voluntary manslaughter, and thus punishable by execution. Although she was penitent and showed great remorse, the remorse did not move the jurors.'

'What happened?' Lucy asked.

'Ultimately, as I recall, the jury found the truth in that second witness, determining the woman guilty. She was hanged soon after.' He rubbed his ear. 'In my commentary, I remember describing the jurisprudence involved, questioning the way the evidence had been brought before the jury, and noting something about witness testimony as well.'

'I remember we discussed this case, Father. The questions you raised were important ones for judges to consider,' Adam said. 'We shall see what Fowler does with this tract.'

'Lucy, was there any mention of blackmailing me? I've yet to hear from the blackmailer again.'

'No, sir. Nothing like that was discussed.' Lucy was still mulling over what Adam had just said. 'I don't understand, sir. Do you mean you are going to let Phineas Fowler publish and sell the tract?' she asked, moving toward the door. 'Who knows what he will say about you this time? We have to stop them!'

Adam stepped in front of the door, effectively blocking her from leaving the magistrate's study. 'Wait, Lucy. There's nothing we can do right now. The constable has been informed, but he will need a warrant to search Fowler's premises for Father's notes and to make an arrest. Right now, the evidence is only hearsay, drawing on what you overheard from the Fowlers' private conversation.'

'We can get more evidence,' Lucy cried.

'Lucy, no,' Adam said sharply. 'Don't even think about it. You need to stay away from the Fowlers.'

His father touched her arm. 'Lucy, I echo my son's concerns. I do not know why the Fowlers would wish ruin upon me; I cannot recall ever having met them. But from their behaviour so far, especially that of Gamel Fowler, I do not want you anywhere near them.'

'Yes, sir,' she whispered. Adam looked at her sceptically, and she forced herself to put a sincere smile on her face. 'I understand, sir.'

Master Hargrave clapped his hands. 'All right, enough of that. Let us discuss something more pleasant.' He handed her a folded piece of paper. 'Please give this to Master Aubrey. I'm inviting all of you – Will and Lach, too – to join us for our Christmas Eve celebration. We should very much like to have you all join us for a bit of merriment and good cheer.'

She accepted the paper and carefully put it in her pocket. 'Thank you kindly, Master Hargrave. I shall extend them the invitation.' After dropping her customary curtsey, Lucy quickly left the Hargraves, already wondering how she might find a way around this new promise to stay away from Phineas Fowler.

*   *   *

Duncan stopped by Master Aubrey's that evening, just as they were finishing dinner. Accepting a piece of apple pie and some cheese, he sat down next to Lach.

'Hank and I went and spoke to Phineas Fowler and that printer, Sam Havisham, this afternoon. They were both solicitous and mannerly in their speech. Fowler, in particular, is quite an artful fellow, is he not?' From the way he said 'artful', Lucy did not think he meant it in a kindly way. He took a bite and, after savouring the taste of the pie for a moment, swallowed. 'Both heartily denied knowing who had provided them with the tracts. Said it was not uncommon for someone to provide such stories anonymously. They'd received one just today, in fact.'

Standing up, Lucy began to stack the dirty plates together. 'That's what he told me as well,' she said. 'I never believed it for a moment. Why would someone simply leave pieces without any expectation of payment? Besides, we know now that he's receiving the magistrate's papers from his father and his brother Gamel. Why could you not ask him directly?'

'I pressed him more, but he insisted that he did not know where they had come from. I could not very well tell him that *someone* eavesdropping on his private conversation' – here he gave Lucy a stern look – 'had heard him say something otherwise.'

'Couldn't you just search the place?' Lach asked. 'Find where they are hiding the rest of the magistrate's papers?'

Duncan scraped the last few crumbs from his plate. 'Unfortunately, while it is a terrible thing that they have been publishing such lies, it is up to the magistrate to speak publicly against his defamation. It would be very hard to justify the necessity for a warrant to search the premises, even though I imagine other magistrates would certainly sympathize with Master Hargrave.'

'Phineas complained to his brother about only getting one at a time,' Lucy said. 'Thus, someone, perhaps his father, has the rest hidden somewhere. Maybe Sid knows more, since he followed Gamel.'

Duncan shook his head. 'No, he said Gamel hopped in a cart shortly after he set out, and he lost the pursuit. No luck there. But we'll keep an eye on him, now that we know where the press is located.' He stood up and pulled on his cloak. 'If we hear from the blackmailer again, perhaps we would have new grounds for such a warrant. Until then, I'm afraid we will have to wait and see what comes next.'

After he left, Lucy turned to Master Aubrey. 'I wrote the tract about the soap-makers' murders,' she said, ignoring the scowl that had appeared on Lach's face. 'Lach helped me. I can set it in the morning, if you like.'

'That's a good lass,' Aubrey said happily. 'Let's see it.'

She retrieved her pocket and stared down at in dismay. The piece wasn't there. Hurriedly, she went through her cloak and dumped out her peddler's bag. 'Oh no!' she exclaimed, slumping back against the bench in dismay. 'I can't find it.'

Lach gave her his cheekiest grin. 'Serves you right,' he said, then stuck out his tongue when Master Aubrey wasn't looking. 'You probably lost it, all that scurrying about you did today.'

A twinge of pain in her hip reminded her of the altercation in front of the Falcon with that odd man. In all the excitement of discovering Havisham and Fowler's press, she'd forgotten all about it. Groaning, she wondered if she'd lost it when the man dumped out her sack into the muddy water. 'It *must* be here.'

She spent the next half hour looking in the kitchen, in her bedchamber, turning over pots in the kitchen, and even checking the privy, to no avail. She even went outside with her cloak and lantern held high and walked up and down Fleet Street in the dark, hoping against hope that her account might be blowing about in the street. Finally, Master Aubrey called her inside and bid her to go to bed.

After she had donned her nightclothes, she sat at her small table, staring forlornly at her paper and quill. 'I'll have to rewrite it,' she said. She rubbed her wrist, already anticipating how sore it would be after penning another lengthy piece. 'I hope I remember all the details.'

She continued to stare at the paper, feeling too disheartened to uncork the jar of ink. 'Tomorrow,' she promised herself, as she blew out her lantern and climbed into bed.

FOURTEEN

Bursts of songs and laughter accompanied Lucy and Will as they walked behind Master Aubrey and Lach, lanterns in hand, to the Hargraves' house the next evening. The King had proclaimed that revellers could once again wassail at the homes of the gentry from Christmas Eve until Twelfth Night. Hearing them now gave her a new sense of hope. The previous Christmas, Londoners had still been shocked and exhausted by the damage of the Great Fire and numbed by sickness and plague in the two years before that. This year, more people were inclined to be merry and full of good cheer.

Although the sun was setting, a light snow was falling, bringing an unexpectedly brilliant sheen to the streets and a pleasant crunch beneath their boots. Lucy smiled at Will. 'It's a shame that Celia could not join us. I know the Hargraves would have welcomed her, too.'

Will shrugged. 'I will see her after the Christmas service tomorrow.'

Some drunken revellers pushed at them from behind, waving their wassailing pots in the air.

'Hey, watch it!' he exclaimed, grabbing Lucy's elbow and pulling her out of their way. 'You almost knocked into my sister.'

'Apologies, fine sir,' one of the men mumbled. Or at least that's what it sounded like; the slurring made it hard to know for certain.

His companion chuckled, swaying. 'How about some wassail for the pot?'

The first man leered at Lucy. 'Or perhaps a kiss for my cheek?'

'Get on with you!' Master Aubrey said, planting himself staunchly between Lucy and the men. 'Before I forget this is a night for being merry.'

Taking the hint, the men staggered off, gripping each other's shoulders. Their antics drew her thoughts to Duncan. He'd probably be dealing with such louts and oafs all night long.

Earlier, she'd stopped by the gaol to bring Duncan and Hank some savoury and sweet pies. Although the magistrate had invited them to his celebration as well, both had declined. 'Too much free-flowing wine and merriment tonight,' Hank had said. 'This will be a night for gadabouts and ruffians. It's our duty to preserve the safety of our streets.' Duncan had just nodded. He hadn't said so, but she knew he did not wish to make merry at the Hargraves'.

When she'd set the pies on a shelf in the gaol, she'd noticed another fragrant-smelling covered basket. 'A comely miss brought that pie by for the constable,' Hank had whispered as she was leaving, giving her a funny waggle of his eyebrows. She knew that there had been other women vying for Duncan's attention, but she'd always been too shy to ask him about it. Besides, she didn't want to start a conversation that she didn't know how to end.

When they arrived at the Hargraves', Lucy saw a few familiar guests, including the Larimers. James Sheridan was off by himself, a glass of sherry in his hand.

Mrs Larimer squealed when she saw them. 'Why, it's the good Master Aubrey and our own Lucy Campion! Sing us a song, would you, Lucy?'

Handing her cloak to Annie, Lucy looked hesitantly around at the others. Everyone was smiling at her, except for Sheridan who wore his habitual sour grimace. She looked back at Mrs Larimer, whose cheeks were as rosy as the wine in her glass.

'Ah, don't be shy, Lucy,' Master Aubrey said gruffly. 'Lach and I will join you. Will, too. How about "Poor Red Robin"?'

Although they'd not all sung together before, Will and Lach possessed pleasant tenor voices and Master Aubrey a rich and resonant bass. Lucy rounded out the merry ballad with her bright soprano. There was great applause when they finished, and she could tell that everyone was pleased.

'Please, enjoy,' Adam said, pointing them towards mugs full of warm mulled wine.

The others reached for a mug, but Lucy hesitated. Seeing that Annie was collecting empty glasses and mugs, she began to follow her back to the kitchen to help with the cleaning.

Adam gently grasped her arm. 'Stay here, please, Lucy. You

are our guest tonight.' Then he whispered in her ear. 'You're no longer a servant here. Please try to remember that.'

Lucy gave him a nervous smile and moved over to stand next to Will and Master Aubrey. It was one thing for Adam to say that she was not a servant, but quite another for her to feel that fully in her bones. Although everyone in the room had known her for some time as a printer's apprentice, and perhaps no longer viewed her as a servant, standing next to Adam as his social equal was something else altogether.

'Tell us, Thomas, how is your dear daughter Sarah doing these days?' Mrs Larimer asked. 'Is she still a – you know . . .?'

'Follower of her conscience?' Master Hargrave replied. 'Yes, she is still a Quaker.' Although he did not frown, Lucy could see his jaw tighten. He did not like discussing Sarah's beliefs or the trouble she got herself into because of them.

Oblivious to her husband poking her, Mrs Larimer continued, 'Does she still speak about "women's speaking justified"?' She giggled. 'I remember her shouting that she was like Esther, delivering her warnings to the king! In front of the church, no less! At least she never took on the sackcloth and ashes like those Quakers used to! Goodness, can you imagine such a sight?'

'I am not pleased that my daughter has become so bold in her speech, but I have come to reflect on her words and I cannot say for certain that all are wrong,' Master Hargrave replied, his manner growing more stiff. 'I do not like the disorder that these Quakers bring to our land, but it is true that some of our ideas should be examined.'

A warmth spread over Lucy when she heard this message and just wished Sarah could be around to hear her father's change in temperament, so openly expressed. Her father had always spoken out against the violence that had been enacted by the crowds against Quakers, but he had administered many punishments to Friends himself in the past.

Thankfully, there was a knock at the door then, and another group of carollers began to sing, keeping everyone laughing and clapping as Annie served more wassail and ale. Lucy sipped her mulled wine, enjoying the warmth of the fire and the good company.

'Tell us a tale, Aubrey!' Mrs Larimer cried, the wine definitely overtaking her now. 'Make it a good and bloody one!'

Not needing to be asked twice, Master Aubrey immediately launched into one of his favourite stories, and then another after that. Lucy always marvelled at his tales, and truly no one, perhaps other than Phineas Fowler, had such a keen grasp of intriguing details, from stories first told before she was born.

At one point, Adam, who'd been standing behind her, whispered in her ear. 'Your Master Aubrey is not just a master printer, but a master storyteller as well.'

There was another knock at the door, and everyone stirred expectantly, hoping for another rousing song from the increasingly tipsy carollers who were still stumbling by.

'Not singers, sir,' Annie called to Master Hargrave, as she carried in a large package tied in string. 'A gift for you.'

She deposited it on the sideboard and picked up one of the empty pitchers to refill in the kitchen.

'A gift? I wonder who sent it.' He sounded excited as he examined the package. It appeared to be a box wrapped in brown paper tied with a thin rope. 'Perhaps there is a letter inside. I need a knife to cut this rope. Annie, can you fetch – oh, she's gone. Lucy dear,' he said, his gaze falling on her, 'could you please fetch me the little knife from my study? My glasses, too, so I might see what I was sent. You know where I keep them.'

'Yes, sir.'

She didn't realize that Adam had slipped out after her and came up behind her. 'I must thank whoever sent Father that present,' he murmured, 'so that I might have a moment alone with you.'

'Oh?'

'I have a gift for you, but I do not want to wait until the New Year to give it to you.' From his pocket, he pulled out a small bag made of green silk.

Lucy put her hand to her lips. 'Thank you, Adam, I did not expect . . .' She began to stammer but stopped when he looked at her with mock sternness. 'I have something for you as well, although I did not bring it with me tonight.'

'Hurry, open your gift! Father is waiting and I know he'll note our absence.'

With trembling fingers, Lucy opened the bag, discovering a lovely jade pendant inside. 'Oh, Adam, how lovely. It's too much! I can't—'

He touched her cheek. 'Please don't injure me by saying you can't accept it. This pendant belonged to my mother, and I know it would please her that you wear it now, for me. I remember her having a special fondness for you.'

'I, as well, for her. But your father, how would he feel if—?'

'Father wholeheartedly agreed with this decision. Please do not disappoint us by refusing this gift.' He reached up and secured the necklace around her neck, touching her skin slightly as he did so. A lump rose in her throat as she remembered Mistress Hargrave. Flighty yet kind. Certainly, she had left this earthly world too soon.

'Beautiful,' he said. His hands were on her shoulders as he stepped back to admire the piece. His eyes met hers then and for a moment she was lost in their deep blue.

Then they heard a loud bellow from the other room. 'I think they are awaiting the knife,' Lucy said, grabbing the small cutting knife from the wooden desk. 'Oh, and your father's glasses.'

She saw that some of the guests had taken their leave in her absence, and Cook, John and Annie had been invited to partake in a glass of wine.

Lucy handed the magistrate the knife and his glasses. Still studying the package, he said to Adam, 'Not the script of anyone I recognize.' Indeed, the hand that had written out Master Hargrave's name was ill indeed. Not an educated hand; that was certain.

He cut the twine and opened the wrapping, and they all peered inside. Three objects were wrapped in grey linen and tied with more twine. 'I have no idea who the sender is,' the magistrate said. Although his tone was jovial, she could hear a slight strain, too. She did not miss Master Hargrave exchange a glance with his son.

They opened the first package which contained two silver candleholders.

'Very elegant,' Cook said approvingly.

'They are quite pretty but . . .' Annie began, but she trailed off, looking worried.

What was wrong? Lucy tried to catch her eye, but Annie was staring at the floor, twisting her hands in front of her.

'Very elegant and pretty, I quite agree,' Master Hargrave said, holding them up for all to see. 'Indeed, I have never received a gift such as these.' He looked sympathetically at his servant. 'Poor Annie is distressed, and I know why.'

'Father? What is it?' Adam asked.

Everyone else peered at the candleholders, trying to figure out what was so odd about them. They were beautiful but ordinary, as far as Lucy could see. Then she peered closer. 'Oh!' she exclaimed softly, clapping her hand over her lips.

'I see Lucy has realized as well. These beautiful candlesticks already belong to me. My late wife selected them herself. More specifically, these were two of the items that were stolen from me recently.'

The joyful mood in the room suddenly became tense.

'Annie, who brought you the package?' Lucy asked. 'Can you describe him?'

Annie's cheeks flushed as she looked tearfully at the magistrate. 'I'm sorry, sir. Just a lad. I should have paid more attention.'

Master Hargrave waved away her distress. 'Don't fret, Annie,' he said kindly as he looked at the packaging again. 'I imagine that my benefactor paid the lad to bring these so-called gifts here. Even if we had questioned him, he might not have been able to shed more light on the package anyway.' He picked up the next package. 'Let us look inside these other packages.'

He picked up the next, which was long and slender, and unwrapped it, revealing two silver serving spoons. Annie gasped.

'Ah, more of my purloined objects, I believe.' Master Hargrave squinted at the stems. 'Indeed. My grandfather's monogram is here, stamped into the silver, is it not? I suppose I should be thankful that no one melted them down.' He picked up the next and carefully pulled away the cloth. 'Ah, as I suspected. The box that I kept on my desk.' He opened the lid, disclosing two more small wrapped packages. 'If I were to surmise, these should be my missing flea glass and my pocket sundial. Let us see if my supposition is correct.'

He opened the first and held up the flea glass. 'I am heartily pleased to have this back in my possession. My spectacles are hardly strong enough for me to see all that I need to see.' He held up the other item, which appeared to be a leather pouch. 'This should be my pocket sundial and yet it strikes me to be the wrong size and shape.'

Carefully, Master Hargrave opened the leather pouch and gently shook the contents into his hand. 'Well, well. What do we have here? This is not one of my possessions.'

He held up his hand for everyone to see. Cradled in his palm was a book-shaped pendant on a silver chain. When he held it up to the light, they could see that the tiny object had been meticulously painted to resemble the spine and cover of an expensive book.

'What a lovely pendant,' Lucy breathed. She'd never seen anything like it.

'Looks like one of those Papist objects,' Annie said, wrinkling her nose. 'Has some saint's bones or clippings in it, I'd wager.'

Master Hargrave frowned. 'I don't think it's a reliquary,' he said, picking up his flea glass. 'Let us see what may be inside. I'd wager that no saint's parts will be found. There must be a clasp – yes, here it is.'

With a slight click, the tiny cover of the book was opened, to reveal two panels of painted images. 'Look, this panel can flip.' Carefully, with the end of his quill, he flipped the page as one might turn the pages of a book, revealing two more delicately painted panels. He held up the flea glass while everyone looked up eagerly. 'These reverse-painted images do not speak to the spiritual or the godly, but rather to the secular.' He held out the flea glass to Adam. 'An exquisite miniature. An expensive piece, I have no doubt. Here, examine it for yourself.'

Adam accepted the flea glass and studied the pendant, and then handed it around. In turn, everyone, even Cook, picked up the flea glass and examined the piece. When it was Lucy's turn, she could see that the first two insets, looking to be two halves of a blue and silver gilded painting, depicted what appeared to be a calf, a bear and two men. When she turned the insert, the two panels depicted a man halfway up a scaffold, his hands tied before him. He was bending down to speak to a woman looking pitifully up at him. There were no words in any of the insets, and no indication of the author's name.

'What do these images mean, I wonder?' Lucy asked.

'Two men, a calf and a bear,' Adam mused. 'That seems familiar. I'm not sure why.'

'Is it familiar?' the magistrate asked. 'My own mind, I fear, is rather blank on what it might mean. The curiosity of the piece is only matched by the strangeness of the gesture.'

'Why give it to you, I wonder?' Lucy said, continuing to examine the pendant. 'Was it simply meant to replace the sundial? Or is there some sort of message there? Yet why give these objects back at all?' She closed her eyes, trying to think. She was glad now that she had only sipped at her wassail. She opened them again. 'We know your assailant was Gamel Fowler, the bookseller's brother, and that he was the one who stole these items from your house.'

'I should think he could easily have earned a pretty penny for the objects he stole,' Cook commented. 'They were quite valuable, were they not? They could have melted down the candlesticks and serving spoons, as you say. Or sold them.'

'Ah, that is so,' the magistrate said, clearly intrigued. 'Does our thief, Mr Gamel Fowler, have a conscience? Is that why he returned nearly everything to me?'

Lucy stared at the items on the table. Was Gamel the type of man who would viciously strike down an older man and then return items he had stolen. She shook her head. 'I doubt it was Gamel. I wager it was a different person entirely – a person with a conscience.'

The magistrate nodded. 'That seems a reasonable supposition. Moreover, there is another intriguing question to consider.'

Lucy thought for a moment. 'What about the items that were *not* returned?' she said. 'Why keep the other pieces?'

The magistrate looked pleased. 'Yes, that is exactly the right question to ask. Annie, do you recall what the other missing objects were? Besides my papers, of course.'

Annie frowned. 'In addition to the pocket sundial, which you already mentioned, sir, I believe you are also missing a small snuff box that you received from your late father. You kept it on your desk. It was also monogrammed.'

'If Gamel Fowler stole the objects, as Sid believes, it does not mean he was the one who returned them to you, sir,' Lucy said.

An image of Phineas Fowler buying the bouquet of dried flowers from the old flower-seller rose in her mind. 'Perhaps it was someone who knew of the crime and wanted to right a wrong. Maybe Phineas sent them back. Gamel may not even know that the objects were returned.'

'Even if Phineas had a call of his conscience and returned these items,' Adam replied, 'he is still benefiting from my father's stolen papers for his own gains.'

The magistrate began to rub his temples with his fingertips. Seeing this, Lucy glanced around at the others. 'We should take our leave,' she said. 'You should rest now, Master Hargrave, so that you may be well for Christmas.'

'Thank you all for a most intriguing evening,' Master Hargrave said, as he walked them to the door. 'It has given me much to ponder.'

'Father's head ached all this morning, so he is still resting,' Adam said, as he and Lucy strolled towards the Hargraves' home, a light snow crunching under their feet. The late-morning Christmas service at St Dunstan's had just concluded and all the parishioners had burst on to the street with collective cheers, some off to go wassailing and carolling again, others off to their cards or to take in a play. Now that their godly obligation was over, everyone had scattered this way and that, eager to partake in another day of merriment and good cheer. Will had headed off to find his Celia, Mary and John went to her sister's house, and Master Aubrey had whisked Lach off for a game of cards at the Cheshire Cheese. Even Annie had pulled Sid away, leaving Lucy alone with Adam. He leaned in toward her. 'He will be glad to see you wearing our gift.'

Her hand flew to her neck. The beautiful necklace was buried under her best dress, close to her throat, so that it would not accidentally catch on something and become lost forever. He must have noticed her wearing it during the service. 'I have something for you both as well.' Shyly, she pulled out a small package wrapped in a scrap of blue silk.

He opened it with great seriousness and then smiled. It was a small wooden tile with a carved image of a man reading a book. She had bought it months ago on a whim, when visiting a carver's shop to get new woodcuts for their press. She'd had to use all the coins she'd been saving to purchase material for a new petticoat. At the time, Adam had not even returned from the colonies, and she had not known when she'd seen him again, or even whether she'd be able to give it to him if he returned.

He traced the carving with one figure. 'I shall have to get another just like this,' he said. 'Only it would be of a comely young woman writing a book. They can sit beside each other on my desk. I like to imagine that's how we might spend our evenings together.'

A warmth spread over Lucy as she thought about what that would be like – to be with Adam so intimately, every evening. Was that how he imagined their future? Without thinking, she reached up and touched his cheek. He grabbed her hand and kissed the back of her fingers.

With a slight gasp, she stepped back, looking around.

'Ah, Lucy, if you could see your expression. I'd fetch the cleric right now if I could, just so you'd accept my attentions.' He laughed gently before tucking her arm in the crook of his elbow. 'The walk is icy here,' he murmured, patting her hand. 'I should not like you to fall.'

'Any more mysterious gifts?' Lucy asked the magistrate when she and Adam arrived at the Hargraves' home.

Master Hargrave was sitting at the kitchen table, the book pendant and flea glass before him. Without asking, Lucy began to stoke the fire in the oven to warm the venison and leek pie that Cook had made for them the night before. He asked a few questions about the service and the biblical passages that the priest had discussed. She remembered how he used to ask such questions of the servants, even when he had attended the sermon, as part of his obligation as the head of the household.

The kitchen door opened, and Annie entered, Sid behind her. They both stopped short, seeing the magistrate and Adam in the kitchen. 'Oh, sir,' Annie cried. 'I hope it is all right if Sid joins us. We had thought we might take in a play, but neither of us had any money.' She paused. 'He has no other place to go at Christmas.'

Master Hargrave inclined his head graciously, as if he had not sentenced Sid to the stocks on more than one occasion. 'Sit down, Sid. Join us.'

The pie in the oven, Lucy sat down beside Adam and picked up the pendant again, studying the images. 'I wonder what the artist was thinking. These images must tell a story of some sort. I know when we select a woodcut for a ballad or true account, we want it to help explain what the tale is about. Even though we have to use the same woodcuts for many different pieces.'

The magistrate nodded. 'I believe that is so, Lucy. The artist is trying to explain something. I do not think these stories come from the Bible.'

'Or the Decameron,' Adam added. 'Or the Canterbury Tales.'

'Nothing related to Greek and Roman stories of their gods either,' Master Hargrave said.

'It doesn't seem like any folk tale I know, either.' Lucy stopped. 'Although . . . a calf and a bear. I feel as if I heard a story at a fair I attended with Sarah. Something about a calf and a bear being switched. Was there something about a thief, too?'

'A calf and a bear and a thief . . .' The magistrate's face cleared. 'Eureka! I know what it refers to!' With that, he scurried out of the room, leaving Adam and Lucy looking after him. A moment later, Master Hargrave returned, a dusty old book in his hands. It was nothing like the penny pieces Lucy sold out on the street. This was a meticulously crafted piece bound in smooth embroidered leather. With a sense of contained triumph, he placed it on the table.

'Aesop's fables?' Lucy asked. She'd seen cheap printed versions of the old storyteller's tales and she was sure Master Aubrey had a copy in the storeroom. 'Those are children's stories, are they not? Morals and lessons.'

'Exactly, Lucy. I've not thought about our good friend Aesop for quite some time. I imagine that the maker of this pendant aimed to send a specific message.' He ran his fingers down the index. 'Ah, here we are. "Two Thieves and a Bear." Two men heard tell of a calf in an ox stall. Thinking they could steal it, they decided that one would go inside the stall and then hand the calf out of the window to the other man. The first man went inside, and the second man waited outside, as promised. A lengthy time passed, but there was no sign of the man inside or the calf.

Fearful, the second man ventured inside, only to discover that his companion was caught in the stall. Not with a small calf, but rather in the embrace of a bear who was part of a travelling circus.'

'A bear!' Annie cried.

'The second man fled, leaving his companion to be dealt with by the owner of the calf and to the mercy of the bear.'

Lucy, Cook and Annie all raised questions at once.

'What does it mean?'

'What's the moral?'

'Why select that scene?'

'I know what it means,' Sid said. '"Don't steal." See, it's simple.'

Lucy shook her head. 'I'm not sure. That would be the lesson for the man who was caught, I suppose. I imagine the message is also supposed to be for the second man. I think it's something different. They assumed the calf would be in the stall, but there was a bear instead. I think the moral might be more like "Expect the unexpected". Or, perhaps "Be prepared".'

Master Hargrave looked pleased. 'I quite agree with you, Lucy. What do we make of the other images?'

'It looks to me that the man is on a scaffold,' she replied, before yielding the flea glass to Annie.

'That woman – maybe it's his sweetheart,' Annie said, peering at the images excitedly. 'Although she looks older. Maybe his mother. I think he's bending down to kiss his mother before he is executed.'

'No, I think the thief is biting her ear off,' Adam said, grimacing. 'Now that we know that these are from Aesop's fables, I recall this one too, I believe.'

'Biting her ear off!' Annie made a gagging sound. 'What is this terrible tale?'

Master Aubrey ran his fingers down the index. 'Perhaps it is this one, called "The Thief and His Mother".'

'That's it. I remember now. When he was a boy, this man stole a book from his schoolmate,' Adam explained. 'Rather than condemning the action as wrong, his mother praised him. Thinking such acts of thievery to be right and just, the man continued to steal until he was caught and sentenced to death for his many thefts.'

Out of the corner of her eye, Lucy noted that Sid was trembling slightly. Without asking for permission, she poured a little more mead for him, which he gulped down. He'd been luckier than other criminals, only spending time in the stocks and in gaol for short stints. Other criminals had not been so lucky. Indeed, had her own brother not almost been hanged as well? That thought still kept her awake at night, even several years later.

Adam was still telling the story. 'As the thief mounted the scaffold to receive his punishment, his mother came to bid him farewell. He leaned down, and rather than kissing her cheek as expected, he bit his mother's ear off. "This terrible occurrence is all your fault," he told her "for not having corrected me as a lad."'

'The moral is "Spare the rod, spoil the child",' Annie said. 'Easy.'

Master Hargrave nodded. 'In essence, yes. Very good, Annie.'

Lucy had picked up the flea glass again and looked back and forth between the panels. 'This pendant contains two accounts of thieves. The first warns the thief to be prepared and to expect the unexpected.'

'While the second story warns that follies must be corrected in youth, lest they lead to calamity later,' Adam continued.

'What is the link between them? Are these Aesop's only tales concerning thieves?' Lucy asked.

'No, there are many,' Master Hargrave said. '"The Thief and a Boy." "The Thief and a Cock." "The Thief and the Innkeeper." Quite a few more tales about thieves.'

'Why these specific tales, then?' Lucy asked. 'Master Hargrave, sir, what do you think?'

'Both illustrate how order and justice can prevail,' he said, appearing deep in thought. 'Although neither in the usual way.'

'Perhaps that's what the thief was trying to tell you,' Lucy said. 'Certainly, the blackmailer has been trying to punish you, even if we think his means and words are unjust.'

The magistrate clucked his tongue. 'We must also keep in mind that my anonymous sender may not have been either the thief Gamel or the blackmailer, but a different individual entirely.'

FIFTEEN

Lucy yawned, carefully placing her tracts back inside her pack. She hadn't been able to garner much of a crowd, even outside the Cheshire Cheese. Everyone was still lulling about after too much yuletide cheer the day before.

'Gather around, gather around!' a familiar voice called. Sure enough, Phineas Fowler had positioned himself a few feet away. Catching her eye, he gave her his usual wink before turning back to the crowd. 'Let me tell you about *The Soap-Makers' Dirty Demise!*'

Lucy gasped, nearly dropping her pack. *Was that her piece? How had Phineas ended up with it?*

Not noticing her reaction, Phineas continued. 'Let me tell you about the true story of how Guy and Mary Donnett, soap-sellers at Pye Corner, did most horrifically die a most horrible and tragic death!'

As he spoke, Lucy stood still, her hand clapped over her mouth. What he was reading was most certainly from the text she had written. Within a few moments, a small but excited crowd had grown around Phineas. Passers-by who had been too busy to listen to Lucy were now jostling each other, trying to get closer.

'Say, I heard about those murders,' a spice-seller said to his friend.

'I did, too.'

'Is he talking about the Donnetts?' she heard people calling. 'He's talking about the soap-maker and his wife!'

'I've been wondering what truly happened!'

'Who killed them? What does he say?'

Lucy's throat tightened as Phineas effortlessly orated the words she had so painstakingly crafted. *How dare he!* She clenched her fists tightly in her skirts as she listened. Word for word, he regaled the small crowd with news of the Donnetts' murders. *Had he stolen the tract from her?* She wanted to scream 'Thief!' at the top of her lungs.

Instead, she forced herself to step back from the crowd, moving against a shadowy wall, as she took deep breaths, trying to control her anger. *How had this happened? How had Phineas received this piece? Had it been stolen from her or—*

She slapped her cheek with a loud groan. She hadn't lost it when the man had dumped her pack in the water. She must have lost it later, when she and Sid were standing outside Havisham's shop, as they spied on him through the opening in the shutters. What had Duncan said about his conversation with Phineas later? *Someone had even left a tract for them that day.* Certainly, she had signed it 'Anonymous'.

'Regardless, how dare he do this?' she grumbled. She watched as the crowd continued to throw coins and stretch out their hands. A small spark of pride rose up inside her, as she watched them clamour for her words. 'It doesn't matter how well he tells the tale,' she muttered. 'It is I who penned the story.'

Within minutes, he only had a few copies left. She crossed her arms as Phineas concluded his sales, still wanting to confront him.

As she was about to approach, she was suddenly beset by doubt. If she challenged him, then he would realize she'd been standing outside the shop. He might figure out she'd been spying on him. How would he react? Especially if he realized it was she who had sent Duncan and Hank to his door. That would give everything away. Best stay silent.

As if he knew she was watching him, he looked at her suddenly and bowed in her direction. Out of habit, she started to drop a curtsey in return, before stopping herself in annoyance. *Why should I curtsey to the man who stole my words?*

Picking up her skirts, she hurried home, tears of frustration mixing with the light mist that began to swirl about her.

'We have your reams of paper,' the elderly deliveryman called. He pointed to the corner of their workroom, close to the second printing press where Lach was working. 'Stack over there as usual?'

'That's fine, Clyde,' Lucy replied, holding open the door to let him and his son unload their cart. When they finished, she handed him the money Master Aubrey had left for the papermakers and bid them to rest. She could tell that Clyde was exhausted. 'Master Aubrey left out a few of our recent publications, if there is something that interests you. Lach, bring them out, would you?'

Lach set the tracts beside them on the bench, and Clyde began to flip through them. His son Dan spoke up for the first time. 'Do you have the one about the woman who killed her midwife?' He snickered. 'Thought the woman had birthed her of a cat? I heard some lads talking about it. Thought maybe you'd been selling that one.'

Lach and Lucy exchanged a glance. Lach had heard all about the trial record that Phineas had received from Gamel.

'He wrote that quick, didn't he?' Lach muttered. 'Must have worked all the way through Christmas to get it done.'

'Especially since he also produced the *other* one,' Lucy whispered back, still feeling bitter that Phineas had printed and sold her piece.

'What now?' Clyde asked.

'Oh, that piece about the murdered midwife was put out by Sam Havisham's shop,' Lucy replied. 'Phineas Fowler would be selling them. Do you know Havisham?'

Clyde scratched his head. 'Havisham's shop? Come to think of it, we just started supplying them with paper again recently.' He scowled. 'Not sure what's going on there.'

'What do you mean?' Lucy asked.

Clyde was not a man to engage in idle chatter, so she was surprised when he answered her. 'Don't get me wrong. I was glad when Havisham reached out to me a few weeks ago. Said he'd found a new partner who would help him publish again. I knew him from before the Fire, you see, and I was heartfelt sorry to hear his presses and livelihood had been lost to the flames.' Clyde sighed. 'I was quite pleased when he told me that he'd been able to get his business operating again.'

He sat back then, with the air of saying all he was going to say. But Lucy didn't want to end the conversation. 'You said you are not sure what is going on there,' she prompted. 'May I ask what you mean by that?'

'Can't say for certain. Something just isn't right. The bookseller – Phineas, you say? He seems like a good enough chap, although a bit too loud for my taste.' He paused. 'Do you know that they all moved in with Havisham? Phineas, brother and father. Act like they own the place, too.'

'Is that so odd?' Lucy asked. 'Lach and I live here with Master Aubrey, and my brother Will lives with me. Is that not the same? Perhaps Mr Havisham needs the rent.'

'No. It is right that a young woman's brother lives with her, if she's employed with two men. Besides, Aubrey invited you, I imagine.' He shook his head. 'From what I saw, those Fowlers had the run of the place. The brother – Gamel, I think – was directing us this way and that. Even told Havisham to get out of the way.' He lowered his voice. 'A shame really. Havisham seemed afraid of them.'

'Why do you say that?' Lucy asked.

'I've known Sam Havisham a long time. Not good friends, but acquainted enough from the years that I believe I have a good measure of him. Before the Fire, he would never have let a man best him in anything. Since his injury,' he said, 'he's let the Fowlers take over. He's become so meek and barely speaks on those occasions when we make our deliveries. The father will stand there in such a menacing way, I hardly dare to ask my old friend how he's doing.' He sighed. 'Sam Havisham may be the master printer, but it is easy to see that someone else is in charge of that shop.'

Lucy and Lach glanced at each other. She could tell Lach was thinking the same thing as her. A master printer was always in charge of his shop. His word was law, too. While Master Aubrey often let them have their way on small things, he was the one who made the decisions about what should be sold and when, overseeing aspects of the production.

Setting his cup on the table, Clyde stood up. 'All right,' he said, gesturing to his son. 'We'll take our leave now, so that we may be back at the mill by the morning.'

After the papermakers left, Lucy began to prepare a ream of paper for the afternoon's printing. She was still thinking about what Clyde had said. 'Could it be true that Mr Havisham is afraid of the Fowlers?'

'Three against one, after all,' Lach replied. 'Maybe he felt he needed Phineas's help so much that he became desperate.'

'It would explain why a reputable printer like Havisham allowed them to print pieces from Master Hargrave's personal notes,' Lucy said. Accidentally, she kicked the table leg. Stifling a yelp of pain, she sat down heavily on the bench to take off her boot and rub her injured toe. She didn't want Lach to mock her pain, since she had brought it on herself. 'It bothers me that those Fowlers can get away with stealing from the magistrate and then profit from his writings.'

Lach muttered something under his breath.

'What did you say? I couldn't hear you.'

He set the type down. 'I said, "Let's steal the papers back."'

Lucy stopped cutting the twine that bound the stack of papers. 'Of all the absurd things . . . Wait, are you serious?'

'I am that. Now that we know all the Fowlers live at Havisham's, it seems we have a real chance. Think about it. When you told me that Gamel seemed to give Phineas the trial notes one at a time, I assumed that Gamel lived somewhere else. That's no longer the case.' He pounded his fist on the table. 'I'm willing to wager on this, Lucy. The magistrate's papers are somewhere in Havisham's house. We just need to look for them. Let's go now.'

Lucy stared at him. There was not even the slightest look of mischief or jest in Lach's expression. It was as though she was looking at a man she'd never met.

Slowly, she replied. 'Phineas may be out selling right now. It doesn't mean that no one is at home.'

Lach shrugged. 'We won't know unless we check.' He stood up, taking their cloaks off the wooden pegs on the wall. He tossed hers to her. 'Come on, Lucy. Master Aubrey isn't expected back until late this afternoon. He will never know we left if we return in time to get our chores done before supper.'

Dumbfounded by Lach's unusual determination, Lucy eyed him as he strode down the street. In all the years she'd known him, she'd never seen him express him such purpose and determination.

'Why are you staring at me?'

'I'm just wondering where the mischievous lad is.'

He straightened his hat. 'Some wrongs need to be righted.'

Reaching Havisham's shop a few minutes later, she and Lach edged close to the windows, trying to peer inside. As before, the shutters were not completely closed, and they could see the room was dark. The fire was not lit in the hearth, and there were no lanterns set out. Straining her ears, she could not hear anyone stirring either.

'The place looks empty,' Lucy whispered. 'Everyone appears to be out.'

'I'd wager Phineas is out selling,' Lach replied. Boldly, he pulled at the front door but grimaced when it wouldn't open. 'You'll have to go in through the window and let me in.'

Lucy felt an uneasy twitch in her gut. She knew that Duncan and the Hargraves would not approve of her breaking into Havisham's shop, but she pushed the feeling away. Lach was right about one thing. They *had* to get the magistrate's stolen papers back. She just couldn't let the magistrate's good reputation be ruined. Not after everything he had done for her.

She glanced up and down the street. There weren't too many people out and about, and no one seemed to be paying them any attention. Lach pushed open the shutters. Bracing herself on the window ledge, Lucy managed to hoist herself up and over, feeling smug that her skirts did not get caught.

'Let me in!' Lach hissed from outside. 'Be quick about it.'

There was an extra key hanging on a ring by the door. Ever since the Great Fire, people had learned to have a second key so they would not get trapped inside, should a conflagration strike again. Quickly, she inserted the key and opened the door for Lach. Shutting the door softly behind him, she held her breath, listening for any sounds from upstairs.

Finally, she exhaled. 'I don't think anyone is here,' she whispered.

'Let's make sure,' Lach said, loudly calling out into the empty room. 'Helloooo!'

'Shush! What are you doing? What if we get caught?' Lucy hissed.

'We'll just say the door was open,' he whispered back. Then he shouted again, 'Helloooo!'

They listened closely but again heard no sound. Lucy began to breathe a little more easily.

Even with the windows mostly shuttered, the room was lit enough that they could walk around without needing to light a candle or find a lantern.

Lucy moved to the printing press. She could see that Phineas was in the process of setting a new piece, which appeared to be the start of a new true account. There was a handwritten page beside it, with the text written out. The handwriting was not familiar, so she assumed it was Phineas's work, not Master Hargrave's. '*Revenge and Murder*,' she read out loud. '*The true account of a man who, after being cozened by his cousin into buying a tavern that collapsed the very next day, did murder that cousin in a most desperate and despicable way.*' Looking through the pages, she frowned when a scurrilous passage about the magistrate caught her eye, this time identifying him by name. A wave of anger passed over her. *How dare he? The magistrate wouldn't have written such a thing.* Phineas must have decided to use one small element of the woman's testimony at trial to craft another sensational true account. That was just too much! She set the piece down with trembling fingers.

She began to look around the room. Similar to Master Aubrey's method, Havisham had hung bags containing printed pieces and tools on nails on the walls. Lucy pointed to the west wall. 'I'll look in these. You take the ones on the other wall.'

Carefully, they began to unhook the bags and rummage through them. Most contained copies of the tracts and ballads she'd seen Phineas selling, although one bag contained the few pieces Fowler had acquired from Lucy. Another bag contained pieces from another printer that Lucy recognized. A few others were stuffed with all sorts of printed tracts and broadsides, most likely whatever Havisham had saved before the Great Fire destroyed his shop. After a few minutes, they had searched every bag to no avail. None contained the magistrate's personal papers.

With a sigh, Lucy replaced the last bag on its peg.

'Where else could the Fowlers be keeping the magistrate's records?' she asked. 'In one of the bedchambers? Or perhaps in the cellar?' That's what Master Aubrey did. Rather than storing dried fruits, vegetables and other foodstuffs in his cellar, he kept most of his enormous collection of tracts, broadsides and ballads in carefully managed crates.

A step at the front door caused them both to freeze. Had Phineas returned?

The sound of a key in the lock compelled Lucy to action. Silently, she grabbed Lach's arm, pulling him off in the direction of the kitchen, praying there was another way out at the back of the building.

They tiptoed into the kitchen, frantically trying to figure out what to do next. A table and chair had been lodged against the back door; they would not be able to move either without making a great deal of noise. *What shall we do?* Lucy asked herself, trying not to panic. *We can't go back. We'll run into Phineas for certain.*

Her eyes fell on the cellar door, which was kept shut by a heavy wooden bar.

She pointed to it. Lach nodded, understanding her intention, and together they carefully slid the bar upward and opened the door to the cellar. Peering down into the darkness, she could just make out several steps leading to the cold recesses below. Taking a deep breath, she grabbed the lantern that hung on a hook by the door and, after quickly lighting it, started down the steps.

Lach came behind her, carefully easing the door shut behind him. A soft thud from the outside made her heart jump in her chest. The bar must have slid back into place.

'You locked us in!' Lucy whispered, shaking his arm.

Lach pulled his arm away. 'If Phineas comes into the kitchen, I think he'd have noticed if the bar was still up,' he whispered back. 'Then he might come down after us.'

'What if we can't get out?' she hissed. 'Then we'll have to call him for help.'

Lach shrugged. Lucy had to admit it was probably quick thinking on his part. 'No matter now,' she conceded, still speaking as softly as she could. 'We'll figure it out later.'

A skittering sound by her feet distracted her, and she clapped her hand over her mouth to keep from yelping out loud. *Rats!*

She began swinging the lantern around to scare the verminous beasts away. Last thing they needed right now was to be bitten by a hungry rat.

Shadows danced all over the stone walls as she moved. Something strange on the wall caught her attention and she stopped the dramatic flailing and held the lantern aloft. 'What *is* all this odd stuff?' she whispered.

Instead of dried meats and fruits and other items that needed to be stored in the cool cellar chambers, here were all number of strange objects, laid out on tables and benches. There were different sorts of tools and instruments, and other curious objects. She walked around, holding the lantern up so that they could both see.

Lach stopped beside a large glass. 'This is a weather glass,' he whispered. Then he pointed at another item. 'That's a candle-dial.'

'Be attentive, Lach,' she scolded. 'We need to find something that can help us get out of here later. I don't want to wait here all night.'

'Do you think you're going to just tiptoe past Phineas?' Lach scoffed. 'That's assuming that the other Fowlers won't be back, too.'

'Hey, you're the one that locked us in here,' Lucy replied. 'Let's just keep looking. If we have to leave in the middle of the night, well, that's what we'll have to do.' A qualm ran over her as she thought about how worried everyone would likely be, if Master Aubrey returned and found both of his apprentices missing, their chores left completely undone.

In the corner, she saw a cellar window, and a feeling of relief stole over her. 'There,' she said. 'Perhaps we can climb out.' She walked down the steps and across the dirt floor. 'Hoist me up, would you? I don't see a ladder or anything to stand on.'

'No way. You're too heavy.'

'What? I am not,' Lucy replied. 'You are but a weakling.'

Their bickering was half-hearted. Lucy knew that, like her, Lach was trying to keep his mind off their current predicament. The Fowlers might not take kindly at all to their illicit presence in their home, and Gamel at least had shown he was not afraid to use violence.

'All right, let's give it a go,' he said, intertwining his fingers and holding them out to her to give her a boost. She pushed the cellar window, but it appeared to have been stuck shut. No amount of pushing or pounding could get the window open. She could feel Lach trembling as he struggled to keep her aloft.

'Let me down!' she called. Without hesitating, Lach practically dropped her to the hard earthen floor.

She scowled at him but pulled herself back up.

Loud shouting from the floor above caused them both to stop moving.

'What's going on?' Lach said, his voice squeaking.

She cocked her head, trying to make out the voices. The sounds were muffled, and she couldn't hear what they were saying. 'It sounds like two men and a woman.' She climbed the steps again, pressing her ear against the door, and Lach did the same.

The voice of Phineas, the troupe player, soared sonorously above the others. 'I demand you leave at once! You have no business here.'

Then the woman's voice rose as well, and her words were clear. 'I shall do no such thing!' she screamed. 'You will pay for what you've done! For the lies you've printed!'

'What lies?' Phineas countered, his voice still easily carrying. 'I am quite certain, Madam, that I do not know to what you refer. I ask that the two of you kindly leave my home. In a generosity of spirit, I shall not pursue with the authorities that you're trespassing in my home.'

'We will not leave!' the woman cried out. 'You have done us a grave injustice, which we shall see rectified. And that you show no remorse – well, we shall show you no . . . mercy . . . in . . . return.' Her last words were punctuated by great heaving gasps.

'Hey, what are you doing with that?' Phineas shouted, now sounding afraid. 'Get away from my press! No! Don't!'

Above, they could hear some tremendous banging sounds, and then a great crash, followed by the sound of something scattering across the room.

'What is happening?' Lach whispered.

'It's the printing press!' Lucy replied softly, placing her hand to her chest. Her heart was aching, feeling a moment's sympathy for the bookseller, thinking how long it would have taken Phineas to set that text. 'The typeface must be everywhere!'

They heard Phineas again. 'I beg of you! Please do not destroy my press!'

'I do not care about this soulless machine!' the woman shrieked back at him. 'This thing destroyed my life! Why could you not have let the past stay where it belonged? You've ruined everything!'

'The truth was already out! It was stated at the trial! I did nothing!' Phineas cried. 'You've no right to take your fury out on me. Woman! I beg you, cease and desist your terrible actions!'

'But you don't understand! P–people didn't know!' The woman shrieked. '*I* didn't know! Now we are humiliated!'

Phineas began to sob. 'I–I'll p–pay you for your suffering! Just give me some time! Anything you ask, I'll grant it to you! Please!' His begging was unbearable to hear, and Lucy had to keep herself from covering her ears with her hands.

'There's nothing can be done now! We'll see you destroyed, too!' the woman screamed back, in full-blown anguish. 'Yes, go ahead! Do it!'

'No, pl–please don't!' Then a dreadful new sound chilled Lucy to her core. It was the muffled thwack of a bar hitting flesh, followed by Phineas's anguished cries.

'I beg you—' His words ended with one last loud cracking sound, and then the sound of a body falling heavily to the floor.

Lucy gripped Lach's arm, and his hand clutched over hers in a shared fear. *What had happened to Phineas? Was he all right? Why wasn't he speaking now?*

There was some shuffling above and some indistinguishable murmurs. Lucy and Lach stared at each other. *What was happening?* The sudden silence was even more distressing than the intense shouting they had just experienced.

Then more footsteps of two people walking around. Finally, the sound of the front door opening and slamming shut.

For a moment, Lucy and Lach just huddled together, stunned by what had just transpired on the floor above.

Finally, Lucy shook free of Lach's hand. 'We have to get out of here.' She grimaced. There was still no sound from the floor above. 'We need to check and see if Phineas is all right.'

Mounting the stairs, Lach rammed his body against the door. 'Oof!' he said, rubbing his shoulder.

'Heavens, Lach! What did you expect? We already know we can't get out of here by brute force. That door is solid oak.' She held up the lantern, looking around as she descended back into the chilly cellar. 'There *must* be something here we can use to open the door.' She cast the candle around, trying to remain calm even though her heart was racing at breakneck speed.

Her eyes fell on a woodworker's square on one of the tables. Picking up the tool, she said, 'Perhaps I can use this to raise the bar of the cellar door.'

'That will never work,' Lach said, grabbing a bevel. 'Try this.'

They went back to the top of the cellar stairs. Lucy held the lantern high, while Lach manipulated the bevel through the crack of the door. She could barely breathe, as she watched him carefully slide the bar upwards, allowing the door to open.

Still holding her breath, Lucy and Lach tiptoed into the kitchen, listening for sounds from the rest of the building. There was an eerie silence that was disconcerting. Lach gripped Lucy's arm as she slowly pushed open the door that led to the workshop.

'Mr Fowler?' Lucy called, her voice sounding strained to her own ears. 'Are you all right? Phineas?'

Stopping still in the doorway, Lucy slowly took it all in. The workshop was in complete disarray, and the small press had been overturned and broken into several pieces. The cases containing the type had been dumped out, the tiny metal slivers strewn all about the room. An inking ball had been cracked open, and a thick smear of ink could be seen across the floor.

Lach tugged on her arm and pointed to the corner. Lucy followed his finger, taking in what he had already seen. An overturned bench was sprawled across the floor, from which two unmoving feet protruded.

'Maybe he is just knocked out?' she said softly, hearing the doubt in her own voice. The stillness was too unnatural. She forced herself forward, Lach staying a prudent step behind.

She stared down at the body, trying to make sense of what she was seeing.

There, Phineas was lying on the floor, a sharp object protruding from his chest, his body still and splayed at an odd angle. There was blood from his skull where he must have hit his head. His eyes were fixed and unstaring. A mallet and ink ball lay beside his unmoving form.

'Is he d–dead?' Lach asked.

Fighting a wave of nausea that flooded over her, Lucy knelt down beside the printer and touched his shoulder, giving the man a little shake. 'Ph–Phineas,' she said, her breath growing ragged. An odd sense of formality stole over in the awareness of his death. Still she could not believe he was dead. 'Mr Fowler? Sir?'

She waved her hand over his mouth and nose. There was no breath of life.

Sitting back on her haunches, she raised both hands to her lips, trying to think. 'What should we do?' She couldn't keep herself from looking down at the dead body. 'Oh, Phineas!'

Unexpectedly, Lach reached down and, putting his hands under her arms, hauled her to her feet. 'Lucy,' he said, giving her a little shake. 'We have to get out of here. What if those people come back?'

Lucy swallowed, trying to keep an overwhelming dizziness at bay. She pressed her hands to her mouth, trying to keep the bile from rising. 'Wait!' she called as he started to open the door. 'Check first. Make sure they are not outside.'

Lach gave her a grim nod. 'Good idea. Last thing we want is for those murderers to know there were witnesses.'

He eased open the door and they peered outside. 'I don't see them; do you?' Lucy whispered.

Lach shook his head. 'No.'

'Let's go. We must fetch the constable. Inform him of what happened.' Her words sounded far steadier and calmer than she felt after they shut the door firmly behind them. She began to walk in the direction of Fleet Street and the constable's gaol. Like her, Lach was deliberate in his steps, as though it was taking everything he had to keep moving.

They walked and walked, trying not to draw any attention from the handful of passers-by on the street. Finally, as they neared Fleet Street, they glanced at each other. The same thought crossed their minds. *Run!*

They did run, stumbling over each other, not looking back, as if the devil himself were after them.

SIXTEEN

'He's over there, behind the bench,' Lucy said, once again swallowing back the bile that had risen in her throat. She leaned against the wall of the printer's shop as Duncan and Hank grimly strode towards the body, the spilled type crunching below their feet as they moved. After Lach and Lucy had arrived at the gaol, stumbling over themselves in their attempt to explain what they had just witnessed, Duncan and Hank had quickly locked down the gaol and followed her back to the printer's shop, with Lach dispatched to bring Dr Larimer to the scene.

The two men studied the body in silence. Lucy took several deep breaths as the enormity of what had just happened began to sink in. It was hard not to think of Phineas. Of the merry twinkle in his eye when he smiled, or the splendid way he would capture his audience. How he had bought the posy of dried flowers from the old woman. How could that vivid and magnetic personality just be gone?

'What manner of instrument is that?' Duncan asked, interrupting her thoughts. When he glanced at her, his face softened at her appearance. 'Lucy, why don't you sit down for a spell? I fear you've had rather a shock.'

'I'm all right,' she said, crossing the room towards them. Being asked such questions made her feel more alert, less numb. She forced herself to look at the long, slender object sticking out of Phineas's chest. The object's wooden handle with its mushroom cap could be seen. 'It's a bodkin,' she said, feeling unsteady again. She rested her hand on the edge of the table. 'We use them when we are composing the text. We can remove or add pieces of type from the composing stick.'

'His assailant must have seized it from the workbench,' Duncan mused. 'This was not planned. Everything occurred in the heat of the moment. A crime of passion.'

'I suppose,' Lucy replied, forcing herself to think back to what she had heard. 'The pair seemed bent on destroying him, the moment they walked into the shop. The woman was quite furious.' She paused. 'I do not know which of them did . . . that.' She gestured feebly towards the bodkin.

'I see,' Duncan replied. 'How about you tell me everything again. Slowly. From the start. Beginning with what you and Lach were doing here. Then you can tell us' – he paused – 'what you were doing while a man was being killed.'

Lucy hung her head at the note of accusation in his voice. In fits and starts, she brokenly explained what had occurred. 'We had it in our heads to steal back Master Hargrave's private notes. We wanted Phineas to stop printing them. It wasn't just that he was profiting from Master Hargrave, but that he was defaming him, too. Then Phineas came back sooner than we expected, so we fled to the kitchen' – she pointed – 'and then we had to hide in the cellar. The latch slid down behind us and we got locked inside. We didn't want to alert Phineas to our presence, so we stayed silent. We heard – everything.' A tear rolled down her face as she thought again about Phineas's shouting and his final anguished cry. 'The intruders left and then we began to figure out how to escape. We were quite frantic. I knew that Phineas needed help and I–I was hoping he was still alive.'

Duncan looked stricken. 'How long before you were able to get out?'

'Maybe another five minutes. Then we found Phineas.' She gulped. 'As you see him here.'

As she was speaking, the door to the shop swung open and a gaunt man, perhaps in his fifties, stood in the doorway. 'What did you say? What's going on?' He looked ashen. 'Who are you?' He looked at Duncan's red coat. 'Why are you here?'

Duncan stepped forward, effectively barring the man from entering the shop. 'I am Constable Duncan. Could you please identify yourself?'

The man gulped, mopping his brow. 'I am Sam Havisham. This is my printing shop.' He looked around in despair. 'What has happened here?'

'What is your relation to Phineas Fowler?' Duncan asked.

Havisham's eyes widened. 'Phineas? He's a printer's assistant. He works for me. Why?' Then peering past the constable, his face suddenly blanched, making him look even more sickly. 'My God! Is that a body?' He began to back away. 'Tell me, it's not . . . Phineas. What happened? Was it an accident?'

Duncan looked at him sternly. 'No, it was not an accident. Phineas Fowler was murdered.'

'Murdered? What? No! How can that be?' Havisham asked, his eyes welling up with tears. He started to shake.

'Duncan,' Lucy whispered, nudging him. The constable nodded at Hank, who stepped forward and led Havisham towards a low bench against the wall, positioned away from the body.

Now seated, the printer leaned his head back against the wall, staring up at the ceiling. 'How did this happen? Who killed Phineas?'

'We were hoping you could tell us,' Duncan replied. 'Was anyone angry with him?'

'Angry enough to kill him?' Havisham shook his head violently. 'No, no. It must have been a thief.'

Duncan glanced at Lucy. She shook her head. They both knew it was not a thief, but he didn't want to give anything away. 'Was anything stolen, sir? Could you check?'

Slowly Havisham looked wanly around. 'I d–don't know. I'll check the money jar.' He crossed the room and crouched down beside a large earthenware jar. It was similar to the container in which Master Aubrey stored his coins. He stared inside it, not saying anything.

'Well?' Duncan asked.

'The money is there. I'd have to count it to be certain, but it looks to be about what it was when I last checked.' He sat on the floor, still cradling the jar. 'I can't think of anyone who would do such a monstrous thing.' Lucy could see now that Havisham was missing some fingers on his right hand. *What sort of calamity had brought that injury about?* she wondered.

Almost as if he had heard her thoughts, he answered her unspoken question. 'These last few years, the good Lord has seen to send me many trials and tribulations.' He stared up at them. 'I caught the sickness before the Great Fire and never rightly recovered. Then, when it was clear that our workshop was likely to be destroyed by the fire, I did my best to save my two presses from being destroyed.' He sighed, regret heavy in the exhalation. 'In the end, as the fire raged all about us, I was only able to save the one, because I hurt myself terribly. My fingers got caught in the gears when I was moving them. The barber-surgeon told me they'd best be removed, after the gangrene set in.' He looked up at them, distraught. 'It was Phineas who helped me. He came to me, asking if he could learn the trade.' He looked helplessly around. 'I had no means to take on an apprentice, so I just took him in without registering him with the Stationers' Company.'

That explains why Master Aubrey has not been able to find anything about him, Lucy thought.

Mr Havisham continued. 'I had to teach Phineas how to set the type because I could no longer use my right hand. Nor could I move or speak with vigour as I once had. I relied so much on Phineas. He had been a gift. An answer to my trials. What am I to do now?'

Spying a cloth on the bench, Lucy crouched beside Havisham, tucking it into his fist. 'The printing press has been knocked over,' she commented. Duncan gave her a warning look, which she acknowledged. She continued blandly. 'The type cases are in complete disarray.'

Havisham looked around, a shadow crossing the printer's face. 'What? Oh, yes, certainly.'

Lucy thought about what she had heard the woman shout at Phineas before he was killed. 'I know you just said that Phineas had no enemies, but do you think someone might have been angry about something he had printed?'

'Something he printed?' Havisham repeated. 'I couldn't say. I have met those who believe that it is an ungodly thing to spread news and true tales. There are others who grow angry when certain truths come to light.'

'Oh?' Duncan asked. 'Has there been anyone recently who held such views?'

He sighed. 'I suppose the magistrates he was writing about might have been angry, particularly Thomas Hargrave. Several of Phineas's recent pieces contained some dangerous finger pointing. I don't know the man himself, but I suppose it could well have needled him. To murder, I could not say.'

Lucy stepped back, aghast at the nature of his speculation.

The magistrate would never do such a terrible thing, no matter how angry he was. She opened her mouth to defend Master Hargrave, but shut it again after Duncan brushed her arm, silently urging her not say anything.

'Why was he writing such things about the magistrate?' Duncan asked. 'I saw a few of those pieces, including one called *The Magistrate's Confession*. Seemed intended to cause his reputation great harm.'

Havisham shrugged. 'I cannot say for sure. I had the feeling that someone was telling him to write these pieces in such a fashion – his father or brother perhaps. Neither seemed to have a particular fondness for the man. For my part, while I didn't much like maligning a man in such a way, I thought that it would . . .' He cast his eyes down.

'Sell more pieces,' Lucy filled in, trying not to show the fury she was experiencing.

'Yes, that is so. I could not run the press without Phineas. I was willing to publish anything he wanted, as long as I could bring in the funds to pay off my debts.' His shoulders sagged a bit. 'Certainly, Phineas always came back with an empty sack and many coins. I thought him my good luck charm, truth be told.' He sighed. 'I fear I was not such a lucky charm to Phineas, poor sot.'

Lucy glanced at the overturned printing press. Fortunately, the content of the text he'd been working on was scattered to the floor, but it would not take long to discover the handwritten pages full of scurrilous charges against the magistrate. She could see the paper overturned on the floor. Casually, she walked over to it and with one foot carefully slid it under a small footed chest where it would not be immediately discovered. In the chaos, it would not even be missed.

The printer continued to stare forlornly at Phineas's prone body, tears forming in his eyes. He did not seem to be listening to Duncan as he spoke, mostly to himself. 'Dear Lord. Whatever am I to do now? I was just getting my livelihood back in order and this terrible thing occurred. I do not know where I will find the strength to start again. I have no one left in this world. No son of my own to teach my trade, or to support me in my need.' His shoulders began to shake.

'We should inform Fowler's family of his death,' Duncan said briskly. 'Where do they live?'

Still seated on the floor, Havisham stretched out his arm to pull out another jar. 'His father and brother live here with me. Matthias and Gamel. I've let them rooms for the past few months,' he said, uncorking the jar and taking a great sip. It smelled like whiskey.

'What? They live here?' Duncan looked towards the stairs. 'Are they here now?'

Havisham shook his head, then took another deep swallow. 'I think it unlikely. They are seldom here during the day.'

'What do they do? Have they a trade?' Duncan asked.

Havisham began to fidget. 'I cannot say. That is, I know nothing of their trade.'

He's hiding something, Lucy thought.

Their conversation ended with the arrival of Doctors Sheridan and Larimer, accompanied by Lach. Sheridan rolled his eyes when he saw Lucy standing there, pressed against the wall. He looked as if he was about to make some cutting remark about Lucy always being on hand for murder when Larimer stopped him.

'Lucy, I think it would be best if you and Lach head home.' He put a gentle hand on both their shoulders in a way that pushed them out of the door. 'Tell Aubrey I've prescribed you both some mead, with a few swallows of whiskey for good measure.'

'Aubrey? You mean my old friend?' Havisham muttered. Then he caught sight of Phineas's body and took another deep swallow from the jar. 'Doctor, why don't you go ahead and prescribe the same thing for me?'

Lucy left Lach, now visibly shaking, to explain everything to Master Aubrey while quaffing down some brandy as she headed over to the Hargraves.

'Phineas Fowler has just been murdered,' she announced as she entered the magistrate's study, too out of sorts and shaken to knock. 'Lach and I witnessed the whole thing.'

'What?' both men exclaimed, standing up abruptly.

Adam nearly leapt to her side. 'Lucy! Are you all right?'

She nodded, but then she began to shake. 'Doctor Larimer

prescribed brandy,' she whispered. 'Or mum-beer. Or any other strong water.' Oddly, she began to giggle.

'Annie!' Master Hargrave shouted. 'Bring us some brandy at once!'

Her legs began to tremble uncontrollably, as the exertions of the last few hours started to catch up with her. She allowed Adam to settle her into a chair. He pulled a blanket over her skirts and knelt down to rub her hands. 'Lucy! What in the world happened?'

Annie came in then, stopping short when she saw Lucy. 'Is Lucy all right, sir?' she asked the magistrate.

'She's had a bit of a shock, Annie. If you would . . .' He gestured to the mug.

'Yes, of course, sir,' Annie said, quickly handing her the mug, which Lucy accepted gratefully. She took a sip, allowing the burning liquid to seize the inside of her throat and warm her body. She suddenly felt as if everything around her was happening at a great distance, as though someone had thrown a blanket around her mind, dulling the sensations. 'I'm fine,' she heard herself murmur before taking another sip of the brandy. Distantly, she heard Annie leave the room, shutting the door gently behind her.

Feeling quite overcome, it still took her a few minutes to speak. She kept her eyes closed, one hand still in Adam's, the other grasping her cup. When she opened them, she could see both Hargraves were watching her anxiously.

'All right, Lucy,' Master Hargrave said, sounding kind but firm. 'We can see you've suffered a great shock. It's time to tell us what happened. Please do not leave anything out. The first thing I need to know is whether the authorities have been notified of Mr Fowler's death.'

Lucy nodded. 'I informed Constable Duncan first thing. The physicians Larimer and Sheridan were both with' – she hesitated, the image of Phineas Fowler's body arising in her thoughts – 'the body when I left.'

'Very good. Now, tell us what happened,' the magistrate asked. 'From the beginning, if you would.'

'We wanted to get your personal papers back from Fowler,' she whispered. A rush of shame caused her to hang her head. 'Lach and I went to his house, thinking we could find the papers and return them to you. When we arrived' – here she gulped, the confession overwhelming her – 'the workshop appeared to be empty, so w–we went inside to look around. We were hoping that your papers might be easy to find.' She hid her face in her hands.

'Oh, Lucy,' Adam said.

'I'm sorry,' she said, feeling her cheeks flame violently.

'All right, never mind that now,' Master Hargrave said. 'What's done is done. Let us hear what happened, if you would. You went inside and . . .'

Taking a deep breath, Lucy continued. 'Then Phineas Fowler returned. We did not know where to hide, but we found the door leading to the cellar. We snuck down the stairs, and then the door latched behind us. We were locked in. We could hear Phineas talking to someone. A woman, who began shouting at him. There was a man, too, but he did not speak much.' Adam's hand tightened on hers, but he didn't say anything.

'We stood at the top of the cellar stairs, and we could hear everything that h–happened.' She began to shake again, and Adam held the cup up to her lips and she took another sip. In deep gulps, she described everything that happened next. When she arrived at the point where they discovered Fowler's body, tears began to flow in earnest. Adam pressed a handkerchief into her hand, watching her anxiously.

Finally, when she blew her nose and looked up, Master Hargrave smiled gently at her. 'That's a good girl.'

'I'm sorry, s–sir. I shouldn't have gone inside the shop. I know you told me not to do anything on my own,' she whispered. 'I just wanted to get those papers back. And Lach was with me. I didn't think—' She broke off. 'I didn't wish to see you harmed any more. That's why we went looking for the papers. You wouldn't think Lach would care about such a thing, but he did.'

Master Hargrave gave her another sad smile. 'Thank you for your loyalty. I am grateful. Indeed, I am gratified that even that red-haired apprentice would get himself in such a snarl on my behalf. Still, pray do not take such troubles again. I should hate to see you come to harm.'

Adam scowled. 'You could have been killed.' He poured himself some brandy and took several deep swallows in quick succession.

Lucy smiled weakly. 'We were not.' She stood up, feeling more revived. 'I've been thinking about what the woman shouted at Phineas. "I blame you for what happened," she said. "Why not let the past stay where it belonged? Why did you taunt us so cruelly?"' Standing with her hand on the magistrate's desk, she closed her eyes, hearing the woman's speech again. 'If I were to wager, she was referring to a piece Phineas published. Perhaps that is why she smashed the press.'

Master Hargrave scratched his cheek. 'That's how it sounds to me as well. Something buried came to light. Something that they published from my personal notes was injurious to that woman.'

'None of these were new stories,' Adam pointed out. 'They all emerged from public trials, all of which transpired before the Great Fire. What's done is done. Why kill the messenger?'

'Perhaps there were some details that had not been known before,' Master Hargrave said. 'However, if Mr Fowler's murder was associated with one of the true tales he published, how can we determine which one? Indeed, there's no way of knowing for certain, at least not before we have more evidence.'

'There was the piece about the players where you were accused of allowing a travesty of justice to occur,' Adam said, setting his cup down. 'Perhaps the victim's family was angry.'

'Maybe we should speak to the family,' Lucy began, but stopped when Adam seized her hand again.

'Lucy, dear. Please think through what you are saying. You *cannot* seek out that family. What if they were responsible for Phineas Fowler's death?' His hand tightened around hers.

She patted it with her other hand before standing up and moving over to prod the fire with the poker. 'There is another thing, too. Phineas was in the process of writing another tract, this one about the magistrate and a ghost.' She paused. The image of Phineas Fowler's lifeless form arose in her mind, and she jammed the poker down on the log, causing embers to stir and fly about. 'When Duncan asked Mr Havisham about who might be angry enough to kill Fowler, he said . . .' She couldn't bring herself to finish the thought.

However, Master Hargrave concluded it for her. 'He said me, did he not?' Without waiting for Lucy to nod, he continued in his dry, thoughtful way. 'It stands to reason. Phineas Fowler has launched an unprovoked attack on my character, and presumably tried to blackmail me. When his attempts failed, he continued to assassinate my character. It stands to reason that I might be provoked enough to murder.'

Lucy whirled around. 'Master Hargrave! That is not possibly true. Constable Duncan would never believe such a thing.'

Master Hargrave raised his hand to calm her. 'Lucy, dear, do not fret. I am just laying out a possible motive, when there are no other apparent suspects.'

'No need to lay yourself out like that,' Lucy said stoutly, causing father and son to smile at her indulgently. She remembered the piece she'd seen Phineas setting. To think the Fowlers still had the magistrate's notes. They *had* to get those pages back. What if Havisham found someone else to print them for him? She couldn't bear to see the magistrate's reputation further injured.

'I wonder what Master Havisham will do now,' she said, sighing. His grief had seemed real, as had his distress at having lost his livelihood. 'He truly relied on Phineas, I think.'

At that moment, an idea came to her. She glanced guiltily towards the Hargraves as if they could read her thoughts, but they both appeared lost in their own silent worlds. Only when she announced she was leaving did Adam snap to attention. 'I will see you home, Lucy.'

They walked home to Aubrey's in silence, Adam heavily supporting Lucy the whole time, as she was suddenly finding it hard to speak and think. When they arrived at the shop, Aubrey and Will were both waiting. Without a word, Will took hold of Lucy's arm and led her to her bedchamber, leaving Adam and Aubrey conversing in low tones.

Will embraced her. 'Get some sleep, little sister,' he said, setting her lantern on the table. 'We'll talk tomorrow.'

Nodding dully, Lucy shut the door behind her. She could hear the muted voices of the others still talking in the kitchen, but she didn't care what they were saying. The events of the day began to overwhelm her, and she blew out her lantern. Without taking off her dress, she lay down on her straw pallet, pulled her blankets over her head and willed herself into a quick dreamless sleep.

SEVENTEEN

The next morning, Sam Havisham stared groggily at Master Aubrey, Lucy and Lach. Although it was nearing nine o'clock, and the tradesmen and merchants had long been bustling, the printer appeared to have only risen when he heard their insistent pounding at his workshop door. He looked from one to the other, with bloodshot eyes and dark circles beneath them, apparently trying to make sense of their presence.

'Shop's closed,' he mumbled, a rank smell of beer emanating from his breath and skin. Clearly, he'd been tippling into the early hours of the morning. He looked as if he'd barely slept.

Master Aubrey held out his hand. 'Sam, my friend. We heard about what happened to Phineas Fowler.'

The printer winced, putting his hand to his head. 'A terrible thing indeed.' He started to close the door.

Lucy prodded Master Aubrey. 'Oh! Er, well, we are here to help you!'

Mr Havisham opened the door a little wider. 'What's that? Help me? With what?' Puzzled, he looked back and forth at Lach and Lucy, his eyes narrowing. 'Hey! Weren't you two at my shop yesterday? You were speaking to the constable. Why were you here at such a time?'

Lucy stepped forward into the door frame, effectively causing Mr Havisham to step back into his shop. 'Yes, sir. We were here. We had stopped by to see you, sir, to renew your old acquaintance with our master. That's when we saw that Mr Fowler was d–dead.' She did not need to fake the tremor in her voice. Coughing, she continued. 'We called the constable.'

Taking another step forward, she entered the shop. Master Aubrey followed her in, Lach more reluctantly. Lucy continued to speak in what she hoped was a soothing manner. 'We are here now because my good Master Aubrey insisted that we help you get your press back up and running.'

She did not dare glance at Master Aubrey when she spoke.

He'd only needed a little convincing after initially resisting, having not wanted to involve himself with another printer's tragedy. 'That is exactly why we should help him,' Lucy had pleaded. 'At the same time, we can get Master Hargrave's private papers back! We must stop this poor treatment.' The linchpin, of course, had been when she promised the printer that she'd write the story of Phineas Fowler's murder. She'd felt a pang of guilt when she thought about earning from Phineas's death but then she remembered how he had passed the soap-seller's tract off as his own. Phineas would understand, she thought. Besides, her priority was to find Master Hargrave's notes, which meant she might never write the piece about Phineas if it ended up too distasteful a tale.

'Get my press running again?' Havisham repeated. 'I don't know. Phineas has not even been buried yet.' He gulped. 'Still, such kindness. To spare two apprentices!' He glanced at his misshapen hand. 'Managing the press is certainly beyond me, I must admit.'

Ignoring the twinge of guilt, Lucy pushed past Havisham and looked around the workroom. Swallowing, she glanced at the corner where they'd found Phineas's corpse. At least someone had scrubbed the blood off the floor, she noted with relief. 'I suppose the first thing we need to do is right the press,' she said. 'Then we can set the type in order in the cases.'

Behind her, Lach made an odd noise. His face was turning an unpleasant shade of green, and he looked about to vomit. 'Are you all right?' she whispered.

He gave her a tight nod in return, before inhaling deeply. He moved over to the printing press, and together they pulled it back to its customary position.

Master Aubrey ran his hands over the machine, gently, as if he were a stable hand checking a horse for injuries. 'I can see that the cover appears to be damaged, but we will have to try a sample to see whether the press still works true and clear.'

'I'll start picking up the type,' Lucy said, taking a small tray from the table. She kneeled down, sweeping up a fistful with her right hand and placing the type into a smaller tray. Painstakingly, she and Lach began the process of placing the tiny pieces of metal into their correct slots.

'Have you a bodkin, sir?' Lach asked the printer. 'The work with the composition stick would go a little easier.'

The printer looked helplessly around. 'A bodkin?' he asked faintly, a sickly expression crossing his face. 'I think it's been . . . misplaced.'

Lucy elbowed Lach. He'd forgotten that Phineas had been stabbed with a bodkin. The constable had likely taken it as evidence. 'Do not worry, sir. We can manage without it.'

Havisham seated himself heavily on a stool in the corner, watching them in a vaguely distracted way.

'Are you all right, sir?' Lucy asked. 'Shall I make you some tea? You look to have a headache.'

'Headache?' Mr Havisham shook his head as if cobwebs had trapped his thoughts. 'No, I don't have a headache. I'm just overcome by this horrible misfortune. Poor, poor Phineas.'

'It sounds as if you knew Mr Fowler for a long time,' Aubrey commented, catching Lucy's meaningful glance. 'Was he apprenticed to you? I do not remember him in your shop, before the Fire. He seemed past the age to become his own master.'

As they spoke, Lucy held up a piece of type to the lantern, trying to decide if it was the number zero or the letter O.

'I didn't know him so very long, actually,' Havisham replied. 'Phineas came to me after the plague took my wife and son, saying he'd like to learn the printer's trade. He could already read and write, I expect because he'd been in a player's troupe when he was a lad. He caught on to everything right quick, too.'

'He lived here with you?' Master Aubrey asked, looking around.

'Yes, along with his brother and father.' An odd expression crossed Havisham's face. 'I had enough rooms for them all and they needed a place to stay after the Fire, so I took them all in.'

'He was not registered with the Stationers' Company as a printer or an apprentice?'

The slight rebuke in Master Aubrey's question seemed to have passed unnoticed by the other printer. 'Indeed, I was just over at the Stationers' Company yesterday before all this.' Havisham gestured wanly in the general direction where Fowler's body had been found. 'Happened that I told them I did have a licence to print, but it was burnt in the Great Fire.' He mopped his head with a sodden handkerchief. 'The Company seems unable to find their own record of my licence. Although the clerks saved the records before the Fire burnt down the Great Hall, it seems that the order is in a bit of a shambles. I was seeking a new licence to produce and sell.' He bent his head. 'Although I don't know how I can do so now. What if the press is completely broken?'

'We could set a mock broadside,' Lucy suggested. She didn't want the man to become too despondent to speak. 'Not a real one, you understand. This will let us see if the press is still working properly. Lach, hand me some woodcuts and text.'

Havisham sighed. 'I should first be grateful if you could see if the press still works. If it doesn't, I'll bid you farewell and a heartfelt thank you for your time.' He pulled out a jug and two mugs, pushing one over to Master Aubrey. 'Your apprentices seem to know what they are doing. Drink with me.'

Master Aubrey accepted the mug and touched it lightly to Havisham's cup. 'Don't mind if I do.'

Silently, Lucy and Lach worked to set random type into the frame. He brought her large woodcuts of garlands, merry maids and cows, as well as letters of different fonts, types and spacers, which she carefully laid out, using the quoin and composition stick.

When she was done, she picked up the ink ball from the floor, carefully removing the dirt stuck to its surface. After dipping it in a small tray of ink, she proceeded to ink the typeface. 'Now we'll lay the paper on top,' she said to Lach, nodding towards the stack of paper behind him.

Lach picked up one of the large sheets of paper and carried it over. She caught hold of the bottom corners and together they laid it carefully over the inked typeset. Grasping the lid of the press, she carefully laid it down on top of the paper and began to roll it out, trying to exert even pressure on the surface as Master Aubrey had taught her.

Then she raised the lid and carefully peeled the paper from the typeface. She and Lach looked it over with a critical eye. There was a whole section where the letters were very faint or missing. 'Maybe a little more ink there the next time, in case there's a slight bend now,' Lach said, pointing to the troublesome spot. 'Otherwise, I think it will work.'

Havisham and Master Aubrey came over to examine the printed sheet. 'Well done,' he said, raising his mug to Master Aubrey. 'You trained your apprentices well.'

In other circumstances, Lucy would have beamed at the approval of another master printer, but now she just gave a tight smile. 'Thank you, sir. We did come here to help. Is there a piece that we could set for you? Perhaps we could complete what Phineas was working on when he was killed?'

Eve as she made the offer, she wished she could bite back her words. The piece Fowler had been setting, *Revenge and Murder*, was another despicable piece that described Master Hargrave's alleged corruption. She'd never set such a piece, no matter how much someone wanted to pay her.

Thankfully, the printer was shaking his head. 'I am not certain I know what he was working on last. I d–did not see any papers. I think the press was still set with the last piece we printed, about the woman who killed the midwife, after thinking she'd birthed her of a cat.' He took another long slurp of his drink. Then, sounding more weary than angry, he added. 'You'd think I'd know what my own shop was printing, would you not?'

'Indeed, I would,' Master Aubrey replied. 'How did such a circumstance arise? As I understand it, Phineas was barely beyond an apprentice. How is it such decisions fell to him, rather than you?'

'What a wretched soul I am!' Havisham replied, rubbing his hands together. 'I needed him to survive; that's what happened. He came, eager to work from the outset, and then, later, became fully supplied of such compelling tales. Is it no wonder I let the business fall to him?'

He looked so pitiful that Lucy couldn't bring herself to feel angry. 'Where did he get these stories and tales, do you know?'

A guilty expression flitted across Havisham's face before disappearing, but he didn't reply.

'Phineas told me once that he had a partner,' Lucy prodded. 'You do not know who it was?'

'Well, his father was the one who had all the stories, which he would then turn into true accounts. I do believe that he fed them to his son one by one. They sometimes fought bitterly about it. Phineas wanted all of them at once, but I imagine that his father held on to them so he could maintain some sort of control over his son.'

'Where did Phineas keep the original accounts after he printed the pieces?' Lucy looked towards the leather pouches hanging on hooks. 'In one of those bags? Perhaps if there was one he was working on, we could help you set it.'

Master Aubrey gave her another warning look. *Stay silent.*

'Those pieces have caused me much trouble.' Havisham shook his head. 'I should have known better than to allow such pieces to be printed in my shop. You have to understand, I did not wish to malign that magistrate. I just felt I had no choice but to comply, as I have no other source of income. How wretched my life has become.'

He stood up then and staggered over to another urn and withdrew some pages that had been rolled into a scroll and tied with a leather string. Inwardly, Lucy smacked her head. Why had she and Lach not looked in the urn when they were there yesterday? Perhaps because Master Aubrey would never have stored pages in such a way, it did not occur to them that someone else would.

He thrust the pages toward Lucy, who recognized the magistrate's careful script immediately.

'This was the last piece Phineas worked on. I know he was going to make it into a tale of how a murdered woman's ghost confronted the man who killed her. Although this is simply an account of a murder trial, like the others were.'

Revenge and Murder. That's what Phineas had titled the piece he'd been working on. She glanced at the space beneath the footed chest where she'd kicked the handwritten piece. She could see the corner of the page where she'd left it.

'I told Phineas I couldn't do it any more,' he said. 'Take it away! I can't even look at it.' He drained his jar in one final gulp and shook it sadly. 'Empty.'

'How about I buy you a drink at the Cheshire Cheese?' Master Aubrey asked, awkwardly patting his shoulder. He gave Lucy a sidelong glance. 'Lucy and Lach can stay here, continue cleaning up. Let me just use the privy first.'

When Master Aubrey left the room to use the chamber pot down the hall, Lach and Lucy returned to sorting the text into the various cases. Havisham remained hunkered on his bench, not saying a word, lost in his own thoughts.

After a few moments of silence, a woman with fiery red hair flung open the shop door, staring at everyone from the doorway. For a moment, she looked around fiercely before striding over to Havisham and planting herself before him. 'I know who killed Phineas!' she proclaimed. 'I shall see justice enacted upon his murderer!'

The three of them all stared at her. Lach's mouth was agape. 'Huh?' he asked.

Lucy swallowed, trying to catch her thoughts after the startling pronouncement.

'My dear Miss Davenport!' the printer exclaimed, finally regaining his voice as he rose to his feet. 'Whatever do you mean?'

'Who killed him, miss?' Lach asked. 'Do tell!'

Ignoring Lach, the woman thrust a paper towards the printer. 'I've written it all out here. Pray, set this piece today so that we can make the truth known to all.' Her smirk, as it stretched across her face, was triumphant. 'This will bring about that man's downfall, once and for all.'

With shaking fingers, Havisham took the paper from Miss Davenport's outstretched grasp and scanned the page. A look of revulsion crossed his face, and he crumpled the paper in his hand and dashed it to the floor. 'Oh, Letitia,' he exclaimed, dropping his earlier formality. 'No. I've had enough of this nonsense. I shall not print such slander.'

'It's not slander,' she shot back. 'I know it to be true.'

'You were not here, were you? You know nothing of what occurred!'

'Tell me what happened then,' she exclaimed. '*You* seem to know.'

Havisham slid back on the bench, shoulders slumping. 'Miss Davenport,' he said, reverting to the more formal address that he'd used when she'd first walked in, 'I know little more than you. I had been to the Stationers' Company. When I came back that afternoon, I discovered the constable here and Phineas' – he gulped before continuing – 'Phineas, dead, on the floor. Killed by our own bodkin. Just there.' He waved his hand dispiritedly in the general direction of where Phineas's body had been discovered. The constable told me so.'

'Then who did do this terrible deed, Sam?' Letitia asked. 'Who was angry with him? A spurned lover? Or perhaps someone's husband? You know what a swain Phineas could be.'

'I don't know!' Havisham replied, sounding despondent. 'How could he have enemies? Letitia, you knew him. He was a friendly, affable soul. Who would have wanted him dead?' He coughed. 'Besides, it may have been a woman who killed him.'

Letitia's eyes narrowed. 'Why do you say that? There was a witness?'

Havisham looked startled. *Don't look at me!* Lucy thought. Beside her, Lach shifted uncomfortably.

'I am not certain,' Havisham said vaguely. 'Someone discovered the body and went to the constable for help.'

Lucy must have made some noise, because suddenly Letitia's eyes were upon her, harsh and sceptical. 'Who's this, Sam?'

'Oh, er, Lach and Lucy. They are apprenticed to Master Aubrey. They stopped by to assist me, as fellow printers with the Stationers' Company.'

'How very helpful,' Letitia replied, her words taking on a slight mocking tone. She fixed her bright green eyes on Lucy's own. 'You seem familiar. Have we met before?'

'I–I don't think so,' Lucy replied, forcing herself not to fidget. There was something disconcerting about the knowing way the woman was regarding her.

'Are you helping with the tract that Phineas did not complete?' she asked, looking around.

Lucy did everything she could not to look at the handwritten account tucked under the chest. She hoped too that Havisham would not mention the piece he'd withdrawn from the urn. 'Not yet. Right now, there is too much to do to sort all the type that was dumped on to the floor by Phineas's assailant.'

'I see,' Letitia said. For a long moment, she stood there, regarding Lucy in a disconcerting way. Finally, with a sniff, she took her leave.

Master Aubrey re-entered the room then. 'Who was that woman, Sam?'

'Letitia Davenport. A friend of the Fowlers, I suppose,' he

said, then added vaguely, 'She sometimes stops by. Offers her thoughts on the pieces.' He buried his head in his hands. 'Nothing has been right these last few months! Nothing has been right since the Fowlers came to live here.' He gulped. 'Now, with Phineas dead, I don't know what to do!'

Master Aubrey put out his hand. 'Let us go have our drink now,' he said firmly. 'We can continue this along the way.'

When the door shut behind them, Lucy picked up the pieces of paper that Havisham had ripped up and strewn about the room, and smoothed them out on the table. Fortunately, they'd only been shredded into four pieces and Miss Davenport's writing, though ill-formed, was not so difficult to read.

'"The Magistrate's Murderous Manner,"' she read, both hands curling into fists. '"How one magistrate did take it on himself to kill the printer for telling the truth of his corruption and lies."' Her hand flew to her chest. 'How could she say such a thing about the magistrate!'

'Perhaps she's the one who wrote such things before,' Lach said, his face twisting into a grimace. Like Lucy, he appeared shocked by the ugly words.

Lucy continued to read out loud. '"Enter the magistrate into the printer's shop of one Phineas Fowler, shaking a true account of his corruption of the law. 'Who are you to expose my corruption in such a way. I shall have you killed!'" Such filthy lies.' She slapped her hand on the paper. 'The magistrate would never do or say such a thing.' She forced herself to take a deep breath and read everything again.

The calming moment allowed her to see the tract differently. Besides the lies, there was something about the tract that seemed strange. 'Why does this tract read so oddly?'

'Sounds like a play,' Lach commented, reading over her shoulder.

Lucy skimmed the piece again. 'That's true. I wonder why?' She tucked it in her bag. 'No matter now, though. I shall bring it to Master Hargrave later. Perhaps he will know who Miss Davenport is, and we might resolve at least one of these vexing questions.' She moved to the stairs.

'What are you going to do now?'

'I'm going to look upstairs,' Lucy said. 'The rest of the magistrate's papers are likely to be in one of the bedchambers.'

'Make sure you pay attention,' Lach said with surprising firmness. 'We don't know how long the Fowlers or Havisham will be out. They won't take too kindly to finding you in their chambers.' Lach's freckles stood out as he frowned at her. 'Just don't do anything your usual idiot self would do.'

'You're the one who got us locked inside the cellar,' Lucy reminded him, smiling at his bullish concern, as she mounted the stairs to the chambers above.

When she reached the first of two landings, Lucy regarded the narrow corridor before her. There was a door on either side and another set of steps at the other end. Idly, she wondered where they exited on to the ground floor, since they might not have decided to hide in the cellar if they'd seen the steps.

Her heart pounding, she put her ear by the first closed door. Silence. Cautiously, she pushed open the door and went inside.

The room was tidy, with only a few pieces of furniture and even fewer personal items in sight. Just a straw pallet, several candles, a small table with a pitcher and basin, and a wooden trunk in one corner, with a short stack of printed accounts on top of it. The small fireplace in the corner appeared to have been recently swept clean. On the wall, someone had pasted several familiar pieces related to the Great Fire, some of which she had sold for Master Aubrey.

Still listening for any noises below, Lucy quickly knelt beside the trunk and glanced at the printed pieces. Mostly printed sermons and religious pieces. Whispering a small prayer for forgiveness, Lucy prized open the trunk, finding it full of sturdy men's clothes and several old and patched blankets. 'Havisham's room, I'd wager,' she murmured to herself as she stepped back into the corridor, shutting the door softly behind her.

She opened the other door, which led into a much more ornate bedchamber. The bed was covered by brightly coloured blankets, with two satin embroidered pillows on one end. The table was full of talcs and notions, perfumed soaps, and even some dried flowers. There was a mirror and comb.

'A woman's bedchamber?' she wondered. She opened the

wardrobe, discovering it full of the tailored jackets favoured by
Phineas, as well as some fine dresses that could only belong to
a very tall woman. There was a basket on the floor of the wardrobe containing woollen hose and nightshirts, as well as some
silk scarves.

Thoughtfully, Lucy shut the door of the wardrobe and looked
around. Like the first bedchamber, which was likely occupied by
Havisham, someone had also pasted ballads and penny pieces
on the walls. Looking more closely, she could see that almost
all were pages from the plays of the Bard and Marlowe. At the
sight of them, a pang of sadness struck her, as she suddenly
recalled the handsome bookseller beautifully orating his penny
pieces. No doubt he'd been a fine player when he performed
with that troupe. 'I hope you'll find your justice, Phineas,' she
whispered. 'In heaven if not on this earthly plane.'

Once again, she stepped out into the corridor and tiptoed past
the privy chamber and up the back stairs to the top floor. There
were two chambers, but the ceiling was sloped in such a way
that both doors were ajar. Cautiously, she cracked open one of
the doors and discovered an even more barren room than that
occupied by Havisham. Beside the pallet, which was covered
with two simple wool blankets, there was a crate. A man's
clothes hung from hooks on the walls – trousers, shirts – and
that was it.

Pushing open the last door, she stared in amazement around
the bedchamber. In addition to the bed and table, two curio
cabinets and a wardrobe were crammed together on either side
of a small fireplace. In every corner, displayed on every surface,
there was a hotchpotch of objects. Small marble statues, birds'
nests, miniature portraits, an assortment of items, including many
odd things she did not even recognize. 'This is akin to what Lach
and I saw in the cellar,' she mused. 'Someone in the household
is a collector of some sort.'

She opened the doors of the first curio cabinet, finding the
three wooden shelves crammed with more strange items. There
were all types of tools and objects, some related to mechanics,
others for sewing, such as scissors and a bodkin. There were no
papers, though, and she shut the doors carefully.

Expecting more of the same, Lucy opened the doors of the

second cabinet, emitting a small gasp when she took it in. This cabinet was full of weapons, mostly axes and heavy blades, as well as a few smaller knives and other sharp objects. There was also a leather hood with spaces cut out for the wearer to see and smell. She jerked away in disgust. An executioner's mask.

Who would collect such morbid objects? Lucy hastily shut the door again. 'No time for that now,' she whispered to herself.

Disappointed that she had not found any of the magistrate's writings, Lucy crept down the stairs, stopping short when she heard Lach speaking loudly from the workroom below.

'I am an apprentice with Master Aubrey's shop,' he was explaining. 'My master thought that Mr Havisham could use some help. I came to clean up the type, while they went to a pub.'

'You may leave now,' she heard a man reply. 'I am mourning my son and we will not be opening the shop for some time.'

That must be Matthias Fowler, Lucy thought, her heart pounding.

'How about I wait until Mr Havisham returns?' Lach asked, filling Lucy with a rush of gratitude. Although he was likely afraid, she knew he did not wish to leave her alone in the house with the Fowlers. 'My master would not be pleased if he thought I had not finished the tasks he had set for me.'

'We'll tell Havisham we asked you to leave,' a younger man said. *Probably Gamel*, Lucy surmised.

There was a shuffling sound and some muffled protests from Lach, and then a loud clap of the front door as it was opened and shut. Lach had likely been pressed out of the shop, causing Lucy's heart to sink. She pressed her hand to her mouth, her heart beating quickly again. *What to do? What to do? What will they do to me if they find me?* She squared her shoulders. *They won't.*

There was the sound of a fist slamming on the table. 'Who killed Phineas, Gamel? I have to know.'

'I don't know, Father, but—'

There was a pause. 'Why that face? Do you know something?'

'Father, I cannot say for sure. Though I recall now that there was a woman looking for Phineas. She kept walking up and down the street, and I heard her enquiring after him.'

'Woman? What woman?'

'I don't know. At the time, I thought little of it. I thought she might have been responding to his charms – you know how Phineas was – but now I wonder. Perhaps she had something to do with his death.'

Lucy froze, wondering if they might be talking about her. Then she shook her head. *No, I never asked anyone about Phineas directly.* Perhaps the woman she and Lach had overheard shouting at Phineas that day had been looking for him beforehand. Stood to reason, certainly.

'I must see justice done for Phineas,' Matthias said. 'I must see his murderer dealt with.'

'Certainly, Father,' Gamel replied. 'I would expect nothing less of you.' He coughed. 'That reminds me, Father. I have something for your collection.'

'For my collection?' Matthias sounded puzzled. 'Oh, I see. Thank you.'

'Does it not please you, Father? I had hoped it might help assuage your sorrow in the smallest way.' Even to Lucy's ears, she could tell Gamel sounded disappointed.

'I just prefer to do my own collecting,' Matthias replied. 'I find excitement in the hunt, not just in the ownership.'

There was another long pause, and Lucy strained to hear any sound from below that might indicate what the pair was doing.

'Let us go and speak with the constable again,' Matthias said. 'I thought he mentioned a witness who said Phineas had been killed by a woman. If we find the witness, we might learn who murdered him.'

Lucy shivered. She knew the constable would never give up her name, but still it was a frightening prospect to think about these men pressing her for information.

'Let me put this upstairs before we depart,' Matthias said.

He's coming upstairs! Lucy thought. Hoping she had guessed right about the rooms, she stepped into chamber that most likely had belonged to Phineas. There would be no place to hide if she was wrong.

She heard Matthias's heavy tread on the steps, and then a pause when he reached the first landing. Had she shut all the doors behind her? Frantically, she tried to recall if she had left everything as she had found it.

Lucy braced herself for the chamber door to open abruptly, hoping that the moment of surprise would be enough to keep her from being trapped. The steps continued up the stairs; above her, she heard the door squeak open and close again.

Then, a few minutes later, she heard Matthias go back down and the shop door slam shut.

Opening the door a crack, she could see the hallway was clear. She slipped out and down the stairs, gasping as she burst through the shop door and back out on to the street.

'It's about time!' Lach muttered to her. Evidently, he'd been concealing himself behind the crates they had hidden behind the other day. Without saying another word, he grabbed her by the hand and hauled her down the street back to the haven of Master Aubrey's workshop.

'I couldn't find Master Hargrave's notes,' she said, panting as they ran. 'They must be well hidden.'

'I thought for sure they were going to find you and kill you,' Lach muttered, when they finally slowed a few blocks away. 'Did you see Phineas's father? If ever there was a man who could kill you with his own eyes, it is him.'

A shiver ran over Lucy and she hugged herself. 'I think you're right,' she said, describing the weapons she'd seen in the curio cabinet.

Lach listened silently as she rattled off all the items she could remember, including the executioner's mask and axe. His face seemed to have paled. 'Those are some odd things to collect,' he said. 'Where are they off to now?'

'They are going to speak with the constable. They are quite determined to find Phineas's killer, although I'm quite afraid of what will happen when they do.'

Lying on her pallet that evening, Lucy could still hear the shouts of revellers on the streets below. The merriment would continue through the end of the week and on until Twelfth Night. Duncan must have his hands full right now. She hoped he'd been able to enjoy a little merriment himself.

She stared at the shadowy ceiling, thinking about everything that had transpired these last few days.

'I can't sleep,' she complained to herself and rolled out of bed, pulling a warm blanket around her. Sitting down at her little table, she turned on the lantern and pulled out the tract Phineas had written from the magistrate's personal notes.

'*Revenge and Murder*,' she read out loud. '*The true account of a man who, after being cozened by his cousin into buying a tavern that collapsed the very next day, did murder that cousin in a most desperate and despicable way.*'

She then began to peruse the magistrate's personal notes that Havisham had pushed towards her earlier. Although Master Hargrave's hand was fine and elegant, he'd written many phrases in Latin, and much of the trial description was accompanied by other difficult and unfamiliar words. She shook her head. 'How am I to make sense of this?'

Still, she tried. Skimming through the different pages, she could see the basic shape of the trial emerge. He'd captured portions of testimony from the witnesses and the defendant, and he appeared to record much of the judge's commentary as well. He'd circled or underlined some phrases, and written comments in the margins. Lucy read one of the comments out loud. "'First, defendant claimed that his cousin had been inhabited by a 'dreadful spirit' and thus deserved to be killed, then defendant claimed he himself had been inhabited by a spirit commanded by a devilish entity, who compelled him to commit the crime. Then he claimed crime of passion. Then he finally offered that, in his rage, he had planned out the cold-hearted killing of his only cousin, for having wronged him. Hardly self-defence.'" Then another question. "'Why has Allerby not noted the clear pre-meditation?'" She lightly knocked her knuckles against her forehead. The magistrate's words were stark, accusatory. No wonder he'd been concerned about his notes falling into the hands of the wrong individuals. 'I'll give them back to Master Hargrave tomorrow,' she promised. She'd stopped by earlier that evening only to discover that he and Adam had taken a short trip to Oxford. As such, she hadn't been able to ask Master Hargrave about Letitia Davenport or give him back the piece she'd found.

She was about to set them aside and blow out the candle when she noticed some faint markings, where someone had lightly underlined certain words. In the margins, a hand different from the magistrate's had written, *This will do.*

She looked through the pages again, noticing other places where words had been slightly marked as well. Everything underlined had been an object.

Then she sat up straight. The Fowlers were indeed interested in curious things. Indeed, hadn't the house been full of strange things? The cellar and the upstairs bedchamber were full of peculiar and interesting objects. What was it Gamel had said to his father earlier, about getting something nice for his collection?

That idea reminded her of the printed collection of curiosities that she'd received from Phineas Fowler the day they met, and she began to rummage through the small box by her bed. She pulled out the list. 'Could this tract be describing his father's own collection?'

Carefully, she unfolded the pages and began to review them, trying to think whether she'd noticed such things at the Fowler's home. 'There were certainly birds' nests and flea glasses, and salt spoons . . . not sure about that . . . not sure about that.' She kept running her finger down the list, trying to note if any of the underlined items appeared on the list.

This time she began to read the items in detail, her index finger pointing to each one at a time. Finally, her finger slowed when she came to a line that had been buried before. *A book-shaped pendant or reliquary, embossed, with Aesop's fables.* She sat back. 'I'd wager this is the same one that Master Aubrey received on Christmas Eve. It *was* from the Fowlers. Which one? Phineas, I assume.' She pushed the thought of Phineas's lifeless, bloodied body out of her mind. She thought instead about how Phineas had bought the posy from the old lady with more coins than required. 'He was a decent man, I think.'

She continued to look at the list, stopping when another item jumped out at her, in a section called *Weapons and Tools.* There was a long list of different types of knives, one flintlock gun, and then a dental pelican. She rubbed her jaw as she studied that one. 'Dental pelican. Used to extract teeth with efficiency.' She paused. 'That's certainly an unusual object. But why is it grouped here under weapons? Very strange.' Her thoughts began to churn then. 'How odd that he had a dental pelican in his possession, and we know one was stolen from the tooth-puller's family.'

She stood up, nearly knocking over her candle. 'Could he be stealing from the victims?' she asked the empty room. Then a strange thought came to her, and she clapped her hand over her mouth. 'No. He's not stealing from the victims. These objects came from the killers.'

She looked back at what had been underlined in the magistrate's notes. 'Was this what he was planning to take next? Or does he have them already?'

Blowing out the lantern, she climbed back into her bed, still thinking. 'I need to speak to Sam Havisham tomorrow. Maybe he has the answers we need.'

Although questions still plagued her, it did not take her long to drop off into a dreamless sleep.

EIGHTEEN

After she'd completed her chores the next morning, and Will and Master Aubrey had both left on different errands, Lucy slid next to Lach on the bench. 'I must tell you something,' she said, pulling out the collection of curiosities. 'Remember this piece from Phineas Fowler? Something struck me about it.'

She tapped the line that described the pendant. 'I'm sure this is the same object that was sent to Master Hargrave,' she said. 'The piece was so unusual – I can't imagine that there would be many like it. Besides, what a coincidence that would be.'

'Hmm, that does seem odd.' Lach scratched his nose as he spoke. 'Do you think this might be describing their own collection?'

'I'm not certain. However, I have the distinct sense that the collection does not belong to Phineas Fowler, but rather to his father, Matthias. I believe we saw a few of these items listed here in the cellar.'

Lach couldn't quite hide his shudder, remembering their time in Havisham's cellar. 'I suppose that could be true,' he said, grunting. 'However, some of these items are not wholly uncommon. Many may own items like those described here.'

She turned the page and pointed to another section. 'What about these?' she asked. 'I saw a few of these too, I swear it. When I was in his bedchamber, looking for the magistrate's notes, I saw them in a cabinet, along with a lot of other strange things I told you about.'

Lach whistled as he looked over the descriptions. 'Are you thinking that Matthias Fowler returned most of the objects that his son had stolen from Master Hargrave? And the pendant – do you suppose it was a gift to make up for what his son had done?'

'Perhaps. I don't know. Someone else could have sent the pendant to Master Hargrave, with or without Matthias's knowledge. When I started examining the collection, I found some other interesting things as well.' Lucy pointed to the description of the dental pelican. 'Look at this one. A dental pelican. See the category it's in?'

'Weapons and tools?' He made a face. 'Since when is a dental tool a weapon?'

'Exactly. Only in the *Tooth-Puller's Tale*,' she replied, pulling on her cloak and gloves. 'I find it very strange it would be listed this way.'

'Where are you going?'

'I'm going to speak to Sam Havisham. I think he knows more about the Fowlers than he has let on. I also want to ask him about what that woman, Letitia Davenport, said to him. About writing of Master Hargrave's so-called "corruption". I've been thinking about her words all night. I can't shake the feeling that she's involved with what happened to Master Hargrave. What is it?'

Lach was staring at her, his mouth slack-jawed. 'You're speaking in jest, are you not? You are not truly talking about returning to Havisham's again?'

'Not to worry, I shall not be very long.' She tapped on the piece of paper on the table. 'Besides, don't you have to set your *Poor Robin's Merriments and Jests*?'

'Lucy, you're going to get yourself killed and I won't write your murder ballad if you do.'

His gruff concern touched her. 'How about this? I'll speak to him only if no one else is there. If not, I'll extend him an invitation to join us for supper tomorrow night. Master Aubrey won't mind, I'm certain.'

'Oh, Lucy. Are you here to help me again?' Havisham asked hopefully when she appeared in the doorway to his shop. He was leaning over the printing press, painstakingly placing the type in the frame with one hand. 'Although, truth be told, I don't think I can keep this up at all. I'll have to see about hiring a new apprentice.'

'I thought you were taking a break from printing,' Lucy commented. She looked around, trying to determine if the Fowlers were around, Lach's warning stark in her thoughts. 'At least that's what Matthias Fowler said yesterday.' She looked at the stacks of papers on the table. 'Are you sorting your inventory? Do you have the source for those other tracts?' she asked. Perhaps there was still a way to retrieve Master Hargrave's stolen notes.

'Those tracts. No, Matthias has them all.' He groaned, and again Lucy could smell the stench of spirits on him. He'd already been tippling, despite the early hour. His next words confirmed her intuition. 'I need a drink. Do you have any ale?'

'No, sir. I d–don't.' She paused, and then asked the question that had plagued her. 'Mr Havisham, sir. Why would Letitia Davenport have written such dreadful lies about the magistrate? She claimed that he had killed Phineas! Why would she say such a thing?'

His face seemed to turn even more grey as she spoke. 'Perhaps it's true. I don't know the magistrate personally. People have always done such terrible things when their reputation is besmirched.'

'It's *not* true. Master Hargrave would never have done such a thing.'

'You are indeed adamant,' he noted, his words slurring slightly. 'You sound so truthful.'

'That's because I am truthful! Master Hargrave is no killer. I am certain of that because—' She checked herself before she could complete her thought, busying herself with straightening one of the piles on the table.

'Because? What were you going to say? You know the truth, don't you, Lucy?' Havisham turned his bloodshot eyes on her. 'You were here that day, weren't you? *You* were the witness, were you not?'

Lucy gulped. 'I told you: we found him dead. Then we summoned the constable.'

Havisham shook his head. 'No, Constable Duncan said there was a witness to the murder. That witness was you, wasn't it? Please, Lucy. Tell me what happened. He was my friend.'

'I d–don't know what happened,' Lucy began, which in some ways was true. She didn't know who the killers were, and she most certainly did not know why they had decided to enact such violence upon Phineas.

Havisham slumped lower on his bench, his body a portrait in sorrow. 'I see.'

Lucy swallowed and then made a swift decision to honour Phineas's life by telling the truth. 'You are right. I did overhear the crime, but I was not in a position to see who killed him,' she said, speaking hurriedly. 'Honestly. That is the truth. I just know that there were two people with Phineas when he died – a man and a woman. But I cannot say for sure who killed him.'

She rubbed her hands on her skirts. 'The woman was angry about one of the pieces he'd published, but I don't know which one enraged her so fully.'

She stopped then, expecting him to ask the obvious next question. *Was there nothing you could do while my friend was being murdered?* He did not. He appeared to be weighing her words.

'Thank you, Lucy.' He held up a familiar crumpled sheet of paper, containing Lucy's true account of the Donnetts' murder. 'I found this one account among his belongings.' He held it out for her to see. 'Very odd – I don't know who gave us this tract about the soap-seller. I don't recognize the handwriting. It is not an educated hand; I can tell you that much.'

Lucy took it, noticing how Phineas had written some notes around her cramped text. On the second page, she saw that he had underlined the passage where she had speculated about the nature of the Donnetts' marriage outside the Fleet Prison. The word *licence* was underlined twice.

'He told me he went and searched out some information on his own, since he felt some things were lacking.'

'Is that so?' Lucy asked, startled. 'Where did he go?'

'He said he'd spoken to Mrs Donnett's sister – Mrs Bainbridge – at length.' Havisham sighed. 'He was so gleeful when he returned, as if he were one of the King's own spies. He'd worked something out.'

'What did he discover?'

'I can't rightfully say. Gamel was here at the time, tried to tease the information out of him. But Phineas just gave that charming smile of his and said we'd all have to wait. Said that there was likely a whole other tale to be told, that he'd set down to write soon.'

'Did he write it?' Lucy asked, growing excited. Perhaps Phineas had recorded his discovery.

Havisham shook his head mournfully. 'No, if he did, I have

not found it.' He rubbed his jaw. 'Though I think Gamel pursued the matter after Phineas was killed.'

'How do you mean?'

'He brought something back for his father this morning. "For your collection," he had said. "that justice might be done."'

'"That justice might be done"?' Lucy repeated. 'What do you think he meant by that?'

'I'm not certain. His father was quite angry, shouting that Gamel did not understand. Said he would find justice for Phineas's death in his own way.'

A chill ran down Lucy's spine. 'I wonder if Gamel had figured something out. I wonder what that item was. What did he do with it, do you know? Does his father have it?'

Havisham gestured wearily towards Matthias's grey coat hanging on a hook by the door. 'He stuffed it in the interior pocket, if I recall.'

Lucy stood up and resolutely began to search Matthias's coat. She expected Havisham to protest, but he let her be.

She withdrew a crumpled and creased document printed on a fine grade of paper. It was a marriage certificate for Guy Donnett of Fetter Lane and Jean Miggs of Tailor Street, issued in June 1645.

'What is this?' she muttered. This was not a licence issued by a Fleet Prison cleric, but a document signed by witnesses and the minister at St Dunstan's church. She looked at the name of the bride again. Jean Miggs. Not Mary.

'Mr Donnett *had* been married before. This must have been the certificate of marriage with his first wife.' She stared at the piece. 'I suppose this explains why he and the second Mrs Donnett got married at the Fleet in such a clandestine way. Certainly, Mrs Bainbridge had not known that her sister's husband had been married before. Although if she had known, she is unlikely to have mentioned it, especially if she had disproved of her sister's match.'

Havisham came to look at the certificate over her shoulder. 'He probably didn't want to deal with his late wife's in-laws any more.' He shrugged. 'I imagine a lot of men might feel that way.'

Lucy carefully tucked the certificate back into Matthias's coat where she had found it, and sat back down at the table. She picked up her own handwritten piece, staring again at the notes Phineas had written. He'd circled the words *marriage licence* and his brother had brought back a marriage certificate for his father.

She then picked up the printed true account and began to read it in more detail. Phineas had added many flourishes and embellishments, making the narrative even more exciting. Nothing seemed all that different from what she had originally written. 'He was saving it all for another true account,' she said, feeling a pang that such a tract would never come to light. She continued to read, then stopped sharply. There was a line she had missed before that Phineas had added to the section where she speculated about the Donnetts' marriage. '"Someone over on Fetter Lane may have much to say about this,"' she read. She put the paper down as she mused over the sentence. 'Fetter Lane? That was Guy Donnett's address on the marriage certificate.'

'What is going on?' Matthias Fowler asked, entering the room from the stairs. Although she'd heard his voice before, this was the first time she'd seen him up close. Perhaps in his mid-fifties, he had sandy grey hair and piercing dark eyes. What had Lach said? He looked like someone who could kill a man with his eyes.

Havisham stepped back and Lucy shifted uncomfortably. She wondered how long Matthias had been listening to their conversation.

'Uh, Lucy, this is Matthias Fowler, the father of Phineas. Matthias, this is Lucy Campion, apprenticed to Master Aubrey. She was here yesterday, helping me sort my trays.'

'What is that?' Matthias asked again, sounding impatient. He was pointing at the piece Lucy had written, lying open on the table.

'We were just talking about how someone gave us this true account for Phineas to print and sell. About the murder of two soap-sellers up on Pye Corner. It was probably the last piece that Phineas ever sold.' Havisham pushed angrily at the offending piece. 'Written by "Anonymous". Didn't even ask for a single farthing.'

'You don't say?' Matthias replied. 'Let me see it.' He proceeded to read it over easily, in the silent manner of those who'd learned to read when they were young. For some reason, Lucy found herself watching the man's face, trying to discern what he was thinking. Although he had seemed angry when he had first picked up the paper, Lucy could now see an excited glint in his eye. She wondered what intrigued him so about the tale.

'A fascinating story,' he said, 'although I'm disappointed that Phineas had spent his time producing this one, when I had other tales on hand waiting for their place in the queue.' He scratched his cheek. 'Still, I am quite struck by this. As I understand, the Donnetts were murdered after Phineas sold a piece mentioning their names. Now Phineas is dead after he sold this piece about their murders.' His laugh was thoroughly unpleasant. 'A most unlikely coincidence, I should say.'

Lucy was overcome with nausea as she absorbed what Matthias had said. Could he be right? Could this piece about the Donnetts' murder have brought about Phineas's own killing? How could that be? She swayed uncomfortably on the bench, a terrible thought overwhelming her. What if she had been the one who had printed and sold the piece? Would Phineas's murderer have tracked her down? Killed her instead of Phineas? She shuddered, looking down.

Lucy stiffened when Matthias gave her a knowing wink. '"There, but for the Grace of God, go I,"' he quoted.

Does he know I wrote the piece? She shivered as a chill ran over her.

His lips still curled, and he carefully folded the piece into squares and placed it in his pocket. 'I am heading out now,' he said, pulling his cloak and hat off the peg by the door. 'There's something I must do.' He swept out of the shop and on to the busy street.

Why had Gamel wanted his father to have that certificate? Why had it made Matthias so angry? She stood up. What was it Havisham had told her about the fight between father and son? 'For your collection,' the son had said, 'that justice might be done.'

Why would he have needed such a piece for his collection? she asked herself, standing at the door. *I need to find out what's on Fetter Lane.*

NINETEEN

Lucy stood where Fleet Street intersected with Fetter Lane, regarding the rows of bustling shops and homes which stretched all the way to Holborn to the north. Fetter Lane was a road that Lucy knew well, having just been at the Falcon the week before. She frowned. It had been at the Falcon that that man had knocked her down and dumped her pieces into the muddy puddle.

Did members of the Donnett family still live on this street? Was that what Phineas had meant by his cryptic words? He'd practically invited his readers to discover the connection for themselves. Perhaps someone here knew something about the Pye Corner deaths. On her way over, she'd hurriedly stopped back at Master Aubrey's and told him to let the constable know. *I'm just going to see what I can find out*, she'd said, even though Lach looked sceptical.

She began to look at the signs above the shops more closely. Most featured pictures of their wares, so that people who could not read could still find the shops they needed readily enough. Many of the signs were dull and cracking, though, from the onslaught of nature's elements, indicating the business had been the same for years, even decades. Although it was chilly, it was not as blustery as it had been, and there were many merchants and tradesmen going about their daily business.

She watched a leather-maker arranging hides on the open shelf in front of his shop, trying to work out a plan. *Should I ask about the Donnetts? He's likely to know.* She started to move towards the man and then stopped, mid-step. *Best be prudent.*

Having decided to get a sense of the street first before making enquiries, she attuned herself to the conversations transpiring around her as she walked alongside the various shops and stalls. Deal-making, friendly haggling, exchanges of coins and merchants' tokens . . . the street was full of life. While not as crowded or bustling as Covent Garden market, most of the people seemed in good spirits, looking forward to another evening of wassailing and merry-making.

One shop towards the end of the street caught her eye, standing out against the liveliness of the street. Black crepe had been wrapped around the old sign, suggesting that someone had recently died. What kind of shop was it?

She glanced around at the merchants and passers-by around her. Surely it would not be strange to simply ask about the shop. She was about to ask an old woman selling beads, when the sight of a familiar figure caused her to gasp. Matthias Fowler was standing a few yards away, speaking to the leather-seller she had just passed. *He must be here for the same reason I am*, she thought. He must want to discover what had so intrigued Phineas in the days before his death.

She stood back against the shadowy wall of a shoemaker's shop, observing the senior Fowler.

Has he seen me? She couldn't say for certain. However, she'd not seen him glance in her direction, appearing to be wholly absorbed in whatever the leather-maker was telling him. Several times the leather-maker ran his hands along the hides, as if explaining something about them.

After listening intently, Matthias then said something that caused the leather-maker to shake his head. With a tip to his hat, Matthias walked slowly away, with none of the vigour once displayed by his son. A moment later, he stopped again, this time to speak to an older woman, who was shaping a clay pot in front of her stall. After he spoke to her, the woman pointed in the direction of the shop with the black crepe strewn over it, across the street from where Lucy was still crouched against the wall. Matthias reached into his pocket and left something in a small pot beside her, probably a coin. Accepting the payment, the potter inclined her head in thanks.

Lucy watched Matthias as he walked over to the shop, first staring up at the crepe-draped sign hanging from the staff above the door, and then poking around the pots and basins stacked in front. He rapped sharply on the front door and then peered in through the shuttered window when no one came to the door.

Impatiently, he jostled the door again and knocked a few more times, his pounding growing increasingly determined. After a minute, he stepped back, shoving his hands into his pockets in resignation. Dejection evident in his slumped form, he turned and crossed the street toward the Falcon.

To her surprise, Matthias did not enter the tavern, but instead positioned himself by some barrels lining the front of the establishment, still gazing at the shop on the other side of the street.

He must be waiting for the shopkeeper to return, she surmised. Even though she was still about thirty yards away from him, she did not want to draw his attention while she had yet to figure out what intrigued him so about the crepe-draped shop. If he was settling in to wait, then she would as well.

Noticing some children kneeling on the ground, in the small space between the shoemaker's and the silk merchant's shop next door, she moved over to see what they were doing, while still keeping a vigilant eye on Matthias.

They were playing cherry-pit, a game that she and Will had once adored, back when they lived in Southwark and well before she had entered service. They'd been quite skilled, often earning a bit of bread or some sweets off the other children. Their mother had not let them play for money, as she feared it would lead to gambling, a vice that would in turn invite Satan into their hearts.

These children apparently had no such qualms, playing for farthings and half-pennies. Just as she and Will used to do, the children would blow on their hands to warm them before rolling the cherry-pits towards the holes in the ground. Inwardly, she groaned every time they missed. Finally, one of the boys landed a cherry-pit in the hole, although Lucy reckoned it was more by chance than anything.

'I got it in the hole!' he exclaimed, clearly delighted. 'Farthings all around!'

Lucy stiffened as Matthias suddenly glanced at them, the children's whooping and clapping catching his attention. Still crouched down, she edged backward until she was in the open doorway of the shoemaker's shop.

Fortunately, he turned back in the direction he'd been facing, and she stood up awkwardly.

'Good day, miss,' the shoemaker called to her from his seat at a workbench, using his awl to poke holes in a bit of leather. All around the room there were rows of shoes and boots, in various stages of completion. Some pairs were old and worn, others looked stiff and unyielding. He gave her a friendly smile. 'In need of new shoes? Or perhaps you need your boots repaired?'

Knowing she needed to explain her presence, Lucy lifted her skirts slightly and presented her foot to the shoemaker so that he could see her shoe. 'I spend so much time walking, I'm rather afraid I've quite worn these out.' She glanced back towards the Falcon. Matthias was still leaning comfortably against the barrel.

Not wanting to leave her vantage point, she pretended not to notice when the shoemaker beckoned her in. Sighing, the man stood up from his bench and knelt down before her, grasping her extended foot with a professional air. 'A well-trod heel, that is certain. Probably will give you some aches and pains in your leg muscles and joints, if you don't get it fixed,' he said, taking in her garb. He stood back up. 'What do you peddle?'

'I'm a bookseller,' she said, peeking back outside. Matthias had not moved from his position behind the barrel, but he was craning his neck in excitement. A man had approached the shop with the proprietary air of an owner, pushing a cart full of crates. He produced a key and went inside.

A moment later, the man came back out, carrying a shovel which he used to push away manure that had been left by some recently passing horses. Matthias was clearly watching the man with interest but had not yet moved from his position.

Lucy studied the man as well. Was there something familiar about him? Something stirred in Lucy as she tried to remember where she might have seen the man before.

'How long have you had a business on this street?' she asked the shoemaker.

'For fifteen years, and my father twenty before me. I thought I'd lose everything in the Great Fire, but the good Lord saw fit to spare my business that day.'

'Tell me, what is that business across the street? The one whose sign is draped in black crepe?'

'Draped in black? Why, that's the Donnetts'. Father and son own the business together. They make soaps and sell them out of their shop.'

'Soap-makers named Donnett? You don't say.' Somehow, this knowledge didn't surprise Lucy very much. It stood to reason

that someone related to Guy Donnett might also have pursued
the soap-making trade, as such occupations often ran in families.
Father and son, the shoemaker had said. Perhaps this business
was owned by Guy Donnett's brother and nephew.

'Did one of the Donnett family die recently?' Lucy asked. 'I
saw the black crepe covering the sign. I assume they are closed
for business right now.'

'Ah, yes, I believe it was the father, the senior Donnett, who
passed away. Something unnatural, I heard.'

'The father? Curious,' Lucy murmured. 'What was unnatural
about his death, if you don't mind me asking.'

'I can't say for sure. I'm not one for gossip, you see. When
my missus was alive, I'd know the whole tale, and then some.'
He chuckled. 'Now, I mostly keep to myself.'

Peering out of the doorway again, Lucy watched as Matthias
crossed the street and spoke to the man. Setting down the shovel,
the man jerked his thumb towards the shop's entrance, and both
men disappeared inside. What was it Phineas had discovered?
What was the man telling Matthias?

'Miss?' The shoemaker was watching her with a puzzled air.
'Do you want to leave those shoes with me? I can fix them while
you wait. Cost just a few pennies. Make them as good as new.'

'Maybe later,' she said. Ignoring the shoemaker's disgruntled
mutterings, she left the shop and quickly crossed the street and
perched by the open window in a way that allowed her to peek
inside.

TWENTY

Matthias was walking about, running his hands along a stack of burnished iron pans. 'I heard tell of a soapmaker Donnett who was killed up on Pye Corner,' he was saying. 'A relative of yours?'

The man spat. 'My father. Guy Donnett.'

Lucy clapped her hand over her mouth. She'd not expected that. Did that mean Guy Donnett had two shops? One here with his son, and the other with his wife at Pye Corner? That seemed rather unusual.

She shut out the thoughts that swirled around her mind so that she could listen.

'Then you are . . . Lionel Donnett?' Matthias asked. He must have learned the man's name during his earlier enquiries.

'Yes. What of it? Why are you asking about my father?'

Matthias did not answer the man's question, evidently having had the same thought as Lucy. 'Business appears to have been fortunate if your father was able to set up two different shops, one with you and one with your . . . stepmother?'

'That woman was not my stepmother!' Lionel said, his jaw clenched. 'She was nothing!' He gestured around the room. '*This* is my father's shop.'

The pure anger on his face jarred a memory for Lucy. Inhaling sharply, she stared at the man. Lionel Donnett was the man who had pushed her down outside the Falcon and dumped her papers into a muddy puddle. She steadied herself against the barrel as she remembered his menacing words: *Stop peddling your lies!*

Inside the shop, Lionel was still speaking in low, angry tones. 'Look around! Everything here belongs to my father and my mother.'

Lucy was still confused. *Had Guy Donnett divorced his first wife?*

Again, Matthias answered her question as he advanced toward

Lionel with a chuckle. 'I see,' he said. 'Must have been a shock to discover your father had married again. A younger, more becoming woman, from what I understand.' He stopped a few inches from Lionel and jabbed a finger into the man's chest. 'My question to you is this . . . Why kill the messenger?'

'Kill the messenger?' Lionel's eyes widened as recognition set in. 'You know about the bookseller?'

Then before Matthias could respond, Lionel picked up a great slab of soap and struck him across the head, knocking him senseless to the ground.

Shocked, Lucy rubbed her eyes, trying to make sense of the assault she had just witnessed. Still reeling, she stepped back unsteadily, toppling against a great stack of crates piled below the window and bringing them all to the ground with a great crash.

Scrambling to her feet, she was about to run away when a heavy hand clamped down on her shoulder and another wrapped across her mouth. 'What have we here?' a woman's harsh voice whispered in her ear. 'A spy?'

Unable to reply, Lucy felt herself forcibly dragged inside the soap-makers' shop.

Lionel, still standing over Matthias's unmoving body, started at the sight of them. 'Ma? What in the world are you doing with that girl?'

'What happened to that man?' his mother demanded at the same time, her hands still clamped heavily around Lucy. 'Whatever you did to him, *she* saw it. Caught her skulking about.'

Lucy began to squirm against her captor, but before she could wrest herself free, Lionel stepped over Matthias's prone body and stuffed a dirty cloth in her mouth, keeping her from shouting. Then he grabbed her jaw painfully and forced her head up. She met his eyes, trying desperately not to show the fear she was feeling.

'Wait a minute. I know her,' he said in surprise. 'She's a bookseller. She was in front of the Falcon the other day, peddling her gossip and lies.' He prodded the still unconscious Matthias with his foot. '*This* one was threatening me about that bookseller. I suppose she and him are working together.' He wagged his finger at Lucy. 'Don't try to deny it. Why else would you both be here?'

Trying to protest through the tightly wadded cloth in her mouth was futile.

Lionel waved his hand at her. 'No matter. I'll take care of you in a moment, after I get the other one out of here first.' With that, he picked up Matthias by his feet and dragged him violently out of the room, not caring that the man's head was being bounced along the ground like a sack of potatoes.

'Why did you come here?' Mrs Donnett pushed Lucy into a chair and held up a soap-cutting knife. 'If you scream, I'll kill you.' She pulled the gag from Lucy's mouth. 'What are you two up to? What business have you here?'

When Lucy didn't reply, the woman yanked at her hair, bringing tears to Lucy's eyes. 'I'm not with him,' Lucy whispered, her words sounding unconvincing even to her own ears. 'I was here to buy some soap. But I wasn't sure if I should go inside when I saw them talking.'

'Liar,' Mrs Donnett snarled. She held the knife against Lucy's throat. 'Tell me or I'll kill you now. Your choice.'

Lucy stopped struggling as she weighed her options. The woman would probably stop her before she got halfway out of the door and she didn't think anyone would hear her if she screamed for help. Had Lach summoned the constable? She couldn't know for sure. Even if he had, would Duncan be able to find her here.

'All right,' she said. 'I came here because I wanted to know the truth for myself.'

'Truth? What truth?' the woman snapped.

'You are Mrs Jean Miggs Donnett, are you not?' she asked, remembering the name and date on the St Dunstan's marriage certificate. 'Guy Donnett's wife. Despite the true account that claimed that *other* woman was his wife.'

Mrs Donnett spat at Lucy's feet. 'She was a harlot who seduced my husband! I am Mrs Donnett! Not her. You have no right to enter my shop and speak of that woman!'

Lucy realized she'd made a misstep and sought to soothe her. 'How terrible that he deceived you in such a way. Weren't you married over twenty years?'

'How did you know that?' Mrs Donnett asked, sounding less surly.

'I heard it mentioned,' Lucy said vaguely. 'You certainly did not deserve such a villainous deception.'

Mrs Donnett sniffed again, indicating tacit agreement. 'I was always a simple God-fearing woman.' Tears showed in her eyes. 'Faithful, loyal.'

'You didn't know, did you? How could you have?' Lucy said. She remembered something that Mrs Bainbridge had said about her sister's husband. 'Your husband probably claimed he was always on long trading trips, did he not? That must have been when he was with his, er, other family. *He* committed bigamy, living a life with another woman. *You* did nothing wrong.'

Mrs Donnett frowned. 'I was utterly deceived by him.'

Even though Lucy knew the answer, she still asked gently. 'What changed? How did you find out? Was it the *Tooth-Puller's Tale*?' At the woman's nod, Lucy continued. 'You must have seen it and realized that your husband had . . . taken another wife, while still being married to *you*. The shame of bigamy must have been . . . tremendous.'

Mrs Donnett began to weep, an ugly, anguished sound. 'I confronted him about it. He just laughed.'

'Why did you just not bring him to court? Surely the courts would have seen your side. He was clearly in the wrong, committing bigamy.'

'He claimed it was not bigamy,' Mrs Donnett said, swiping angrily at her tears. 'He told me that the priest who married us was not truly a man of God, that he was a trickster. It was *my* marriage that was the lie.'

'*She* was the legal wife? You were not?' Lucy stared at her. Then, before she could stop herself said, 'You must have been furious!'

'We both were!' Mrs Donnett brought her fist heavily down on the table. A frightened expression crossed her face.

'You *both* were furious. You mean your son Lionel was furious, too,' Lucy said slowly as something began to work itself out in her mind. 'He must have been angry that his mother was so deceived, but also that he was deceived as well.' Her voice dropped as the realization that had been bubbling up inside her finally emerged as a coherent thought. 'It was your son who killed them.'

Mrs Donnett's face said it all. 'I never thought he'd do such

a terrible thing, you have to believe me. But when a man learns—'
She broke off when Lionel re-entered the room, putting her hand
back on Lucy's shoulder.

'Finish your thought, Mother. When a son learns he is a bastard,
and his father made his mother into a whore, well, certainly, he
gets very angry indeed.'

'You must have been even more angry when the bookseller
published the piece about their murders,' Lucy said, trying to
keep them talking. 'You couldn't bear that he had put your shame
out in the world, for all to see.'

'I warned him to stop spreading lies about my family, about
my husband,' Mrs Donnett said. 'He called them a "loving
God-fearing couple"! Such a lie!'

Lucy felt a pang, thinking how she was the one who had
penned those words following what Mrs Bainbridge had said of
the couple. 'You warned him,' she repeated. Then, unable to
refrain, added, 'Was that all?'

Lionel Donnett looked her up and down, in a way that made
her thoroughly uneasy. 'I think it's time we decide what to do
about our uninvited guests, don't you, Mother?'

As he moved toward her, Lucy stomped hard on Mrs Donnett's
foot, breaking free of her grip and pushing herself towards the
door. She'd almost made it when something heavy struck her
over the head. A sickening sensation overwhelmed her, and she
was unable to resist as Mrs Donnett tied her hands and feet with
a bit of rope. As she moaned, the dirty cloth was stuffed in her
mouth again.

Hauling her over his shoulder like a sack of meal, Lionel
stalked out of the room and dumped her in a chilly back room.

For a moment, Lucy lay dazed on the floor, trying to figure out what
to do. Painfully, she looked around, noticing that Matthias was
trussed up beside her. The room they were lying in had only one
window high up on the wall, letting in a small amount of light. She
could see that it was a storeroom of sorts, full of crates and bins.
Along one wall was a workbench and a pitcher. There were unlit
lanterns hanging from the wall. The hustle and bustle from the
street outside was muted, and it would be hard to attract attention.
She couldn't hear anything from the Donnetts in the other room.

With distaste, she managed to spit out the dirty cloth. Matthias had revived and already pushed the cloth out of his mouth.

Lucy struggled to sit up. Her mouth dry and sore, she struggled to speak. 'We need to get out of here. We need to untie ourselves first, I think.' She began to wriggle her wrists, hoping to pull one of her hands free of the knots. 'Or else they might kill us when they return. I know they are trying to figure out what to do with us.'

He was still lying there, looking calm.

'You'd rather wait here for them to kill us?' she asked, still tugging at her wrists.

'No, I'd rather stay alive. Ah, the delicious irony.' He gave a grim chuckle, suggesting a joke that only he understood.

'Why were you here anyway? To kill them? To get revenge for Phineas?'

'That would be murder, my dear.'

Matthias's mocking coolness irritated her, and she returned to looking around the room.

'I've witnessed death many times. Seeing you die will not bother me a bit.' He chuckled again. 'Although, truth be told, I'd appreciate a little more ceremony. Feel free to begin your final confessions.'

'My final confession? Whatever do you mean? I have done nothing wrong,' Lucy said. Since she was unable to untie her own bonds, she dragged herself across the floor towards him, putting her bound hands by his. 'You'll need to untie me.'

'No confessions at all? Perhaps you've not killed anyone. What about lies? Surely you've had a few of those.'

Lucy could hear herself promising the Hargraves that she would not bring herself into another perilous position. *That was a lie of sorts, was it not?* She sighed. 'Please. Try to untie me.'

He held out his wrists. 'Untie *me*.'

Reluctantly, she reached up to the ends dangling off the knot. 'You said you've witnessed death many times. In battle? During the plague?'

He chuckled grimly. 'Both in battle and from sickness. However, I was referring to the gallows. Killed them myself.'

Their fingers touched then, and Lucy rolled away from him in disgust. He rolled over to face her when she spoke. 'You were a hangman.'

'Yes. Trained by Jack Ketch himself.' He grimaced. 'Although I was nothing like that bumbling fool.'

Lucy fell silent, her mind conjuring the image of the executioner at the gallows. Although she was often sent to the hanging tree or Newgate to sell murder ballads and dying confessions to the crowds, she usually avoided watching the spectacle itself. Sometimes the executioners wore black hoods, like the one she'd seen in his bedchamber, but just as often they did not. Usually, they did their grim work in silence, carrying out whatever sentence had been meted out to the condemned. They stayed in the shadows while the criminals cried out their laments and remained to collect the bodies for burial at Houndsditch. Only when the execution was botched, and the hanged did not die, did they take a more central role. On such occasions, the fickle crowds would clamour for the executioner to be merciful, and he would pull on the body of the condemned or call on young boys to do it for him. Lucy had seen such a botched execution once and it still bothered her. She shivered.

'I see that look of disgust in your eyes,' Matthias said, his eyes flitting towards the ceiling. 'The likes of you will never understand. You will cheer on death, but you do not wish to know the executioner.'

'I never cheered on death.' Lucy pulled herself up into a sitting position and scooted backwards until she reached the wall. Sniffing deeply, she caught the pungent smell of lye, but then something far sweeter. Rosemary? Lavender?

'Perhaps not. You excite and inflame with your true accounts and murder ballads,' Matthias replied, watching her idly all the while. 'Perhaps as much as any staged spectacle that I offered. Are we so different?'

She whipped her head around to glare at him. 'I have never taken a life, nor delighted in its loss.' Using the wall as leverage, she managed to get herself into a standing position. As she had hoped, she could see bits of soap all around the workbench. Spying a pitcher and basin on a table, she hopped across the room, being careful not to catch her skirts.

Matthias continued to talk, almost sounding as if he was reminiscing. 'There was a skill to being an executioner, you know, which most people refuse to acknowledge. A skill in managing the spectacle as well.'

The basin was empty, but the pitcher was full of water. Leaning over, Lucy managed to knock the pitcher over on the table so that some of the water spilled into the basin. There was a dead spider floating there. She remembered when the old woman had pointed to the shrivelled spider on the church's sundial. 'Something ill is coming,' she had crooned.

She forced herself to reply to Matthias, despite the disturbing nature of his words. 'Is that so?'

'Indeed. I always knew how long it would take someone to die. Sometimes it depended on the way they approached death.'

Curious in spite of herself, Lucy could not refrain from asking, 'What do you mean?'

'Many of the condemned were heroic in their refusal to voice their lamentation and inner turmoil. I, in turn, made their deaths heroic.'

Heroic? His words were disturbing and yet she knew his occupation, while not an honourable one, was a necessary part of the legal system. Bending over, she managed to position the lavender-smelling soap between her chin and shoulder. Moving with excruciating slowness, she managed to drop it into the half-filled basin.

Matthias continued to reminisce about his terrible doings. 'I also enjoyed seeing the arrogant and mighty men cut down to size, seeing them rendered pitiful. I have memories of them all.' He frowned. 'Then, of course, there were those who escaped their sentence. As "I and my gallows moan."'

'I know that one, too,' Lucy said. Then she continued to recite.

> Excepting when
> The thieves and magistrates made a truce,
> Saving some criminals from the noose,
> Thereby I was of no use.
> I and my gallows moan.

'Yes, well done,' he said, sounding pleased. '*The Cry of the Hangman*. Phineas wrote that one about me. He knows I did not like to be denied seeing justice done.'

Another line of the ballad flew to her lips without thinking. '"In secret the accursed may pass me bribes, although not always enough to save their cowardly lives."'

The man clicked his teeth. 'Most hangmen take bribes, to assure a faster and easier death. Less pain, I would tell them. I never took money.'

'What did you take, then?' Grimacing, she raised her hands behind her back and tried to grasp the soap in her hands. It slipped out of her hands and slid across the table and on to the floor. She reached for another piece of soap to put into the water.

She remembered the underlined words in the magistrate's personal trial notes. The stories of the stolen objects. 'You took mementos from the killers. Why?'

'For my collection.' Matthias grunted heavily as he pushed himself to a standing position as she had done. 'Looks as though you'll need my help before you turn all the water over.' He hopped over so that he was directly beside her, reaching out to steady the basin.

'I don't understand. Why would you wish to remember them? Did you think they were so right that you needed something to remember them by?'

'I cannot fully explain it. There was something, deep inside me, urging me to remember them. That I could remember the names and actions of the men and women I executed at the hanging tree.'

'Why would you want to do such a . . . thing?' She almost said 'dreadful', but she stopped herself just in time, not wanting to antagonize him more.

'You cannot understand what it means to take a life. It is something I hope you will never understand.'

Finally, Lucy managed to position her wrists so that she could rub the soap on the ropes. Biting her lip against the pain, she awkwardly moved the rope binding her wrists against the soap. Would this even work? 'Why have there been no collections of curiosities or advice about how to escape from being bound?'

Matthias gave a snort that sounded almost like a real laugh. 'If we should get free, I promise I'll write that very piece for you. *A Hornbook for Hostages*.'

Lucy rolled her eyes at the thought. At least the tight binds were finally loosening. She returned to their discussion. 'Do you mean that you want to remember their crimes – their murderous actions – so you can remember your sense of justice?'

Matthias's eyes opened. For a moment, he didn't say anything, but she could see his jaw twitch, and the muscles in his neck moving as he swallowed. 'Yes. I had to remember that I was the necessary sword of justice. That I was there to help restore order when the world has been turned upside down.'

The ropes were definitely loosening now. She still had more questions of Matthias before she could think about how to escape. 'Why did you steal from Master Hargrave? Why did you want him to be ill-treated and maligned?'

'It is not as you think.' Matthias sighed. 'A few weeks ago, my younger son, Gamel, and I were together in a tavern, when we happened to hear your Master Hargrave speaking to that other judge. We heard him say he'd been writing down his thoughts on the trials he'd attended. My son thought this could help out Phineas and Master Havisham. As you know, Sam had lost his printing shop during the Great Fire, and they had just started his press again. I thought surely these true accounts would liven his work, and they most certainly did. Havisham told us he'd never seen someone sell so well.'

'Gamel was the one who stole from Master Hargrave. He struck him over the head!' Lucy exclaimed. 'The magistrate could have been killed!'

'Ah, he's fine, is he not?' Matthias scoffed. 'Besides, I gave him a good scolding about the other objects, which I thought was an unnecessary excess. Besides, none was particularly notable or curious. I returned them on Christmas Eve, with a gift of my own.'

'The book pendant?'

'You know about that.' Again, he sounded pleased. 'I thought the magistrate would appreciate it. I chose it for my collection years ago.' He paused. 'You look disgusted. I should say that I have two collections. One is as I have described to you – the curious objects from murderers. The other is simply a collection of the curious and strange – odd items, natural and mechanical alike, that appealed to me. The pendant that I gave to Master Hargrave was one such item. I'd picked it up from a German tradesman, and the panels had very much appealed to my sense of justice. I thought the magistrate would be able to relate as well.' He frowned. 'I had never intended Phineas to describe all parts of my collection, but despite the scolding I gave him, the damage was done, and news of collection was out in the world.'

Lucy continued to pinch and pull at the ropes. 'You say that you asked Gamel to steal the magistrate's notes to help Phineas create true accounts of murders and trials and get him back on his feet.'

'That is so.'

'You had another reason, did you not?' She thought about the underlined words. 'Why steal from murderers who'd long been executed? Those accounts were all from before the Great Fire and many even before the plague.'

'There were some individuals I never collected from. It bothered me.'

With a great sigh, Lucy slipped the rope off and she could move her arms again. Quickly, she knelt down to untie the ropes around her ankles.

'Are you going to let me free?' Matthias asked, watching her. 'You might need me.'

Lucy hesitated. The door was still locked from the outside, but escape might be easier if they were both unfettered.

'I'm not a murderer, you know. I may have killed many people, but those deaths were all sanctioned by court and king. I'm not going to hurt you.' His voice caught. 'I'm not a bad man.'

'Why did you become an executioner?' Lucy whispered. The raw pain on the man's face was difficult to bear.

Matthias scratched his head. 'It's a long story, best told over a drink.'

'Tell me now,' Lucy insisted. 'Or I won't untie you. I'll leave you here.'

His shoulders sagged a bit. 'My wife died just a few days after giving birth to Gamel. Life became more difficult. It was hard to make ends meet, and with my uncle and father, I began to steal to get enough food on the table for my two boys. We began to hold up merchants as they travelled outside of London. We picked ones well laden with goods but poorly protected.' He paused. 'For a while, our small takes were satisfying, and I was able to provide sufficiently for my boys.'

'What happened then?' Lucy asked, intrigued in spite of the urgency of their situation. She did not hear anything from the corridor.

'Eventually, we were caught. Highway robbery. Our crimes were deemed violent enough that we were condemned to hang.' He fell silent. 'I thought I would never see Phineas and Gamel again and I was at my wit's end, full of consternation and grief over the impoverished life they would surely lead upon my shameful execution as a criminal.' He broke off.

'Well, what happened?'

'The magistrate offered us each a choice.'

'What was the choice?' Lucy demanded.

Matthias's voice was hollow when he replied. 'He said, "You may live and receive a full pardon for your actions, as long as you execute the other two."'

'What? What magistrate would set such an outlandish proposition?' Lucy asked, indignant. 'I don't believe it.'

'I wish it were not so. They needed another hangman.' He sighed. 'My father refused immediately. My uncle did not waver either. I began to weep, because, God help me, I wanted to live. I wanted my boys to live.'

'You took the deal.' She untied him, with several hard yanks of the rope.

'My father and uncle both urged me to live, and to raise my boys.' He swallowed, rubbing his wrists together. 'I know it is not believable to an outsider's ears, but they both begged me. Better that at least one of us live, than all three of us die.'

She couldn't bring herself to look at him, feeling emotion from his story washing over her.

'I took up the mantle of executioner and I killed them both. One after the other. An axe to the back of the head, in front of the magistrate. First my uncle, then my father. I was then pardoned as promised and began my days as a hangman.'

Lucy stood stock still.

'Not a day has gone by that I have not thought of this decision. Should I have refused? Many a night I think so. My two boys, growing up in the shadow of my shame, my occupation that others view as so dishonourable.' His eyes glistened. 'Then I looked at my boys. My boys who were alive because I was there to take care of them. I knew in my heart that I had done what was right. The dishonour was in the magistrate who asked me to do such a terrible thing. I have done my part to regain order in this world and put things to right. I was doing the work of God and king, and that may not be gainsaid.'

Lucy stepped away as he reminisced, his eyes half closing.

'My collection began that night, with a necklace we had stolen in the robbery. I knew where my father had hidden it. At first it was a memento of him, a reminder of how he had saved me. Then it became a reminder of how I had killed him instead.'

As he untied the rope around his ankles, Lucy regarded him warily, unsure of whether she had made the right decision.

'Later, I was always uneasy about the execution until I had an object from the killer. For me, it was a reminder that they deserved to die. I did not want anything from their victims – why would I? Usually, they were innocents, undeserving of their fate. I could only do my job well when I had something to remind me that these criminals had done something unspeakable and deserved to be executed.'

'You are no longer a hangman.'

'Am I not? Is that something that changes in a man? I should say, once a hangman, always one.'

'Are you planning to murder them for killing Phineas?'

'Murder them? No. I was here to warn them.'

Hearing a sound in the hallway, Lucy braced herself to run and defend herself in any way she could. She didn't see any weapons but there was a cloth bag of soaps that could provide a hefty punch as needed.

The door opened, and Mrs Donnett was standing there, a knife in her hand. 'You untied yourselves,' she said, sounding confused. 'How did you manage that?'

'Let us go!' Lucy pleaded.

'You'll turn us in! We'll be tried and hanged for certain.'

'That is likely so,' Matthias said. 'Why did you kill my son?'

The woman began to weep. 'Why did he have to print those

stories? Say those terrible things about my husband marrying and living with another woman.'

Then they heard a scuffling sound from the hallway.

'Ma,' Lionel called from down the hallway.

'What is it? I'm busy!'

'This can't wait,' he said, appearing in the doorway.

To everyone's great surprise, Gamel Fowler emerged from behind him, a flintlock pistol at Lionel's back.

Matthias, with unexpected speed and force, suddenly lunged forward and knocked Mrs Donnett to the ground.

Gamel looked at his father approvingly. 'Tie her up, Father.'

Matthias began to tie Mrs Donnett, his knee to her back, wrapping her arms and legs with the same twine that had just bound Lucy. Then he began to tie up Lionel as well. The man did not move as he was being bound but stared at them with hate in his eyes.

'Let me go,' Lucy said. 'I will inform the constable at once.'

Gamel waved the flintlock at her. She saw now that he had a second gun holstered on his leg. 'You're not going anywhere, miss.'

'Gamel, what are you doing?' Matthias asked.

'I plan to execute them.' He pointed to his gun. 'Each is loaded. It shall not take long.'

'What?' Lucy exclaimed. 'You can't murder them.'

'I didn't say murder. I said execute.'

'I cannot let you do that,' Lucy protested.

'I'm afraid you can do nothing to stop us,' Matthias replied. 'However, Gamel, we must first allow them their dying confessions. As we would with any execution.' He pointed to some paper and a quill on the table. 'Lucy, fetch the paper. You shall capture their true testimony before they are executed for killing Gamel's older brother.'

'Was everything you said before a lie?' she said desperately.

His look was inscrutable. 'Remember what I told you.'

'Let's get on with it,' Gamel said, waving the flintlock around, causing everyone to flinch.

With shaking fingers, Lucy sat down and picked up the quill and dipped it in the ink. She'd taken a dying confession once before, but of a very different sort, in a very different context. 'Please begin,' she whispered to Mrs Donnett. 'From the beginning.'

Her voice quavering, Mrs Donnett began to speak, telling the story of how she had met Guy Donnett when he was a young man. 'He'd begun to court me straightaway,' she said, sounding more pleading than proud as she began a long narrative leading to how she had killed her husband, the other Mrs Donnett and, later, Phineas.

As she spoke, Gamel paced the room. Clearly, recording this confession had not been in his plans. But Matthias prompted Mrs Donnett throughout, clearly well versed in how to structure dying testimonies. Offer a bit of background about the accused. Describe the circumstances leading to the crime. Provide sensational details of the crime itself. Finally, conclude with abject grief and remorse, and a plan to beg for mercy in Heaven.

As she captured Mrs Donnett's confession, Lucy continued to ponder what Matthias had told her earlier. Why had he insisted that he was not there to enact revenge, or justice for that matter. *Why had he said he was there to warn the Donnetts? Warn them about what?*

'Did you record that last part, Lucy?' Matthias said, sounding irritated. 'You look a bit scatter-brained.'

'I did,' Lucy replied, stretching her fingers. She read back what Mrs Donnett had said. '"Thus, I do repent of killing my husband and his harlot,"' she said, glancing at the woman. With her scowl and arms crossed tightly across her chest, she looked as sorely unrepentant as she sounded. She held out the pen. 'You must put your mark.'

Resentfully, the woman took the quill pen from Lucy and haltingly signed her initials. *J.M.D.*

'You, too,' Lucy said, pushing the other paper towards Lionel Donnett.

Showing more comfort with the quill, he angrily scrawled his full name next to his mother's initials.

A distant pounding at the front door of the shop caused them all to look around. Lucy opened her mouth to scream for help, but Gamel waved the flintlock in front of her. 'Not a word from you.'

Matthias moved past his son. 'I shall check on this.'

A moment later, Lucy heard him saying, 'This way, Constable.' At the rumble of two familiar voices, she sank back in relief.

'What is going on?' Gamel cried, as the door burst open, to reveal Duncan and Hank standing behind Matthias.

Duncan took in the scene at once, his eyes narrowing when he saw the flintlock in Gamel's hand. 'Drop your gun,' he ordered.

Gamel didn't move, instead staring at his father in disbelief. 'What is going on? Why did you bring them back here?'

Matthias stood directly in front of Gamel and stared into his eyes. Then, reaching out, he gently removed the gun from his son's grip. 'Constable, these two people killed the Donnetts at Pye Corner. She was married to Mr Donnett and didn't like that he had another family.' The former hangman's mocking laugh turned angry, and he shook his fist at the soap-makers. 'They also killed my dear son Phineas in his own printer's shop.'

Matthias stood up and faced Duncan. 'They also kept the young lady here and me hostage. I demand that you arrest them and have them stand trial. My son Gamel and I have done nothing wrong. We are the victims in all of this.'

'Except that you came here to execute the Donnetts!' Lucy exclaimed, grabbing his arm. 'And your son assaulted Master Hargrave and stole his belongings, threatened him with blackmail, and wrote terrible things about him! How can you say you have done nothing wrong?'

Matthias shook off her arm but didn't reply.

Duncan's eyes flitted over Lucy anxiously. 'What does he mean, you were held hostage? Are you hurt?'

'I am all right, Constable,' she said, smiling weakly. She suddenly felt exhausted from what she'd undergone in the last hour, and wearily sat back down. 'Indeed, as Mr Fowler has said, these two are your murderers, twice over.' Wanly, she waved the still drying page in the air. 'This account contains their full confession.' She scowled in the direction of the Fowlers. 'And those two are not so innocent either.'

'Constable, tell us, how did you come to be here? Did you receive a message of some sort?' Matthias asked, with a smirk towards Lucy.

'Lach told you, didn't he?' Lucy said. 'I asked him to fetch you.'

Duncan and Hank looked puzzled.

'Lach? No,' Duncan replied. 'A woman potter came to our

gaol a little while ago, informing us that there were murderers living in this house. We might not have come, but she insisted, saying that a man had paid her a tidy sum, warning that another murder might occur if we were not quick.'

Dumbfounded, Lucy stared at Matthias. 'It was you. You sent that woman for help. That's why you had me write their confessions. To give the constable enough time to get here, before something h–happened.' She fumbled for words. 'Why? You told me you did not care if they killed me.'

Matthias glanced at his son, and Lucy understood. 'You said you were here to warn them.' Warn them that his son was coming to kill them. She could read the plea in his eyes. *I could not let my son commit murder. I could not bear to see my son hang for murder.*

Duncan picked up one of the papers Lucy had written. 'These are signed confessions?' he asked, incredulously skimming Lucy's uneven script. Then he gestured to Hank. 'Help me secure them to bring them back to the gaol. Mrs Jean Donnett, Mr Lionel Donnett. I hereby arrest you for the murders of Guy and Mary Donnett, soap-makers, as well as for Phineas Fowler, printer and bookseller.'

Hank reached down to haul Mrs Donnett to her feet. 'All right, ma'am. Let us go.'

'Would you be so good as to let me take my medicine first?' Mrs Donnett asked, looking somewhat forlorn. 'I need to take it before you drag me off to gaol.'

Lionel looked up. 'Mother!'

She gave him a wan smile. 'I shall not be a moment.' To Hank she said, 'I keep it in the kitchen.'

Duncan nodded for Hank to untie the woman and accompany her to the kitchen. He crouched beside Lucy. 'Are you all right? Shall I take you to Larimer?'

'I am fine. I'm just glad this ordeal is behind us.'

For a short while, they all fell into silence, Gamel and Matthias sitting shoulder to shoulder without speaking, and Lionel looking inexplicably forlorn from his space in the corner.

Then a great shout and crashing sound from another room caused them all to start. Lionel put his head in his hands.

'What is it?' Duncan called, leaping to his feet. 'Hank? What is going on?'

A few moments later, Hank appeared in the doorway, looking grey. 'I'm sorry, sir. Mrs Donnett just took her own life.' He held up a vial. 'Rat poison, I'm supposing. She went and swallowed it all before I could stop her. Convulsed for a bit and then died.'

Lucy's hand flew to her chest. *Self-murder! Only the good Lord would judge her now.*

In his corner, Lionel began to quietly weep. 'I knew that was her intention. The final humiliation of imprisonment and a trial. And then a public hanging. She could not bear it.' He slammed his fist on the ground. 'This is all my father's fault! He brought this on himself! I have no remorse that he was killed, seeing all that his deception and lies have wrought.' He pointed at the confession on the table. 'And you, miss! Publish her account. Show the world how she was wronged, from her own words. Let people see that justice truly prevailed.'

Matthias stood up and towered over Lionel. Hank and Duncan tensed, not sure what he was about to do. But the man just bared at his teeth in the grimmest semblance of a smile and pointed to Lionel's neck. 'The only true justice is at the hanging tree. You shall know the weight of it soon enough.'

TWENTY-ONE

Lucy sat at Master Aubrey's kitchen table, tapping her spoon against the table. There'd been so much excitement these last few days that she hadn't realized that one thing was still nagging at her. Why had Letitia Davenport written such terrible things about the magistrate?

She spread the tracts that Phineas had printed, focusing on the ones where the magistrate had been mentioned. The first few had spoken disparagingly of the magistrate but did not directly malign him. But *The Magistrate's Confession* was different. This was the one that had been published after the failed attempt at blackmail. She read the full title out loud. '*The Magistrate's Confession, Or, Foiled No More – A True Account of how a Magistrate who did know a Certain Truth of Murder did seek to Repress it.*' This seemed more in the vein of what Miss Davenport had tried to publish about the magistrate later.

What was it Havisham had said about Miss Davenport? That she'd known the Fowlers since their days in the theatre. Slowly, Lucy read parts of the tract out loud. '"Henry Fortenberry, a player with the Swan Theatre, did kill another player, Winston Scott, whilst they were playing together with foils, before an upcoming performance."'

Thoughtfully, she continued, stopping at the description of Scott's wife. Her eyes narrowed.

Lucy and Adam stood by the playhouse in Covent Garden. A sign near the door announced the *The Maid's Tragedy* with a list of the players below. Lucy pointed to the actor playing Melantius. 'That's him,' she said. 'Mr Pepys was correct.'

The previous afternoon, after Lucy had raised her suspicions to the Hargraves, the magistrate had immediately sent a message around to his friend Sam Pepys, a frequent theatregoer, enquiring where a certain player might be performing. After a flurry of messages between them, Pepys had suggested that they try the newer playhouse on Drury Lane. Adam had insisted that he accompany Lucy, and she had readily acquiesced. Ever since her ill treatment at the hands of the Donnetts, he'd been highly attentive, though thankfully not stifling. They had not had much time together recently anyway, and she welcomed his company.

'Doors open at two o'clock today,' a paunchy theatre hand called to them. He was feeding a small dog from his hand by the playhouse entrance. 'First performance at three. Come back later.'

'We just want to speak to someone,' Adam stated. 'It shall not take long.'

The man shook his head. 'Troupe is rehearsing now.'

Lucy jumped in. 'No, we'd like to speak to the wife of one the players. Mrs Fortenberry. We heard that she often watches her husband practise. We won't disturb the rehearsal.'

The man took in Adam's gentlemanly bearing and Lucy's modest dress. 'All right, I saw her earlier. Go on in. Don't make a nuisance of yourselves.'

Entering the playhouse, they walked through the vestibule and into the main theatre area. Lucy had seen a performance at this theatre before, but it was still hard not to marvel at the grandeur, and without crowds in attendance it was easier to take in the details. They moved towards the long rows of green baize-covered benches that extended throughout the pit, which were reserved for people of quality. She'd never been so close to the stage before.

A few players were on the stage shouting their lines, apparently rehearsing a dramatic court scene. One of the actors spoke, his voice tight with controlled emotion.

> You do me wrong,
> A most unmanly one, and I am slow
> In taking vengeance but be well advis'd.

Lucy touched Adam's sleeve. 'There she is.'

In the pit, about halfway from the stage, midway down one of the rows, a red-haired woman sat by herself, intently watching the rehearsal. Giving Adam a nod, Lucy went down one end of the aisle, while he advanced from the other, so they could seat themselves on either side of the woman.

'Mrs Fortenberry,' Lucy said quietly. 'Or shall I say Miss Davenport?'

The woman looked up and stared at Lucy. 'Y–you!' She was about to run but Adam sat beside her, effectively blocking her way. She slumped back on the bench. The players on the stage continued with the scene, oblivious to the drama playing out in the pit.

Lucy pulled out the crumpled piece of paper that the woman had tossed on to Havisham's workshop floor. 'Do you remember this?'

Mrs Fortenberry sniffed. 'What of it?'

Lucy pointed to the angry lines that spoke of Master Hargrave's alleged corruption and his motive for murdering Phineas Fowler. 'Why did you write such terrible lies about the magistrate?'

'Who says they are lies?'

'Phineas was killed by someone else,' Lucy replied quietly. 'As I suspect you already knew, even when you wrote this piece about him. It was wrong for you to try to clumsily place the blame on Master Hargrave, this man's father.'

'I don't care. Hargrave let a grave miscarriage of justice pass!' she whispered fiercely, tears rising in her eyes. She poked Adam's arm. 'My husband was murdered in plain sight, on a stage like that one there, in front of me! We all believed it to be an accident, and it was not. Your father knew the truth and chose to suppress it, to save his friend's reputation. Thus, I wanted to see him ruined, as I have been ruined.'

Striving to remain calm, Adam spoke carefully. 'Mrs Fortenberry, my father simply noted some places where the testimony might have been probed. There was nothing he could have done. He did not deserve the wrong you have done to him.'

'Do you not understand the terrible wrong that has been done to me?' she asked, touching her throat. With her other hand, she pointed at the player who was currently prancing about a woman seated on a throne-like chair. 'That man, there. Playing the role of Melantius! Henry Fortenberry!' She spat. 'He calls himself my husband, but he only acquired that position after taking my true husband's life.

'In one dreadful blow, he slayed my husband as they practised a duel on stage. Everyone saw it. We all believed that it was a terrible accident, I more than anyone. He wept and was so despondent over taking the life of his dearest friend, and we were also quick to offer him solace. I did not see then the true depth of what he had done. The play that he was performing in his own mind!' She swallowed. 'Not only did he take my husband's life, but later, after he was swiftly acquitted, he was given his best roles, for which he had been secretly practising.' Her chest rose and fell as she struggled to speak through short gasped-out words. 'He coveted me, too. In my sorrow and loneliness and misplaced trust, I did agree to wed him. Much to my eternal regret.'

Adam and Lucy exchanged a glance. It was hard not to feel a pang at the woman's distress.

'I truly thought Fortenberry was my husband's most dear friend. I thought he married me to protect me, to give me life after my beloved one's passing. I never believed that he would have done such a thing on purpose.' Tears began to slip down her cheeks. 'Do you know what hell it has been for me, knowing that I must live as a wife to my dear husband's murderer? Watch him demean my husband's roles?' She wiped the tears angrily. 'He cannot be tried for his crime again. How can I not blame the magistrate, once murder did out?'

'It was not my father's fault. You have no right to blackmail or malign him in such a way.' Adam's fist tightened. 'You must publish an apology.'

The woman sagged in her seat, defeat written all over her body. 'Publish an apology? Why should I? Indeed, who will apologize to me for allowing me to marry my husband's murderer?' She patted her stomach, in a way that seemed more like a slap than a tender caress. 'For bearing his child?'

Lucy tried a different tack, still bothered by some missing pieces of the story. 'How did you come to know Phineas?' she asked. 'He must have shown you the magistrate's notes. Is that when you decided to blackmail the justices Hargrave and Allerby?'

'I've known Phineas for a long time, even when I was a player myself a short while, these last few years, when the King allowed women to perform on stage. He was one of the few people who I'd shared my suspicions about my husband with. He came to me about a month ago, saying that he'd come into possession of a magistrate's personal papers, and there was one that concerned the trial around my late husband's death. He was as disgusted and dismayed by this gross miscarriage as I was.' She sighed. 'I told him what to write, and he did it. As for the blackmail, I just wanted the justices to squirm.'

For a moment, the three sat in silence, watching the players on stage grow more heated in their roles. 'Why did you not follow through on the blackmail?' Lucy asked. 'Why did you never try to extort more from them?'

'When I went to retrieve the package that day, I realized at the last moment that the site was being watched.' She gave a rueful cluck of her tongue. 'Somehow I did not expect that the magistrates would contact the constable after I told them not to. Still, I managed to turn it around.'

'By following the constable?' Lucy realized. 'You were the one who eavesdropped on our conversation at Master Aubrey's shop, isn't that so?'

Mrs Fortenberry chuckled, sounding genuinely amused for the first time. 'I admit, I was curious to see what the constable would do. I imagined he would go to see Hargrave or Allerby. I certainly never expected that he would go to your printer's shop, and I was intrigued by why you seemed to know so much about it.'

Adam coughed as she continued. 'That's why I knew later, when I saw you at Havisham's shop, that you were more involved than you let on.' She gave Lucy another curious glance. 'After Phineas published *The Magistrate's Confession*, I suddenly felt that was all I needed. I only wished for the justices to experience some humiliation, which pales in comparison to the devastation I felt when finding that my husband's killing had not been accidental at all. That I, of all people, had defended him. It was because of my testimony that everyone was convinced. I had heard the whispers later, but by then there was nothing I could do.' She smoothed down her skirts. 'That's why I didn't blackmail them further.'

She exhaled. 'You *must* understand that I had nothing to do with Phineas's death. I did not wish anyone dead.' A tear trickled down her cheek. Even though the woman had been a stage

performer, her honesty seemed authentic. She slumped even
further in her seat. 'I see now that my anger was misplaced,' she
added, looking up at Adam. 'I shall send an apology to your
father. You may choose to publish it as you please.'

Her husband looked over in their direction then and gave them
a courtly flourish. In his fine clothes, he appeared to be a
gentleman of quality, handsome and of noble mind and body.

Indeed, nothing could be further than the truth, Lucy thought.

Adam swore under his breath, perhaps thinking the same thing.
'Let's go,' he said to Lucy.

They left the theatre then, Mrs Fortenberry still holding her
hand to stomach, as she watched the players perform upon the
stage.

Sid set his wassail bowl of lamb's-wool down on the table, as
drops of the mulled ale drink trailed down his cheek. 'Wipe my
face, my lady,' he called to Annie. He'd found both the dried
bean and dried pea in the king's cake and pronounced himself
the Lord of Misrule and Annie his Queen, following the Twelfth
Night custom. Then, a faint flush rising in his cheeks, when he
glanced around at Master Hargrave, he added in a far humbler
tone, 'If you would be so kind.'

The magistrate just waved his goblet. 'It's your evening, Sid.
You may be as impudent as you like.'

Annie tossed her head. 'Only if it agrees with me.'

The Hargraves' house was full tonight, with servants, friends
and family all laughing and merry-making and drinking together.
In the morning, everything would go back to how it was, social
standings duly recognized and accorded. Tonight, though, the
world was purposely upside down.

Lucy went over to where Master Hargrave, Adam and Allerby
were engaged in quiet conversation, staying aside from the more
frivolous happenings around them. She held out two copies of
the tract that she'd printed earlier, which she would begin selling
in the morning. 'Here you are, sir. The apology to you from
Letitia Davenport, writing as Mrs Fortenberry.'

A slight glimmer shone in Master Hargrave's eye as he read
aloud what she had titled the piece. '*A New Mirror for the
Magistrates; Or, Standards Set by a Most Reputable and Wise*

Magistrate, Recently Vilified in the Press.' He coughed. 'Thank you, Lucy. Your words have humbled me indeed.'

Unexpectedly, Allerby reached for Lucy's hand and pressed it to his lips, before giving her a little bow. 'Thank you, my dear. Thomas has informed me how you tracked that wretched black-mailer down and convinced her to issue her apology. I should never have thought that a servant would be so inclined to help a man of our station.' He looked at the cavorting around him. 'Perhaps on a night like this I should be more inclined. You have given me much to think about.'

Adam pressed his hand against her back. 'Let me echo my father's thanks, Lucy,' he said softly in her ear. 'And Allerby's admiration.'

'Constable Duncan,' Master Hargrave called past them, catching sight of the constable and Hank joining the festivities. 'I am so glad you have joined us. Pray, have something to eat and drink. Mister Allerby just brought some news that I've been waiting to share with everyone.'

'What is it, sir?' Duncan asked, accepting a mug of wassail from Annie.

'It seems we have a new executioner at Newgate,' Master Hargrave replied, his expression inscrutable. 'An acquaintance of sorts.'

'An acquaintance? Who is it?' Lucy asked.

'Mr Donnett's son. Lionel Donnett,' Allerby replied.

Lucy clapped her hand over her mouth. She could tell that the others were as startled as she.

'How did that come about?' Duncan asked.

Lucy leaned forward as well, her own thoughts churning. She had a sense of how such a thing might have transpired. Indeed, Allerby's next words confirmed it.

'Donnett's sentence was commuted in exchange for being a hangman,' he explained. 'Since his mother had already poisoned herself, he did not need to worry that he would have to execute her. I suppose he thought it worth taking on such an occupation, to save his own life.'

As the others drifted away into conversation, Lucy stood by the window watching the softly falling snow, pondering Donnett's fate. She shivered, her hands tightening around her warm mug.

'Are you cold, Lucy?' Duncan asked, appearing at her side.

'I was just thinking about Lionel Donnett and the life of a hangman. Had Matthias Fowler suggested it to him, knowing there was an opening? Or did he try to deter him?' Softly, she whispered the last rhyme of *The Cry of the Hangman.*

> Though their ghastly corpses invade my sleep,
> Righteous justice has been my lot to keep.
>   I and my gallows moan.

Duncan was silent for a moment as the morbid words hung over the air, at odds with the merriment around them. 'I suppose, for Matthias, being a hangman was a type of calling,' he said. 'I can see why he collected those objects from the criminals he executed, although I had at first thought it to be very odd indeed. He used them to remind himself that his role in the legal system was as important as mine or Adam's. I imagine, though, that sometimes that might be hard to remember, especially when the dead invade the dreams.' He gave a short laugh. 'Enough of this, Lucy. I noticed you've been wearing a very lovely pendant of late. A gift perhaps?' His question was full of meaning, and he searched her face as she sought to reply.

A blush rising in her face, she touched her throat. 'From Adam. It had once belonged to his mother, my late mistress. Master Hargrave approved,' she added hastily. She began to stumble for words. 'He thought, they thought . . .'

He sighed, a look of disappointment crossing his face before he could hide it. 'I see. I thought that might be the case.' He stepped back from her. 'Lucy, please do not be concerned. It pleases me no end that the Hargraves have embraced you as they have. I know that Master Hargrave views you as a daughter and Master Adam views you as . . . well, I do not need to express that in words. There was a time I worried that you'd not be accepted by their set, but my heart has grown appeased lately on that point. I am no longer so aggrieved.' He smiled in his old boyish way. 'However, as I told you before, I will persevere until I hear you commit your troth.'

Her eyes filled with sudden tears. 'I do not think—'

He held up his hand, his smile still gentle. 'Let us wait and see.'

Shortly before midnight, Adam came looking for her. 'Let me walk you home,' he said, holding out her cloak.

They stepped out into the lightly falling snow. Shouts of merriment could be heard all around them in the distance, but there was quiet between them. He held out the lantern, so that a soft glow was cast about them. He held out his arm to her and, without saying anything, tucked her hand in the crook of his elbow.

'Sid and Annie can only rule for another fifteen minutes,' she said, shyly accepting the gesture.

He chuckled. 'I think they've been enjoying the world turned upside down.'

They walked slowly back. She was surprised when he led her to St Dunstan's churchyard, instead of back to Master Aubrey's. After leading her over to the sundial in the church garden, he paused. 'You know, you've turned my world upside down. I've known it for several years now, ever since you took care of us all during the plague. When I was away in the colonies, I could only think of you. I thought perhaps we could make a fresh start there together, but maybe we can do that here now.'

He set the lantern on the sundial and pulled a small satin bag out of his pocket. He opened it and pulled out a gold posy ring. 'There's an inscription in here. "Love does prevail." I chose it myself, because that's what I believe.'

'Oh Adam, I—'

He gripped her by the shoulders and looked down at her. 'Lucy, I know you are concerned that we come from different walks of life. I know at times you have not been treated as you ought, and I am heartfelt sorry for that. You have already carved out your own space, as a writer and maker of books. Can you not allow such a thing for us as well?'

Tears started to slip down her face as he took her hands gently in his own, placing the ring on her finger. 'With this ring, I pledge you my troth. Will you accept it?'

Too overcome to speak, she could only manage the slightest of nods. He placed his hands on her face and kissed her.

She looked down at the sundial. '*Life passes like the shadow*,' she whispered. 'At the time I thought it was a warning of sorts.'

He traced the engraved words as she had just done. 'I suppose, in some ways, it is a warning. I think you could look at it as a reminder, that we must seize the day, and not live either in regret or worry about what has passed or what could pass. We've survived plague, fire, death and disaster. Now it's a time for renewal.' He kissed her nose. 'There's a world waiting for us, Lucy.'

Standing on her tiptoes, she leaned up to kiss him, startling them both with her ardour. Smiling up at him, she took his hand and led him out of the churchyard. 'A new world indeed.'

AUTHOR'S NOTE

I've long been interested in how disorder and order played out in seventeenth-century England, particularly in the spectacle surrounding public executions. Put simply, as historians have long understood, criminal acts like murder were acts of disorder, while the public execution was the primary means to re-establish order, and right the world turned upside down. In *The Cry of the Hangman*, I wanted to explore the role of the executioner as a necessary instrument of law and justice, while also thinking about what kind of individuals actually occupied this position. While the image of a hood-wearing hangman is a common image in the popular imagination, historian Gerald Robin explains that such figures were not actually anonymous and did not wear hoods and masks, and most people knew who they were. I reference Jack Ketch, the infamous executioner of Newgate, who was regularly alleged to be a bumbling fool, but it's hard to know the truth of it. We do know that there were accounts of criminals – or more likely their families and friends – bribing the hangman before the execution, because it was apparently quite easy to botch an execution. While the ballad at the heart of this story was written by me, I borrowed the linguistic style and refrain 'I and my gallows groan' from *The Hang-Mans Last Will and Testament: With His Legacy to the Nine Worthies* (London 1660).

I was also interested in examining order and disorder through another lens – the legality or illegality of marriage, especially in terms of what constituted bigamy and clandestine marriage. As historian Jeremy Boulton and others have noted, there appeared to have been an increase of clandestine marriages, carried out at such places as Fleet prison, that were conducted outside of ecclesiastical jurisdiction, throughout the seventeenth century and only suppressed with the Hardwicke Act of 1753. Similarly, although bigamy was frowned upon, it was not all that uncommon either. While some bigamy cases did come to trial, it seems there were also mutual agreements to separate since divorce could be difficult and expensive to achieve. Many of these clandestine marriages may have been second marriages, since without banns being read they could be easier to keep hidden from families and neighbours.

Lastly, I was also interested in the order and organization associated with published collections of curiosities and curios. I drew the accounts described in this book from several fascinating collections from the period including, *A Rich Cabinet with Variety of Inventions: Unlock'd and open'd, for the Recreation of Ingenious Spirits in their vacant hours* (1668), published by J.W. 'A lover of artificial collectibles.' I also liked the ones that did not contain physical objects, such as *The Court of Curiosities and the Cabinet of Rarities with the New Way of Wooing* (1685). They helped inform the types of objects and ideas that I thought someone might collect.

ACKNOWLEDGEMENTS

I started writing *The Cry of the Hangman* in May 2020, about two months into the worldwide pandemic brought about by the coronavirus. All my usual writing establishments – coffee shops, bookstores, libraries, bars – were closed and I was forced to do most of my writing on the living room sofa or in my thirteen-year-old's Star Wars themed bedroom. For a few months, over spring and summer, I was fortunate to find a secluded, albeit spider-infested, picnic table off of Lake Michigan. (Those spiders are why I start my book off as I do.) But it was a true joy to immerse myself back in Lucy's world, when the 'real world' got too intense.

To that end, I want to thank the crime fiction community generally (far too long a list to mention everyone!) – especially Sisters in Crime Chicagoland and the Super Secret Fringe Group (you know who you are!) – whether it was cocktail hours on zoom, virtual conferences and book events, Netflix parties, or just communing through social media, you collectively helped me keep the crazies at bay and get this book written. But there were a number of individuals who helped support me as I wrote this book under such incredibly trying circumstances, including Lori Rader-Day, Erica Ruth Neubauer, Tracy Clark, Mia Manansala, Alexia Gordon, Jess Lourie, Ed Aymer, Alex Segura, Terri Bischoff, Laurie Chandlar, Jamie Freveletti, Julie Hyzy and Claire O'Donahue. I'd also like to thank my wonderful agent, David Hale Smith and Naomi Eisenbeiss, especially for hosting virtual happy hours that helped me feel connected and supported by other writers.

I'd like to thank my talented editors Rachel Slatter and Natasha Bell, along with the rest of the Severn House team, for the thought and care you took in bringing *The Cry of the Hangman* to light.

And certainly, I need to thank my wonderful children, Alex and Quentin, for being such thoughtful, caring and resilient kids, especially while dealing from so many disappointments over the past year and a half. And poor Quentin never complained even when I had to start working on the book in his bedroom on early Saturday mornings when he was still trying to sleep. I love and appreciate both of you.

Lastly, as always, I must thank my wonderfully supportive husband, Matt Kelley, who always helped me find space and time to write, even when we had to creatively rotate around the house or pretend that I was actually at a coffee shop or pub. Thanks for always being willing to give me extensive feedback on my drafts, and for letting me know when my characters do or say something that seems a bit out of whack. There's no one I'd rather survive a pandemic with – I couldn't do this all without you!